WASPS AMONG

THE IVY

Wasps Among the Ivy

Copyright 2017 Barry Lees.

ISBN   978-1-9997928-0-0

All of the characters in this book are fictitious. Although reference is made to some real events, any similarity to any persons, living or dead, is purely coincidental.

Cover image by Lidia Ranns.

Also by Barry Lees available on Kindle Books.

This City of Lies

The Governor's Man

By Sword and Feather

Exiles from a Torn Province

Track and Eliminate

The Blue, the Green and the Dead

For Mum

CHAPTER ONE

'Whoa, half way the-re, whoa, livin' on a pra-yer!'

In the bar of the University Student's Union, amidst the thumping din of rock music, an important transaction was taking place.

"Take my hand and we'll make it I swe-ar, whoa, livin' on a pra-yer!'

In a huddle of fourteen people, all seated around a long, low table and where conversation could only take place with mouths up to ears and the next person along could know nothing of it, Luke was assuring his newest customer of the quality of the merchandise he had on sale.

"It's the business, mate." He waxed lyrically about his own product. "Top quality, no shit or nothing."

When introduced by a mutual acquaintance only two minutes previously, his prospective client had called himself Dammo. He was a pale-skinned young man in denim with a first attempt at a beard struggling to grow from his chin. He smelled of joss sticks, body odour and clothes overdue for washing. He nodded and leaned back. Luke leaned forward to hear his request.

"Let's have a look at it then," he proposed with ill-concealed zeal. Luke had formed the opinion that Dammo had originated in Yorkshire, not that Luke was any expert.

Accents and dialects from across the country and beyond were frequently heard in that student environment.

"Not here," he said as though Dammo needed some rudimentary tuition in such matters of discretion.

"Where then?" appealed Dammo.

"Go to the girls' loo," said Luke in all seriousness.

"Did you say the girls' loo?" The student thought his limited hearing was playing tricks on him, or Luke was. Luke provided the requisite reassurance.

"Blonde girl, red top, stands outside it, she'll sort you out. Her name's Candice, tell her Luke sent you."

"Okay, thanks."

The youth finished the last inch from his bottle of beer and got up from the table. A 'Ban-the-bomb' medallion swung on a string from his skinny neck. Luke turned and initiated another conversation of a similar nature with the person sitting next to him on the other side.

Dammo crossed the wooden section of the floor which had been intended for dancing although nobody was dancing at that time. Luke glanced up and watched him go toward the toilets, but he went into the Gents, to Luke's annoyance. A minute later he emerged, adjusting his trouser zip and wiping his hands on his hips. He went to the ladies' toilet where the blonde described by Luke was standing, leaning on the wall next to the door, red top and disinterested manner. She was slim and would have been pretty if she had been fully awake.

"Are you, erm, Candice?" asked Dammo tentatively.

6

"Might be," she said without looking at him, "depends."

"Can you sort me out with some, erm, you know?"

She was about to terminate the conversation rudely when he added.

"Luke sent me. He said you'd sort me out."

That changed things. Now, she took the trouble to look at him. They both looked across at Luke who had been loosely monitoring the situation. Luke nodded. Candice grabbed Dammo's denim jacket and said,

"Come in here."

She pushed open the door to the ladies' toilet and dragged him in behind her. Three young women were huddled around one of three sinks. They barely noticed that anyone had entered the room. Candice and Dammo disappeared into a cubicle. Dammo looked bewildered as Candice demanded to know what he wanted.

"Got any coke?" he asked.

"Shhh!" she urged him. She had become considerably more animated than she had been outside. "Quiet! Sure, I've got anything you want. Show me some cash."

Dammo reached into his back pocket and produced three grubby and crumpled ten pound notes. He straightened them and showed her, clearly demonstrating his inability to negotiate.

"Is that all you've got?" she said dismissively.

"Yeah, gimme thirty quid's worth, alright?" His voice was becoming more feint.

Candice reached into the front of her jeans and pulled out a small, clear plastic bag of white powder. The bag was the roughly cut-off corner of a larger bag and was less than two inches long. She snatched the money and handed over the bag.

"When you need some more, speak to Luke, okay?"

"Sure, ta," said the now delighted Dammo. He waited as she unbolted the cubicle door and walked out, leaving him to follow on. She resumed her place against the wall outside the ladies' toilet and Dammo went back into the gents. Candice caught Luke's attention and nodded her message that the transaction was successful. Luke was busy preparing their next customer.

Seven minutes later, a fully kitted-out Police Support Unit burst into the S.U. bar. The lights came up and the music went off. A stunned clientele struggled to take in what was happening, seventy-eight young people rooted to their respective positions. Luke was the first to realise the gravity of the situation. He stood up and ran toward the toilets, pushing drifting punters aside in his haste. He caught sight of Candice who stood frozen against the wall unable to respond. Luke darted toward her but he was hacked to the ground by a six-foot-five police constable in a shiny black jacket and visored helmet.

Candice sprang into life on seeing Luke being pushed face-down to the floor. His arms were handcuffed behind him and his face was obscured by the big cop and another similarly attired female officer. Candice knew that she could do nothing to help him. She dashed into the ladies' toilet and clambered up onto a window ledge, pushing open the window, she poured herself through it and dropped into the alley at the rear as she heard frantic movement from inside the ladies' room together with authoritative voices calling out orders and answering them. Candice tried to run and pull out the remaining tiny bags of differing substances at the same time. She dropped the wraps and reached another alley leading into total darkness. She took off, running into empty washing lines and metal dustbins, driven solely by the need to get away and with no thought of where she was going.

A light from an upstairs window illuminated the alley enough for her to make out a road ahead. She stopped at the edge of the alley wall and peered out onto the street. Panting and desperate she ran on across the street intending to seek further secretion in the alley opposite, but she never reached it.

A police dog handler had released the hound from the back of the S.U. bar and it needed little light to find its quarry. The German shepherd sank its teeth into Candice's right arm as it had been rewarded for doing, for real and when simulated, every day of its working life. It held on until the handler and two other uniformed cops caught up and took her into custody.

The wounds in her forearms were less serious than the scene suggested and the substances she still had swimming around her bloodstream served to numb the pain to some degree.

"You're nicked, love!" uttered a policeman, who was also out of breath.

"What, what have I done?" pleaded Candice, who had been fully briefed as to what not to say in such circumstances.

"Supplying controlled drugs. You don't have to say anything . . ." but the rest of that speech was not being absorbed by her. She was placed in a police van and taken to Casualty then onto the police detention block where Luke was already being strip searched. The search of Candice's underwear revealed that she had, in her haste, been unable to discard all of her merchandise. Two tiny bags, one of heroin and one of cocaine, were still there.

Meanwhile, in a different police station, Dammo was undergoing a detailed grilling of a different kind. He was writing his own statement of evidence as two plain-clothes detectives were arranging storage for the sound-recording equipment that had been concealed in his clothing. The Detective Inspector had carried out a debriefing session which had gone to plan. Before the night was through, Dammo had assumed his real identity and returned to the police station where he was normally based some twenty-five miles away.

*

In the soundproofed interview room at the central police station, Candice sat slumped on a metal chair and listened to a recording of a conversation she had had earlier. It had not at any point crossed her mind that it may have been recorded. The background sound was the muffled, thumping bass beat of the music in the S.U. bar, but the words spoken by both participants were easily made out.

"Got any coke?"

"Shhh! Quiet! . . . Sure, I've got anything you want. Show me some cash."

Candice dipped her face into her hands in despair. That guy was working for the cops and she had fallen for it. The tape recording went on.

"Is that all you've got?"

"Yeah, gimme thirty quid's worth, alright?"

"When you need some more, speak to Luke, okay?"

"Sure, ta."

Candice had not only implicated herself, she had put Luke well and truly in the dock too. She knew that he would be played that tape and possibly more like it. She felt foolish, having always taken law-breaking lightly. She was staring down the barrels of an actual prison sentence.

The interviewing officer switched off the tape and briefly glanced at his papers before asking.

"Well Candice?"

"Well what?"

"Do you accept that you are the person speaking on that tape-recording?"

"I'm not saying anything until I've spoken to Luke."

"Oh!" said the police officer leaning back in his chair. "So, you agree that you and Luke are known to each other."

"I don't agree to anything." Her tone became more defensive, desperately so.

"So well-acquainted that you have to consult him before you say anything, it seems?"

The interviewer was holding all of the good cards whilst Candice had nothing to use to defend herself.

"What do you want to say to Luke, eh Candice? Is it that you want to know what he's saying about you in another interview room in this building right now?"

Candice was thinking of Luke's instructions to her not to do anything without him knowing about it and that he was to do the same with her. That agreement did not work in police custody, it required an uninterrupted line of communication. She resolved to not answer any further questions.

Luke's interview had run differently to that of Candice. The quality of the conversation on the tape-recording had been heavily affected by the loud music and the interviewing officer had read from Dammo's statement instead. Luke took heart from the poor quality of the taped conversation. He couldn't be charged on that. It could have been anybody talking. The tape player was paused whilst Luke denied all wrongdoing in the S.U. bar. He hoped that Candice had remembered to stick to the plan too. The last thing he needed was for her to crack and start telling them everything. She wouldn't do that, they trusted each other.

The interviewing officer switched on the tape again. Luke heard Dammo and Candice in conversation in the cubicle of the ladies' toilet.

"Got any coke?"

"Shhh! Quiet! . . . Sure, I've got anything you want. Show me some cash."

"Is that all you've got?"

"Yeah, gimme thirty quid's worth, alright?"

"When you need some more, speak to Luke, okay?"

The interviewer stopped the recording, rewound it and played the last part again.

"When you need some more, speak to Luke, okay?"

Luke's heart sank and his skin ran cold. He need not have worried that she would implicate him in her interview at the police station – she had done that several hours ago in the toilet in the S.U. bar.

"Do you want to hear that bit again Luke?" asked the interviewer who was calmly pressing home his advantage.

Luke looked at the floor between his shoeless feet. He let out a deep lung-full of air and looked up.

"I want to talk to the Drugs Squad. I have something they'll want to hear."

CHAPTER TWO

The family were from a mining village in Derbyshire. Luke's older brother, like their father, were coal miners and his mother worked on the till at the Co-op. He saw his father's health gradually deteriorate with an assortment of restrictive lung conditions and his brother, who was only two tears older then Luke, go from a sporty and good-natured schoolboy to a depressed and belligerent young man, quick to resort to violence in the pubs of the neighbourhood. Luke was not certain as to why his role models had caused him such disappointment, but he was adamant that he was not going to go down the mine. That was one common denominator which could not be dismissed.

Thankfully for him, Luke had a realistic aim to pursue. His school achievements were impressive without applying much effort on his part. Whilst most of the kids from the village concluded their education at the age of sixteen, the nearest sixth-form college being twelve miles away, Luke's grades inspired his head-teacher to explore what help could be afforded him in order to continue his education. The parish priest managed to tap into a fund which existed to benefit promising Christian students. All Luke had to do was include an element of religious study to his further education programme and the fund would pay for his transport to the college. Luke was not the first kid from that village to study beyond the age of sixteen, but his family behaved as though he was.

He settled into college activities with the sole motivation of seeking an escape route to a better life than going down a mine. His studies bored him, but he had the foresight to realise what was laid out for him should he fail in his academic pursuits. The college was a staging post for bigger and better things, not just a temporary change from the norms of his upbringing. He 'gave unto Caesar' as his negligible religious studies had provided him the vocabulary for, satisfying his tutors at a canter whilst finding his own forms of entertainment. This could be placed in one of two categories: girls and cannabis. Given a straight choice between the two, he would go for the cannabis nine times out of ten.

He achieved sufficient grades to be offered a place at a university of modest status, to the east of Manchester city centre. His mother wanted a street party. Luke managed to talk his parents out of that idea. Instead he convinced them that any such expense should be redirected toward helping him to fit in to student life in Manchester. New clothes, books, etc. were how he had described his wish-list and his wishes were duly granted. He took the money made available and went to the city. Within a fortnight he was smoking heroin, by Christmas he was injecting it.

*

'A trust-fund princess' was how one loose acquaintance had observed Candice Kendal. Another had referred to her as 'a spoilt brat with no grasp on reality.' She had been blessed with the finer things in life but seemed to appreciate none of them. Whilst she was undoubtedly pretty, expensively turned-out and lavishly funded, she effused an air of terminal boredom.

Candice was an only child, born after her mother's three miscarriages and, according to her parents, clearly the result of a miracle. Her mother had never had any paid employment, instead investing her time cossetting the child from imagined harm at every second of the day or night. Holidays in St Moritz which were supposed to enhance skiing skills invariably failed to progress anyone from occupying the nursery slopes. Candice found them boring too. The house in Tuscany evoked similar feelings in her. Meanwhile, her father spent little time at whatever house his wife and daughter happened to be occupying. He enjoyed membership on an exclusive London gentlemen's club and the charms of a series of discretely selected mistresses.

As owners of vast swathes of farmland, the family income was considerable and not at risk. Inheritance tax was the chief enemy and a team of accountants battled continually against it. They usually came off best. The main family home, on the outskirts of Harrogate in North Yorkshire, was an eight-bedroomed manor house which had been in her father's family since 1810. The house had a staff of nine; a nanny (the faces changed each time Candice ceased to approve,) two housekeepers, two gardeners, a cook, a handyman (whose duties also including driving the family around) and a stablehand. During her childhood, Candice took ownership of four ponies, each in turn being larger as the child grew. She won countless rosettes for her equestrian activities which were invariably collected by other people owing to her abject lack of interest in them. On her seventeenth birthday she was presented with a new Special Edition, Mini convertible. She didn't like it. The day after, it was replaced by a Lotus.

Candice found boarding school only slightly more interesting. This was because she found herself in the company of like-minded people. Her estrangement from her mother brought on bouts of depression, but only for her mother. Candice's attitude changed little. What did occur was a change of values for Candice. She realised how tame her life had been, how her constant state of ennui was the fault of her idiotic parents and not hers. She resolved to take control of her own amusement and make the most of the parental tolerance she had been cursed with. When the opportunity to go to university was discussed, she was offered the Sorbonne, New York or any number of esteemed seats of learning. She wanted none of them. Instead she wished to go to somewhere which would strike alarm into the hearts of her family, a place so low in social merit that her existence there would set her apart from her peers as being daring and 'her own person.' She chose Manchester.

Hell bent on seizing the chance to do anything to embarrass her parents, Candice embarked on a campaign of uncivil disobedience. She was arrested for several instances of drunken antics, including kicking over a motorcycle whilst the rider was waiting at a traffic light and smashing a shop window with a dustbin lid. There was no reason for either offence. She just felt like it. The student village, motorists, the police and shopkeepers were relieved when Candice ceased to come to their attention. She had discovered other ways to transgress, ways which would stretch her mind in a manner previously unimagined. The consumption of class A controlled drugs was an activity which was best done behind closed doors. She needed drugs and someone to get it for her. She also needed someone to share the experience with. She found both in the thin lad from Derbyshire who had attended some of her classes before his appearances had become a rarity.

Candice and Luke became a couple, albeit for unwholesome reasons. From inauspicious beginnings, they grew to rely on and trust each other to facilitate their common aims. For the first time in their respective lives they had someone that they needed and who needed them. An inter-dependent union of two who were together in the cesspool of their making, because they were too miserable to be apart.

Luke had initially acquired his fixes from a fellow student at the university. He was an overseas student and had returned to his home country leaving Luke to seek new sources. Some sales outlets were very low down the pyramid of retail, users running only enough errands to pay for their own drugs. Although this could be said of Luke, he considered himself to belong above that level. He was more intelligent and, to some extent, educated. Those worker-bees were unreliable, and Luke wanted to get what he wanted when he wanted it. That meant aiming slightly higher up the chain. When Candice came along, he wanted to impress her with his ability to get her what she wanted, and largely did so.

When it came to buying drugs, the presence of Candice was both a blessing and a curse. Whilst her good looks made men fawn over her and behave irrationally in their attempts to ingratiate themselves, the savvy drug dealers suspected that she was not what she seemed and tended to hold back their merchandise in the interests of self-preservation. A workable level of trust was established by engaging in the communal consumption of narcotics, although Luke kept a level of awareness at such times. A good-looking girl who was stoned and unable to protect herself in the company of men who knew that they were all living outside the law presented a risk he was not willing to take, even if she was oblivious to it.

It has often been said that drug dealers are like grey hairs – if you take one out, two more appear. Luke and Candice had taken to dealing drugs for the sole purpose of paying for their own consumption. Soon behind with their finances, despite the hurried sale of a damaged Lotus sports car, they were recruited by a local dealer called Mark Masood, mainly because of their ability to move freely in the student community without raising suspicion. All drugs supplied were to be sold and the resultant cash was collected by their supplier at varying places, but this took place virtually every day.

All Luke and Candice knew was their own place in that seedy pyramid of trade. They sold to people who consumed the goods and they collected and remitted the proceeds to their supplier without question, receiving their own reward in tiny bags rather than in cash. It barely occurred to them that there was a larger economic picture and their supplier was merely a bit player in that. On one occasion when Masood was himself less compos mentis than he should have been, he tried to impress them by telling them that he was of high status in the world of narcotic commerce in Manchester. He claimed to be a close personal associate of Mally himself.

There was no way Masood would back up this claim by providing any evidence of his friendship with Mally, but it opened Luke and Candice to the concept that, in that sphere, knowledge was power. Knowing someone, or knowing of someone, carried some currency. That asset could be kept ready for a rainy day. As they sat in their respective cells of that police station, looking down the barrels of prison sentences and the inevitable separation from each other, that rainy day had arrived. Anything they had which could mitigate the grimness of their short-term future had to be used.

They were quick to offer up Mark Masood to the man from the Drugs Squad. Detective Constable Russell Warren let nothing of his thoughts appear on his face as he listened to what they had to offer by way of bargaining chips. He could target Masood anytime he wanted but he was more interested in bigger fish. When Luke and Candice added that Masood was in the inner circle of a man known as Mally, Warren was unable to suppress a slight elevation of his eyebrows. Luke and Candice took heart from this. That little snippet of knowledge they had gleaned in a moment of weakness from Masood was of value and they knew it.

Warren was not interested in catching Masood dealing drugs to users. There were other local teams of police officers who could gather evidence and take Masood out. Warren was more interested in nailing Masood then turning him to inform on Mally, real name Gavin Malligan, who was a scalp worth hunting. Firstly, Warren had to arrange a sting on Masood, then repeat the process to get Malligan.

*

"I'm going to run through the plan one more time. Are you listening, both of you?" said D.C. Russell Warren to the sorry pair seated in near darkness in the back of an unmarked police car. Luke Gould and Candice Kendal sat in silence, each gazing out of their respective windows. They nodded acknowledgement and Warren continued.

"As you have both met our man before, there shouldn't be any difficulty in starting the conversation. Who's going to do the talking?"

They looked at each other with sad resignation of their predicament. It fell to Luke to volunteer.

"I'll do it," he mumbled.

"Okay, you have been together when you have bought gear from Masood so it will appear normal to him this time. The only difference is that you will have a recording device, Luke. The conversation should be more about what he has to say than what you say, clear?"

"Yeah."

He was visibly nervous. His lower lip trembled as did his fingers. Candice Kendal did the same.

"What if it goes wrong?" she asked, darting her eyes between the policeman, her boyfriend and the empty blackness of the side window. "What if he realises what we're doing?"

"My team and I will be monitoring the conversation throughout. We will intervene if it gets dangerous."

Warren's team consisted of a techie guy who was to operate the transmission and recording of conversations and the CCTV filming of the meeting and a Support Unit team, in two vehicles, which were positioned nearby.

The set-up was arranged by calls made from and to public call boxes. It was to take place at midnight on the car park of a supermarket, behind the petrol kiosk. It was skirted by thick bushes separating the car park from an industrial estate. Recent intelligence had revealed that Masood was using a brown Toyota Celica, although he changed vehicles frequently in order to avoid police attention.

Candice and Luke were driven to the edge of the housing estate next to the supermarket. They tested the recording equipment and set off to walk through the estate. The emergency word they had been given was 'Disneyland' although neither could think of an appropriate context in which to introduce it, should the need for subtlety arise. With hearts pounding and dry mouths they said nothing to each other, not because they were being recorded but because they were too nervous to speak.

Would Masood smell a rat? He was no fool. What he was likely to do to them if, or more realistically when, he knew what they had done was too grim a prospect to contemplate. They turned left at a junction and passed a row of six shops, only two of which were functional. They left the street and crossed wasteland towards the night lights of the supermarket. They reached the arranged point and waited.

After ten minutes, a car's headlights shone on them on main beam, making Candice look away and Luke cover his eyes with his forearm. The car slowly purred up to them and the lights were extinguished. The night-vision CCTV cameras homed in on the car. The remote recording equipment picked up Luke's voice.

"It's not him!" he whispered, "It's not Mark Masood."

Warren was about to pull the plug and abort the mission. No indication had been forthcoming which would indicate that Masood was in the habit of delegating. Luke spoke again.

"There's some older bloke driving and there's somebody in the car with him."

Candice's heart and breathing came to a virtual stop. She knew that Luke was to do the talking which was just as well because she was unable to speak.

Warren and the technician operating the recording devices sat in another car. Warren stared intently at the green-lit image on the monitoring screen. The speaker relayed the conversation going on behind the petrol station kiosk. Luke spoke first.

"Hiya!" he said in a pitch somewhat higher than he had intended. "Alright?"

There was no answer for ten seconds, then a deep, voice said,

"Have you got my money?"

From his remote position, Warren sat up and intensely listened to the words of the driver of the Toyota. Did he have a Welsh accent?

"Erm, we usually speak to Mark."

"Well, that's good, because he answers to me." The menace in the voice of the Welshman made Luke as nervous as Candice already was. Warren suspected who it was, but the transmitted conversation alone was not enough for him to be certain.

"Who are you?" asked Luke, already regretting asking.

"My money?" The man was not going to be answering the questions.

Luke's stomach was doing gymnastics. Whoever that guy was, he was not to be trifled with.

"Sure, yeah." Luke scrambled around in his pockets for the cash he was to hand over. The sound equipment produced a noise like a thunderstorm.

"Here's four hundred quid."

He held out the money toward the open window of the car. The man took it and began counting it in his lap in the car. Warren could not see his face on the screen. The passenger had a hood raised over his head. Luke and Candice could not see the passenger's face, but they could see the barrel of a handgun sticking out of his coat and pointing at them.

"Get him out of the car." said Warren knowing full-well that Luke could not hear him. He also wanted both of them out of the car in case they tried to make a dash for it, which depended on how well Luke Gould performed his act of self-preservation.

"What happened at the university bar last night?" asked the man.

"What do you mean?"

"Don't play stupid with me you little bastard. That club you're supposed to sell in, it got raided."

"What? By the police?" squeaked Luke.

"No, by the fucking Salvation Army, you prick! I asked you what happened!"

"We don't know, it must have been after we left," offered Luke, hoping that their new boss would join in with their good fortune and relief.

The car door clicked open and it swung wide making Luke step back. Candice did the same. She stood behind Luke, unintentionally shielding herself. The Welshman stepped out of the car and rested his arm across the top of the opened door.

"Christ! It's him, it's Malligan!" exclaimed Warren, wishing that he had arranged a bigger team. He wasn't to know that his big target would turn up in person.

"Two got arrested. Lucky that wasn't you, eh?" Malligan said.

"Yeah, we'd sold some stuff there, maybe the people we sold to got locked up."

"Maybe, maybe," contemplated Malligan, "or maybe someone is dealing on your patch."

"I can't see that happening," said Luke.

"There's more," said Malligan, feeding out information on a drip. "The ones that got arrested, one lad and one girl. Coincidence, right?"

"Well, yeah, I suppose," said Luke.

"What about you Princess? What have you got to say?"

Candice tensed at every atom of her body. Malligan had the ability to chill her with his presence but when he spoke to her, especially in the tone of suspicion he was using, she felt exposed and defenceless.

"Well?" he insisted.

"N, nothing," she uttered. It sprang to her mind to utter the safety word. It was the only way to call for help, summon 'International Rescue,' to put an end to this unbearable fear. If she had only remembered what the safety word was, she would have blurted it out in an instant.

"Now we have a problem," said Malligan ominously. "Correction, you two have a problem."

"It wasn't us, seriously, it must have been someone else," pleaded Luke with increasing involuntary vibrato in his voice.

"If that's true, well, you were lucky, weren't you? Very lucky."

He paused as he lit a cigarette. The flame from the lighter momentarily distorted the image on the monitor in Warren's car.

"Damn, what's that?" he asked.

"It's just a flame, he's lit a fag, it's alright," the technician calmly explained. "It's clear again, look."

Warren let out a breath but remained on edge. The speaker relayed Malligan's words once more.

"But if it isn't true . . . and I do hope for your sake it was, then you have not only lied to me, but you are out of the pokey already and coming to see me. This isn't good."

He smoked in long drags, bringing the fierce orange glow of his cigarette to take on the form of a weapon.

Malligan threw away his cigarette and grabbed Luke by the collar of his jacket. He pushed him over the side of the car and began to search inside his clothing. He soon found the base-set taped to the small of his back and the wire connecting to a tiny microphone sewn into the button strip on his shirt. Malligan ripped it off and threw it onto the ground.

"Big mistake, boy."

The scrambled cacophony on the speaker made Warren spring into action.

"Strike, strike, strike," he shouted into the closed channel radio set. The two Support Unit vans stirred instantly from 'pause mode' and fired up their engines. The monitor screen became distorted again with a powerful light far greater than the cigarette lighter had caused.

"Oh shit, he's moving, the car's moving," he said before grabbing the radio set again.

"He's moving, don't let him get out onto the road."

"Got that," replied the front seat passenger of the police van.

Warren too was accelerating through the gears, but an unmarked car cannot command compliance from other motorists on its way to an urgent job. The screen trained on the scene at the back of the petrol station faded in and out as the signal wavered. In moments of clarity it showed that Malligan's car had gone and so had Luke and Candice. The Support Unit vans arrived at the scene and confirmed that there was nobody there. No vehicles or people had been seen leaving the supermarket car park as the team had entered. The update was transmitted to Warren.

"Search the car park, there has to be another way out," he ordered as his car finally came within sight of the supermarket complex.

The Support Unit spread out and commenced searching. Warren switched on another police radio, interrupted the current transmission and demanded that the Toyota be circulated for sightings immediately, life-threatening situation, priority one.

Nothing was coming from the search of the car park until, after three minutes which seemed like three weeks, a message came through that a fence panel had been removed allowing vehicular egress onto the landfill site behind the supermarket.

"Get onto the site, seal off the exits, we need more patrols here." Warren's voice gave away his lack of control over the situation. The Duty Inspector was pressing him for another update as to what the nature of the incident was and exactly whose life was in danger. There had been a 'need-to-know' approach to the operation and the local uniformed cops were deemed to be out of that loop.

Warren did not try to explain, it was too complicated to do so and there wasn't time. He didn't have to when, through the opened window of the car, he heard a scream. The piercing, terror-stricken note hung across the night air for several seconds then it came again, a woman's shriek, a panicking, desperate response to something horrific. Warren had only one thought . . . Candice!

Police vans, cars and running cops in boiler suits poured around and across the darkened surface of the landfill site. An access path for wagons afforded some passage through but there was no clue as to where the scream had come from.

"There's someone," called out a female officer in uniform before relaying that information formally over the airwaves. "Over there, on the hill, there's someone moving, confirm it's not one of ours."

"It's not one of ours," confirmed a colleague. "Close in and identify."

The cordon of cops approached the figure bearing torches. Warren ran to the hill where this sighting had occurred.

"One detained. Please find out what for," asked a patrol.

"Who is it?" demanded Warren.

"Gavin Malligan," answered the cop over the radio. "and he has blood on his face and clothing."

"Arrest him!" shouted Warren over the airwave

"There's a car further up the hill," said another voice.

"Get a van here for Malligan," ordered Warren, "and get up to that car, there are two people unaccounted for yet and a second suspect."

All cops not involved in the detention of Malligan dashed to the car. Warren got there fourth. He snatched a torch from another cop and shone it inside the car. In the front seats there was nobody, but in the back seats there were two people. Candice sat shivering and transfixed. Her eyes widened and her mouth hung open, lips and chin trembling, and her manner was detached from the reality of her situation. Next to her sat Luke. Upright and with his head leaning into the rear doorpost away from the side Warren where was standing. There was blood all over both of them. The front seat passenger had gone.

"Candice, Luke, what happened?" said Warren unable to think of anything more suitable to say.

Candice did not look at him. She stared forward and mumbled incoherent humming sounds. Luke's face was turned away. Warren knelt on the driver's seat and reached into the back seat. He touched Luke on the arm, gently then firmly.

"Luke, speak to me," appealed Warren

Luke's head and torso rolled slowly across until he rested on Candice's lap. She still did not look anywhere.

Warren's breath was halted. Luke's eyes were fixed open, lifeless. An old, tape-handled machete was buried in his neck.

CHAPTER THREE

Police headquarters was a complex of jumbled buildings in what had been a deer park until it had been commandeered by the authorities as a satellite army training centre at the outset of WW2. The government simply did not give it back to its original owners. It was made up of a hotchpotch of architecture ranging aesthetically from beautiful Georgian stone to hideous grey prefabricated panels of the 1960s. The building which had cost the most was a steel and blue-tinted glass affair with a revolving door and air-conditioning units adorning the outer panels.

Inside and beyond the beech-wood reception desk, which looked like a hotel lobby staffed by airline cabin crew, ran four curved corridors of off-white and flecked walls and insipid, orange carpet. The second corridor on the left led to a wider waiting area and made the place look like a Harley Street clinic. Six velour covered chairs surrounded a coffee table which had never housed any coffee. Sitting in the corner alone was Detective Constable Russell Warren.

A haircut, a shave and a dark blue suit that had not been worn for at least five years told a story of the rarity of his presence there. The covert nature of the work he has been doing had meant that it was not appropriate for him to be seen at the H.Q. complex. One stray photograph by a speculative reporter and his work would have impossible.

The still of the corridor was broken by the dull sound of hurried footsteps on carpet. Appearing at the seating zone was a flustered young man in a shiny suit carrying a burgundy leather document case which was tucked under one arm as the other struggled to place a constabulary lanyard over his head. Attached to the lanyard was a day-visitor pass.

"D.C. Warren?" asked the visitor, who looked about twenty-one.

"Yes, who are you?" asked Warren already forming his own opinion as to the answer.

"Julian Bensley, I'm with Mead-Farringtone."

He wrestled a business card from the outer pocket of his jacket and handed it over. It confirmed what he had said and added that he held a law degree and was an associate solicitor with the Manchester legal firm. Warren revised his assessment of Bensley's age on the premise that you can't be a solicitor at twenty-one, even an associate solicitor.

Bensley put down the document case on the coffee table and unclipped the edge to open it.

"I've been assigned your case so I am representing your interests in the disciplinary sense at present. Don't worry, the Police Federation are covering our costs."

Warren vaguely recalled a Federation Rep. saying something about getting him some legal support, but it was one of many conversations which took place in the immediate aftermath of the death of Luke Gould. He could not remember all of the content of such exchanges at the time, and some of them not at all. Warren watched

Bensley fumbling around inside the case whilst trying to retrieve a pen from the inside pocket of his jacket which would not keep still for him. He did not inspire much confidence in his latest client. Still, he thought, at least he was not paying the hourly rate demanded by lawyers. Federation funds would be covering that.

Bensley examined several pro-forma documents before finding the relevant one.

"Ah, here it is," he said with some relief. He placed it on the table in front of Warren on the top of a two-year-old magazine dedicated to the restoration of classic cars. "If I can just get you to sign this here and here please."

Warren examined the paper and saw that it contained a great deal of miniscule printed content.

"Am I supposed to read all of this?" he asked with implied incredulity.

"That's entirely up to you D.C. Warren. It's just that I can't represent you until I have your signature here and here." He clicked the biro into action-mode as though it was a gun hammer being cocked and ready to fire.

"Fine," said Warren, who had diminishing faith in the individual sent to look after his legal interests. Whilst he had believed that Bensley was a law graduate, he found it more difficult to believe that he was capable of rendering him any real assistance. Manners alone prevented him from saying so.

Bensley held the paper in place until Warren had signed in both spaces. The completed form was dated and returned to the document case. Bensley summarised the proceedings as he understood them to be.

"Right, as I have been briefed, the police operation which resulted in the death of one Luke Gould was conceived and carried out largely by yourself. Is that correct?"

"Yes, that's right." Warren briefly thought about the line of supervisors who had authorised the sting operation and how none of them were there at the hearing. Bensley pressed on.

"The Coroner's inquest into Mr Gould's death and the murder case against one Gavin Malligan are both ongoing and are to be treated separately from the disciplinary proceedings we are here for today, okay?"

"I get that, yes." Warren knew that he sounded intolerant but was unable to motivate himself to alter his tone. It was unlikely to have been spotted by Bensley anyway.

"There is also the criminal matter of a drugs supply charge against Miss Candice Kendal. The CPS are considering whether or not to go ahead with that due to the tragic circumstances."

Warren saw no need to add to that and Bensley did not pause to allow him to anyway.

"Today's hearing will decide if it is appropriate that you be found to have breached the police disciplinary code. The allegation is that you put two people in mortal danger in order to effect the arrest of a known violent criminal. One of those people was killed as a result of that police operation."

"I followed all appropriate safety guidelines Mr Bensley."

"That is what this case hangs on, D.C. Warren. If we can establish that that you did carry out all reasonable measures and the death could not have been foreseen, there are no grounds for a finding of guilt on your part. However, if the panel decide that you could have done more, so to speak, they could bring in a decision . . . otherwise."

"And if it doesn't go my way, what am I looking at here?"

"There are a range of options, all the way from giving words of advice to immediate dismissal from the police service. Let's hope that doesn't happen." He ended on what he hoped was a lighter note.

Bensley stood and went to the door leading to the conference room being utilised for the hearing, assuring Warren that he would find out what was happening and report back to him.

Warren picked up the classic car restoration magazine but could not muster any interest in its glossy pages. There had been a time, in his teenage years, when he would have taken a keen interest in car publications. He had completed an apprenticeship at an engineering company and had built and raced stock cars at a club until he left to join the police at the age of twenty-one. He had been selected for transfer to the C.I.D. at twenty-six and moved onto the drugs squad at thirty. According to the last girlfriend he had had, a bank clerk called Rachel, he was obsessed with his work. It came first, last and everywhere in between.

Warren had been described by his peers and supervisors as being difficult to work with. What he saw as a commitment to getting the job done was seen by others as an obsession. He stayed later than anyone else and rarely socialised off duty. One Detective Inspector had warned him that he would 'burn himself out' if he continued to function as he was doing. Rachel had expressed similar views. She had been with him since his stock car days and the change in him had been a progressive spiral toward her leaving. She had since met a nice chap from a building society, and with him had led a more sedate and predictable life. Warren rarely thought about her, which had been the case for some time before she had decided to go.

Sitting outside the 'Headmaster's Office' awaiting the decision as to whether he could continue as a police officer, or if he could, in what capacity, he pondered the situation his life was in and how it had got there. He was not to know that Gavin Malligan, a known violent offender and big-time drug dealer, would turn up in person. He had done what he could with the intelligence available to him. Surely, they couldn't hang him up to dry for that. He couldn't deny that the blame had to be placed on somebody and all of the decisions made in respect of that disastrous sting operation had been made by him.

*

Upon hearing that his daughter had been in trouble with the police over drugs, Jonathan Kendal had initially refused to do anything to help her. She was, he had judged, an adult and capable of functioning without parental assistance. She was also an embarrassment to him, and he was quite prepared to never set eyes on her again. It was only at the insistence of his highly emotional wife that he had reluctantly taken some action. Denise Kendal had wailed and howled like a demented she-wolf, casting an intolerable gloom over their show-piece home near Harrogate. Jonathan was prevented from enjoying the less-family-orientated comforts he was used to in London, such was the strength of Denise's campaign. He could not see an end to it and in the sole interest of some peace he had engaged the services of an expensive London lawyer to represent Candice. Her brief was to keep Candice out of jail.

"Candice Kendal!" called the court usher.

Her voice echoed along the chair-lined corridor of the courthouse. Candice rose from her seat along with the drugs counsellor who called herself Cilla but was really named Marjorie. They entered the court and were guided to sit together on two movable chairs placed between the dock and the front advocate's table. A curt nod of approval and reassurance from Candice's lawyer, then the judge's door opened causing all present to rise.

Once in position in his seat, everyone else resumed theirs. The court clerk asked Candice to stand and confirm who she was before he commenced reading out the formal indictment. It related to her being concerned in the supply of a class A controlled drug.

"How do you plead?" he asked dispassionately.

"Guilty!" she answered lifelessly, like a spent force deprived of oxygen.

"Sit please," said the clerk.

Because she was due to give witness evidence in a forthcoming murder trial, Candice's court hearing was moved to a Crown Court in another county. It therefore avoided much of the press attention it would have received in the Crown Court in Manchester. Her guilty plea also served to make it less of a spectacle. The hearing began with a summary of the offences she faced, delivered by a prosecuting lawyer who appeared to have other cases weighing more heavily on his mind.

Candice's legal representative had organised an elaborate and impassioned plea for leniency for the defendant. Within minutes of the opening oratory of the case for her freedom, the untrained onlooker could have been forgiven for seeing Candice as the victim of a crime and not the perpetrator. Lured into the seedy world of drug abuse, cast aside by a cold and uncaring family (overlooking the vast sums of money being spent by that family on the wigged and gowned mouthpiece who was condemning their meanness) and drifted into the shame and degradation of the underbelly of society – a lamb in the lion's den of vile criminal masterminds.

Candice's appearance was an important element of the hearts-and-minds campaign unfolding in the courtroom. She wore a knitted cardigan, the like of which she had never worn in her life, a buttoned-up white blouse and a maxi-length, pleated skirt with sensible shoes. Her hair was tied back in a ponytail and she wore a pair of spectacles loaned to her by the lawyer's assistant for image purposes only. She came across as the epitome of a nice young woman who had been naïve and unlucky, preyed upon by the unscrupulous wolves of the drugs world, as the overly wordy lawyer had painted her. The judge would take some convincing of this.

The lawyer retuned her approach in light of the presence of a magistrate sitting in accompaniment to the professional judge. In a gesture intended to show that judges were not too far removed from normality, it had become the practice for magistrates to be included in the proceedings in the Crown Court, albeit not in any decision-making capacity. Knowing that it was compulsory for the Judge to consult the J.P. before reaching any decisions, Candice's barrister hoped that the J.P could be talked round to Candice's legal team's way of thinking and subsequently influence the judge's decision on sentencing. It could, gauged the lawyer, be like having someone on the defence team in the judge's chambers.

The underlying aim was to convince the court that Candice was like their daughter, niece, neighbour, teenaged friend, anyone who made a connection and reminded them of someone they felt obliged to help rather than punish.

Candice sat and her barrister stood. Occasionally glancing at the handwritten notes on her table, she summarised the circumstances of her client's sad tale. A well-brought-up, young lady from the countryside, cast adrift in the seedy squalor of the inner city, agreeing, under considerable peer-pressure to the consumption of narcotics in order to fit in with her new-found friends. Addicted and vulnerable, she was virtually forced to act as a mule for the distribution of drugs on the university campuses of the city. Her boyfriend had been largely responsible for her fall from social grace. Too proud and independent to ask for help but still claiming to have been manipulated by others, Candice, through her legal representative, pleaded numerous strands of mitigation in the sentencing options. The big one, the ace card, was delivered slowly and with acute deliberation. It relayed the trauma of seeing her boyfriend being hacked to death by a maniac with a machete, fearing that she was to be the next to suffer that fate and the subsequent nightmares and symptoms of bereavement.

The lawyer took the court on a journey of high drama, twists and turns and crafted empathy, steering her enraptured audience through the degradation of drug addiction to the redemption of rehabilitation and counselling. The girl could be clean for good, if only she was given a chance.

The court rose and the judge and magistrate adjourned to the privacy of the comfortable chambers behind the courtroom. Twenty minutes later, they returned to deliver a sentence. The judge did the talking whilst the magistrate did the benign smiling. Candice was given a suspended sentence on the drug dealing indictment. She was also ordered to comply with the Probation Service on a drugs rehabilitation programme and complete four hundred hours of community service of a kind chosen by her probation officer.

Jonathan Kendal's money had achieved the version of justice his wife had intended it to achieve. His home-life was no less stressful but his releases in the capital were once again open for him to enjoy.

CHAPTER FOUR

Gavin Malligan was the son of an Irish-born prostitute. In the early 1950s she had been a teenaged housemaid who naively fell for the charm of her landowner employer. She was instantly dismissed upon announcing her pregnancy. She left Gorey in County Wexford to go to London to have an abortion. She met a man on the ferry from Dun Laoghaire to Holyhead and never reached London. He took her to Cardiff where she got her wish, albeit in a damp basement beneath a second-hand goods shop. Indebted to her new gentleman friend and keen to experience anything that did not remind her of Gorey, she soon became dependent on opium and alcohol.

Because these things required paying for, she was put to work serving the needs of visiting seafarers. Whilst she worked and took her leisure in the pubs surrounding Cardiff docks, her practices surrounding self-preservation continued to be slack. Pregnant again but with less idea of who was responsible than she had been in Ireland, she left it too late for even the backstreet scraper to do anything about. She gave birth to Gavin on the kitchen floor of the unkempt home of a fellow streetwalker, giving him the name of one of the few men she had entertained whose name had lingered in her memory, although nothing else of him did.

She initially responded well to motherhood, making a noble attempt at clean living. With her excesses curtailed, she took a job as a school dinner lady. It was not to last. She returned to the streets and to drug abuse, even more voraciously than before, appearing to her peers to be hell bent on making up for lost time. She died of a drug overdose when Gavin was two.

Gavin's first foster parents had both been schoolteachers. They already had a daughter who was three years older than he was. Their ideal was to complete their family despite medical obstacles preventing a second child. Gavin was told that their house was his home and that they were his family now. Gavin was nearly three years old and showed no inclination to integrate. He resisted the cajoling, rewarding or denial of nice treats and did precisely what he pleased. Anything that was bought for him was systematically destroyed without any gesture toward explanation.

When the girl he had been encouraged to call his sister suffered a broken arm when Gavin pushed her off a wall, Gavin was counselled and asked to apologise. He refused. When he hit her in the head with the handlebars he had pulled off a bicycle, causing a hairline fracture of her skull, the social services were asked to take him away, a move which brought no protest from Gavin. The hapless family accepted that they were a one-child unit from then on. Gavin was told that the house was no longer his home and that they were no longer his family.

The second fostering exercise was to an army household. The man of the house was a twenty-year veteran, serving overseas through several campaigns during and after the war. His wife was a cleaner at the council offices. They had never been able to have children of their own so, in their forties, Gavin represented their last chance at a family as they perceived it should be. Gavin was told that that house was his home and that they were his family now. The soldier was, not surprisingly, disciplined and regimented in his daily routines and outlook on life. He tried to instil these ethics into Gavin but without success.

When Gavin's behaviour warranted it, he was taken aside and swiftly beaten with his foster-father's trouser belt. He displayed no emotion, nor any contrition. Frustrated and exasperated at making no headway in moulding Gavin into a child they could like, the soldier and the cleaner increased the degrees of punishment, hoping to find his breaking point. This equine approach just made him more wild, aggressive and destructive. Fatalities were narrowly avoided when he set fire to the lounge curtains. The fire was contained, and the soldier and the cleaner were able to resume living in the house. Gavin was told that that house was not his home and that they were not his family now. Gavin went to live somewhere else. They did not enquire where.

At the age of six, Gavin Malligan was placed in the first of his local authority run children's homes. He was assured by the social workers that he would be safe there. It was out of Cardiff, up in the semi-rural town of Brecon. It was populated with kids from across Wales, each with their own story, troubles and needs. Gavin saw it as just another temporary domicile and saw no reason to adapt his previous conduct whilst resident there. What he had not considered was that there were many bigger kids there, each with their own opinion as to how smaller kids should be treated. He was slapped and kicked for no better reason than he was there. The staff, rather than try to afford protection to their most vulnerable charges, were considerably worse.

An ethos of superiority through brutality was in place in order to gain sufficient compliance to achieve functionality in the place. The plain fact the Gavin was not bothered by any of the summary punishments was an insult to some and a threat to the power of others. He had to be forced to comply. Weekends spent in an understairs cupboard without light, food or drink tested him and did bring some semblance of hierarchy to him. He was at the bottom of it and he had nothing with which to challenge that. He was up against people, both adults and children, who were stronger than him. From the age of eight he was abused on a daily basis.

A fifteen-year-old boy from Swansea arrived at the home and soon singled out Gavin for his preferred choice of power-play. After one illicit encounter which involved Gavin being removed forcibly from his bed and being tied to a wall-rack in the gym store room, he suffered internal injuries which were explained by the staff as being self-inflicted and resulted in his swift return to the home as before and all of the abuse that came with it. Nobody would believe him now.

Gavin Malligan harboured thoughts of revenge and escape. His plan was to inflict greater suffering on those who had wronged him than that he had endured, then disappear and live wild, unaffected by the rules of a society he had never fitted in with. It was not simply his tormentor who was to be the target of his venom. Everyone who had lied to him about their home being his home, that he would be safe and those who had lied about the internal injuries he had suffered as being inflicted by himself, all liars! Anyone who lied to him was going to pay the price that these people had set. That children's home contained nothing and nobody who should be spared.

At the age of thirteen, he ran away and went to live hand-to-mouth with a prostitute friend of his late mother's. In a hovel of a dockside brothel in Cardiff, he did odd jobs for the women there and contributed when called upon to satisfy the needs of clients with unusual preferences. He had done it before, and he was not bothered by it. At least he was getting money for doing it.

When he could pass for an adult, he went on the road, committing petty thefts in order to eat and progressing to house burglary and robbery with violence. At the age of fifteen, the resentment he had willingly maintained toward the occupants of the children's home at Brecon, manifest itself in an eruption of his anger. He perpetrated a night-time arson attack, razing the building to the ground whilst watching from an elevated and unseen position on a nearby hill. He later heard that nobody had been killed in the fire and his thirst for vengeance remained unquenched. When he later heard that several of the residents and staff had moved to alternative council-run homes, he pledged to himself to find them and put right the wrongs of his childhood.

Three more children's homes in Wales were torched. One resulted in five fatalities. Gavin was never caught for any of them. He was, however, apprehended following a crime spree in England, which spanned Shropshire, Cheshire and Manchester. Whilst each of the police forces managed to pool their resources and send him to prison, no contact or link was made to the arsons in Wales. They remained unsolved.

Released into the new community of Manchester and placed in a halfway house by the probation service, he realised the increased potential of the City as compare to his previous environments. Manchester had more people, more crime and more addicts than he had known in Wales. Realising the money and status in dealing drugs, he started by running errands for a dealer then took over when the dealer got busted by the police, snapping up the needy customers and increasing prices whilst decreasing the potent content of the product.

Any dissent was met with an iron fist. He was known to use a sharp knife to score a line down the limbs of non-payers. Even after assembling a team of willing underlings, he frequently insisting on performing the act himself. He amused himself by speaking to the transgressor in a manner befitting a paediatrician soothing the fears of a small patient before switching in a heartbeat into an intimidatingly angry persona. The use of a sharp knife, whilst satisfactorily effective, was far from unique. He decided that his identity as a big-time player needed something else. When he held his first machete, it gave him a supreme sense of power. When he first cut another human being with it, that feeling sent him into ecstasy.

The first recipient of his new status symbol was a small-time dealer and addict called Timmins, who came from Moss Side. Upon failing to remit the required amount of cash, Malligan and four subordinates tracked him down whilst leaving his family home and took him for a drive to an underused part of industrial Salford. He was stripped naked and held by the arms and legs whilst Malligan slowly sliced into his skin with the machete. The lines ran the full length of his body from his neck to the soles of his feet. The incisions were repeated, in parallel, with clinical intensity, one centimetre away from the first cut, making any subsequent attempt at stitching the wounds impossible. Finally hurled into the River Irwell, where the wounds would inevitably be exposed to untold levels of infection, the debtor was rescued by a passer-by and hospitalised. As he gradually recovered from his injuries, his debt accrued interest. Malligan's interest in him also remained undiminished. Faced with further corrective measures, Timmins persuaded his parents to sell their car and other items of value in order to pay back the money.

Gavin Malligan built up a team of addicts desperate for the services he provided. He knew that the world he had chosen to exist in had its challenges. Other dealers posed a greater threat than the police. At least the police were unlikely to slit his throat as he slept. Keen to stay one or two steps ahead of the pack, Malligan deployed his posse to systematically inform on the rivals to the police. It didn't work every time, but when it did, he was swift to claim the client base build up by the newly incarcerated former dealer.

Sufficient information was gathered by the intelligence arm within the police to identify that Malligan was a player with ambition. He had no Achilles heel such as a wife or other family, he had no home or status in the traditional sense. His possessions appeared to be those of a pauper whilst his assets grew, and prosperity abounded.

He was approached by many people with requests for drugs. Introductions had to be investigated and he deployed his longer-serving minions to enquire as to the potential purchaser's authenticity. The possibility always existed that the buyer was an undercover police officer, or worse still, sent by a rival dealer. The usual screening process was to arrange for the buyer to commit an offence that was too serious for an undercover police officer to be able to justify. Killing two birds with one stone and resisting his urges to inflict the injuries personally, he ordered the physical corrections that were due to poor payers or those who had had their stash confiscated by the authorities to be administered by the new ones. This also served to demonstrate what they could expect should they fail in their obligations. Despite this atmosphere of high violence, the customers just kept on coming.

*

Police Constable Russell Warren reported for duty in newly issued uniform as he had been required to do at his new station, forty miles from his last one. The patrol sergeant took him into the office and welcomed him cordially. There was, as often happens in a hierarchical framework, a sense of shame and resultant pity when an officer who had been deemed to have been successful at something, finds himself down the snake to the bottom of the pile once again. The sergeant maintained a tone of benevolence toward the new man, although, unlike Warren, he knew that the management had other plans for him and that he was to be posted away from there very soon. That decision was to be disclosed to Warren by the Superintendent, who awaited him in an upstairs office.

Warren was escorted there and introduced by the sergeant. The Superintendent was named Brian Henville. He was in his late forties, well-groomed and habitually turned out in immaculate uniform and glass-finish, polished shoes. His mousey hair, thinning on the top, was cut as was the trend in the 1940s and his steel-rimmed spectacles complied with official police standards. He sat at his desk and when the sergeant knocked, entered and introduced P.C. Russell Warren, he remained seated. Warren stepped forward to shake the hand of the Superintendent. Henville looked at Warren's hand then down at the papers stacked neatly in front of him on the desk. His expression was less than welcoming.

"Sit down," he ordered and waved the sergeant away. Warren sat on the only chair on his side of the desk. It positioned him lower than the chair occupied by Henville. Once the door was closed, Henville wasted no time in expressing how he felt about the newest member of his staff.

"I won't beat about the bush Warren. I am fully aware of the circumstances which have brought about your transfer from the Drugs Squad, how your incompetence cost the life of an informant. I didn't want you here. I don't want the failures and rejects from other departments. This is not a dustbin for all of the inept officers of the county."

Warren hardly anticipated a tickertape welcome, but a prejudicially negative assessment of his character was something of a surprise. The guy was going to be a dream to work for.

"I try to embrace a challenge rather than avoid it, that's just my way," said Henville rising from his seat and turning to look out of the window in a statesman-like pose, "and what to do with you is a challenge I am willing to take on."

Warren was considering counting all of the insults he was receiving from this small-minded, self-important man.

"Don't think you're the first de-motivated, failed, specialised officer I have had to rehabilitate, oh no! There have been many, you're no different, ten-a-penny, people like that."

Warren decided that there were too many insults to count so he decided not to.

"I have two problems facing me this week, you are one of them."

There he goes again.

"The other is a duty that nobody wants to do. An important posting which needs to be approached with professionalism and commitment but, due to, erm, cultural obstacles, I have no volunteers for. Now, I have the power to order anyone I think fit to do that job, but why should I send an officer who has done nothing wrong to carry out such a role? No, beggars can't be choosers. You are to commence duty today on your new beat and you are in no position to object."

Warren tried to imagine a beat so unappealing that the boss was treating it as a sentence for the guilty. He could not produce any such possibilities in his mind. Henville paused for dramatic effect before delivering the verdict.

"You are to take up the vacant post at Heavem Hospital."

"A hospital?" he said, giving away his lack of awareness of the true picture, "Why would a hospital require a police officer of their own?"

Henville smiled a sardonic, twisted grimace. That Warren did not know what it meant to be given that role brought him a great sense of power, like a roman emperor about to signal the brutal demise of a slave.

"Don't worry, you will be fully apprised of the challenge that awaits you. Let's just say it will be very different from your Drugs Squad experiences."

"Okay, I get it, I get the bum job nobody wants. That's my punishment. I have a compromise in mind," said Warren in a tone of informality which was not to Henville's liking.

The Superintendent curled his lip to show his distaste, both for Warren and what he was about to suggest. Curiosity alone made him ask,

"Let's hear it."

"I don't intend to spend the remainder of my police service patrolling some hospital. I propose that we set a timescale for me to return to detective duties, dependent on my making a go of the hospital job, of course."

Henville stared intently for a few seconds before breathing in sharply. "You are in no position to bargain with me PC Warren, but, alright! I will support your return to the C.I.D. if you perform your role to my satisfaction."

Henville had no intention of playing fair but he thought it would encourage some productivity from Warren if he was allowed to believe that he was.

"Thank you, shall we agree on six months?" offered Warren. Henville was taken aback at the audacity.

"Twelve."

"Okay," said Warren and he stood up. "Will that be all then?"

"Yes. See the desk sergeant downstairs for your instructions."

Warren left the office thinking how supercilious Henville was, whilst Henville thought how arrogant Warren was. Warren went to the duty sergeant and told him what the meeting had been about.

"I'm going to be working at Heavem Hospital," he said.

"Oh!" started the sergeant, "Good luck with that place."

"Why, what's wrong with it? It's a hospital, right?"

"Oh yes . . . but it's much more than that."

*

PC Russell Warren was driven through the shopping hub then the industrial estates away from the main roads leading in and out of the town. The buildings became gradually less intensely placed until they ended altogether. Out of town and along hedgerow-lined country lanes, he began to wonder how far from the rest of humanity this hospital actually was. The road wound around crop-yielding fields firstly on the flat then ascending a steady incline, zig-zagging up the sloping side of a tree-covered fell. Fleeting glimpses through sporadic gaps in the hedges revealed commanding views but Warren's mind was on other things.

At the wheel was the patrol sergeant, an old cop by the name of Vinnie Davies, who had seen it all and was now nearing retirement. Warren found him agreeable company and put this down to the late-service apathy which made disliking people rather pointless along with most other aspects of the job. Davies asked about Warren's previous postings and mentioned people who they would have been mutually acquainted with. As they had worked at opposite ends of the county for all of their respective service, there were very few common links.

The road continued to rise, and the bends became sharper to cater for the incline. Wooded areas came and went and brought a relative darkness which, along with the twists and turns of the road, served to disorientate Warren. Davies did impart some encouraging snippets, such as that the Heavem job came with a flat for Warren's sole use. That would be welcomed, as the commute from his current accommodation would have been expensive and exhausting. It was also explained that this was a solo post. Officers could be called upon to assist him where needed but they were seven miles away at least so don't expect a swift response. Warren pictured a hospital ward full of half-dead patients having their temperatures taken by Wagnerian matrons. He could not perceive any immediate threat which might call for an urgent response from the town.

The road levelled off and passed through a more structured avenue of trees, each one the same distance from the next. The light from the cloudy sky flicked on and off as the tree branches allowed. An opening in the road ahead looked like a junction but without any road markings. The tree branches receded to give an aura of grandeur to the clearing. The car entered the ring of brightness and turned left to face a giant pair of gates, wrought-iron, black, ornately crafted and imposing. They were held up by two granite pillars, weathered and moss-covered with old-fashioned lamps set too high for anyone to reach. Davies stopped the car in view of a CCTV camera. He waited as the gates slowly crept open to allow their access.

The car hummed along a curved path of neatly trimmed splashes of greenery. It opened out onto a broad expanse of gravelled car park in front of a gothic palace of alarming size. Four floors high and, due to the dense foliage, wider than could be taken in from one static viewpoint. A grand protrusion of an entrance arch jutted out over the car park, held up by Greek pillars. The building was mesmerising with all but the doorway and windows covered with wall-climbing greenery, dotted with tiny pink and white blooms.

"Wow!" he exclaimed to Davies, "That's impressive."

"What has impressed you about it?" said Davies with undisguised cynicism.

"The ivy, all up the walls, it's pretty spectacular, don't you think?" The old sergeant was harder to please. He took in a heavy, slow breath and let it out equally slowly.

"It might look pretty but don't be fooled, lad. There are wasps in there and if you aren't careful, you might get stung."

Warren looked at Davies to help him to decide what he had meant. He gave nothing away in his expression. Was it to be taken literally or was there something deeper? Warren took longer to notice the six-metre high security fence which ran all around and out of sight at one side but not the other.

"Why would they need a huge fence like that? Who would break into a hospital?" he asked. Davies smiled.

"It's not to keep people out, son." Warren processed this information then said.

"What sort of hospital is this, Sarge?"

"For the mentally disturbed," answered Davies, "from the slightly mad to the downright crazy!"

Davies' layman's diagnosis created pictures in Warren's head, some from old pictures of a Georgian or Victorian bedlam, some from movies including 'One flew over the Cuckoo's Nest' and the rest were all from horror films. He had never worked a beat which contained any form of mental hospital before and he did not know what to make of it at all. He gained some perspective by reminding himself that the deal was for twelve months only. How hard could it be?

Vinnie Davies was known to some of the staff. No formal reception or other screening process took place. They entered the main building under the grand stone portico then walked along a corridor of high ceilings and old ornate plasterwork. The first port of call was the Operations Centre, part control room, part CCTV monitoring station and part planning department on the scale of the cabinet war rooms. Davies spotted the person he had come to find.

"Hello Heather," he said to a tall, bespectacled, middle-aged woman with short grey hair and a cigarette between her fingers, emitting smoke into her own face. "This is PC Russell Warren, he's the new beat constable for Heavem. Russell, this is Heather Fellhouse, she runs the place."

Heather switched her cigarette into her other hand and greeted Warren with an enthusiastic handshake.

"Hello Russell, who have you upset to get sent here?" Her quip may have been light-hearted, or maybe it carried too much truth in it to be humorous. That she was smiling, albeit in a jaded and fatigued manner, convinced Warren that she was at least trying to achieve levity.

"I just got lucky. I suppose." He gauged that she would be on the correct wavelength to appreciate irony. She was.

"Give me a minute and I'll give you the grand tour," she said before gathering her key chain and attaching it to the belt loop on her trousers. She slipped on a formal suit jacket to finish the corporate manager look and gave some indication of her planned activities to other members of staff. Vinnie Davies settled down to enjoy coffee. He had no reason to undergo the instructional oratory that Warren was about to hear.

Heather Fellhouse exuded competence of the sort that came of necessity in adverse circumstances. Warren gleaned that she was the sort of manager who did not miss any detail and did not forget what they were all there to do. Not the person to get on the wrong side of either. She had a no-nonsense manner which colleagues would either love or hate. This trait engendered a feeling of kindred spirit for him. She walked with some urgency along the corridor, pointing out the facilities and departments she had decided were of use to him to know. They passed out of the rear of the main building and into a wide, square expanse of grass, level at first but rising up a steady slope to a sandstone monument with a stained-glass window dominating its upper layer.

Heather distracted him momentarily.

"I take it that you are an experienced policeman?" she asked as a casual enquiry as to his professional antecedents. He read her intentions and obliged her with a summary of the towns and departments he had served in before asking her, albeit more directly, to so the same.

"Health authority admin originally, some project work, quite enjoyed that. Got promoted to something expensive and got sent here when my job disappeared in the 'black hole' of reorganisation. That was seven years ago. The challenge now is to keep the lid on this place until it's polite to finish. I won't be staying any longer. It's aged me by twenty years coming here." The humour she had earlier demonstrated was evidently absent from her words.

"Tell me about Heavem Hospital," he asked. Heather paused, in her stride and her conversation, to settle herself to answer that question.

"To call it a mental hospital is insufficient, it's much more than that. There are patients here who have spent decades just existing, they've never known anything else, tragic in some cases. Others have been born with any range of disabilities, mental and physical for some, poor souls. There are the ones who think they are Jesus, whilst some opt for Napoleon. We had one who was convinced he was a fish. Many of them can't function even at a basic level: feeding, toileting, breathing, you know?"

"I'm beginning to," offered Warren out of respect.

"There are wards for people who were born like that, you know, mentally handicapped, and wards for those who have become like that after accidents or illnesses that have caused brain damage. Then there are the 'voices in my head' lot. God only knows what's going on there. There are the ones who have tried to kill themselves. You have probably come across them in your time, I shouldn't wonder. They go into the wards for patients who they haven't decided about yet. Either way, you'll see it all here, in all of its glory.

"The ones who are obvious, they aren't the problem. You know where you are with them. The one's that I can't get my head around are those who look normal but don't say much. They are the ones who terrify me, you know?"

They crossed the expanse diagonally and entered a two-storey building of matching blackened sandstone. The doors were unlocked and locked again once they were inside.

"Then there's the kids' unit," she added.

"There are sick kids here?" he asked with some undisguised incredulity.

"Sort of. It's a children's home but for troubled children, behavioural problems mostly. There are hardly any in it at the moment, so they use the space to house kids who are just in need of somewhere to live, nothing wrong with them in my humble opinion. The psychiatrists would be able to explain it all in more detail, but they are kids and they are here. That's all I am sure of in that respect. The whole place has the atmosphere of a prison, that's on account of The Garrin Unit of course, but we have to try and make the youngsters feel like they aren't in one. Bloody impossible, in my experience but there you are."

"What's the Garrin Unit?" asked Warren in the course of amassing necessary information. Heather stopped walking and looked at him.

"Has nobody told you?" she said, expressing difficulty in accepting his lack of awareness.

"Erm, no," he said, appealing for her to enlighten him.

"It's high security, the reason for all the high fences and locked doors. All of the people in there are violent offenders who have been diagnosed as having some mental incapacity. The Garrin is the biggest problem in the hospital. Without that it might be manageable. As it is, with underfunding, understaffing and cutting corners everywhere, this place is a disaster waiting to happen."

"How do you mean, Heather?"

"I mean that there are some seriously dangerous people in The Garrin, people who should be in Broadmoor or Rampton. They put them in here to save money, I suppose. It's a poor substitute for the real thing."

Warren thought about the assessment Heather had presented him with as she continued to enlighten him about the different sides of the high fences and how on one side they were trying to kill themselves whilst on the other side they were trying to kill other people. It was a high-security prison inside a mental hospital, treating patients for complex disorders as well as incarcerating dangerous criminals. It was beginning to become clear why the running of such an establishment was as difficult as Heather had suggested. Warren was eager to know his place in this mix.

"What sort of things am I likely to be dealing with Heather?"

"On a good day, perhaps one of the kids might run off and you can catch them before they get too far. The family visits to The Garrin Unit can turn up some interesting stuff, especially when they are searched going in and coming out. Thankfully, most of them don't have any family who will have anything to do with them. There can be flashpoints of violence, often with no warning or reason. Some patients who haven't taken their meds can do things which would have ordinary people locked up and forgotten about."

"Such as?" he ventured.

"Sexual assault! That happens. Hard to deal with when both the attacker and the victim are incapable of expressing themselves. Perhaps I'm painting a gloomy picture for you on your first day. Sorry about that. I'd like to be balanced about it but there isn't much to be optimistic about. There's even a drugs and alcohol rehabilitation unit, The Bowers. The fact is that this place is for any soul who can't be allowed to exist in society where normal people are."

Warren thought that Heather's opinion could be applied on a wider scale. The staff may also belong away from the real world. He was now one of that breed. Superintendent Henville's difficulty in recruiting a volunteer to the Heavem Hospital beat was becoming abundantly clear.

Heather pointed out some of the buildings and their particular functions. Warren took in most of it but missed large parts. One part that did surprise him was Heather's revelation that there were still padded cells and straight-jackets available for use. She wafted a cigarette in a barely committed manner in the direction of the ward where that sort of thing took place. The images his brain produced sent a shudder through Warren. He had never thought that such things were real and still operating in Britain. This was the 1980s for Christ's sake.

"You need to meet the medical people. That's a must. Med. records are important too. If they like you, they'll tell you everything you need to know about the patients." Heather imparted advice in large amounts, although only small amounts were sinking in with him.

"And if they don't like me?"

"Aha! I speak hypothetically, there's usually a good exchange of information. You'll be fine in that respect. Bob was instrumental in establishing that."

"Bob? Who's Bob?" asked Warren. Heather stopped in her stride again.

"Oh dear, they really haven't told you anything, have they?" She paused and continued. "PC Bob Tasker worked this beat for years. Poor Bob."

Warren overlooked the 'Poor Bob' quip and focussed on a possible source of advice to enable him to hit the ground running.

"I'd like to meet with Bob, is he still around here?"

"No Russell, he isn't. Bob died a month ago. He committed suicide."

Warren's tour of the hospital departments took on a more desperate air, desperate in every aspect. He did not know enough about the late PC Bob Tasker to be able to form a balanced opinion. All he could think about was that he had worked this beat with all of its frustrations and challenges. Is that what Heavem beat does to people? He was determined to avoid taking on any unnecessary pressures, to keep a professional distance from the human tragedies which unfolded behind every door of this place.

"Oh! And there's something I ought to point out, Russell," she said.

"What's that?"

"Although you are quite right to call it Heavem, that's not what the locals call it."

"And what do the locals call it?"

"They call it Heaven!"

CHAPTER FIVE

Heather explained some folklore about the original sign across the gates got damaged in a storm which removed the end part of the letter M, making it an N, but she rationalised this by adding that few of the people around then could read so it probably was not true. Warren pondered instead on the irony. How a place which, to many, would be seen as a 'hell on earth' could be referred to as Heaven gave him a feeling of self-preservation through humour. Whatever gets you through the day.

The tour took over an hour and still did not cover every aspect of Heavem's functions. There was a commercial garden centre where patients cultivated plants to sell to the public elsewhere. Rows of greenhouses filled an expanse the size of a football pitch as human drones shuffled in and out pulling low trolleys of pot-plants and bags of compost. There was a laundry block which also took in paying customers such as hotels' linen and sports teams' kits. Heavem had a man in a van for this purpose. It was a far from welcoming environment for the public to visit. A sandstone church sat mournfully amid a copse of oak and sycamore trees, its windows unwashed behind protective wire mesh. Behind that was the Children's Unit, a sad attempt at a modern box of a building, two floors of prefabricated beige panels with matching cabin-lodge bedroom blocks next to it. Warren entered one of the oldest buildings and saw that it contained several wards as one would expect a hospital to look. Stairwells and more high ceilings, crumbling plasterwork invariably painted pale green and poorly illuminated corridors branched off in all directions. Grey-faced and medicated individuals shuffled by, some mumbling unintelligible syllables to themselves whilst some side-stepped as though they knew the path across a minefield.

Heather showed Warren everything she could in the time she had. All of it was accessed without a key. The secure parts would have to wait until another day. Finally, she took him along a single-track road through the woods to the back of the estate. There, close to the high fence of the maximum-security facility, was a row of twenty semi-detached houses, each with a garage and a front garden. Between the gaps, Warren saw that there were rear gardens too which all had hedges across the bottom to afford some privacy from prying eyes beyond the fence. Heather led him to the last house which had two doorbells indicating that it was divided into two flats. She opened the door to the stairs leading to the higher level, which was to be Warren's accommodation, should he wish to use it.

The flat was furnished with items which were old but still serviceable. It was better than a long commute. The tour over, Warren was taken back to the operations centre where he was given some keys to the flat and a small office in the main building. Sergeant Vinnie Davies was draining his third mug of coffee and getting ready to leave. Warren waited in a staff room containing a dining table, five chairs, three settees and a sink and kettle. Wired into the wall over the sink was a speaker with an on/off switch and nothing else. Music was coming from the speaker: a swing-band number that Warren was vaguely aware that he had heard before, but he couldn't name the tune or the performer. When the music ended, the velvet smooth voice of a man began speaking. Warren picked up a magazine in the manner of a dentist's waiting room. He flicked through it absent-mindedly. His attention strayed from the radio until he heard the word 'Heaven' being spoken. Recalling what Heather had told him about the local application of the word, he realised that it was a hospital radio station. He listened more intently and the voice said,

"There's a new face in Heaven from today, we've finally got a replacement for the late PC Bob Tasker, poor Bob. We miss you. But, when the odds are stacked against you . . . The new copper on the Heaven beat is called PC Russell Warren. We here at Heaven Radio wish PC Warren all the luck in the world. Oh boy are you going to need it!"

Apart from on police radio transmissions, Warren had never been mentioned on any form of broadcasting medium before. It felt strange. His previous work had required him to go to great lengths to keep his identity a closely guarded secret. Public acknowledgment was unhelpful in a Drugs Squad.

Davies drove Warren back out through the magnificent gates and along the wooded road towards town, explaining on the way that there was no police car available, but he could use his own car and claim a mileage allowance albeit frugally. Warren tried to put the information of the day into some order, hoping to make it all make sense. It was too much to expect that to happen in one day. Perhaps the next day would be less bewildering.

*

"So," began the silk-trimmed Q.C. as he flicked through case papers with impeccably manicured fingers, "is he mad or is he bad?"

The conference table in the barrister's chambers had served as the hub of many such pre-hearing discussions. Principal contributors included the briefing CPS lawyer and the Detective Inspector accompanied by the Detective Constable who had assembled the case papers. His role was to fill the gaps in the D.I.'s knowledge of the less compelling or otherwise interesting elements of the case. The barrister's question was in response to the introduction of the interim psychiatric report on the defendant Gavin Malligan. It had been a wordy document, including the examining doctor's impressive list of qualifications, the method of conducting the examination and the conclusions. The non-medical people present, which was everyone, skipped directly to the concluding opinion. It mentioned some psychosis which Malligan could have or might not have. Whilst he was a sociopath with advanced criminal tendencies, there was some suggestion that his troubled upbringing was a contributory factor. The issues of most importance to the prosecution were; could it be used by the defence team to establish that Malligan was not responsible for his actions when he had killed Luke Gould, and what could be done to counter that assertion? The consultation in the chambers took twenty-five minutes and was called to a halt to allow for another case to be deliberated in a similar fashion. Prosecutions were reviewed and debated in a 'production line' manner and nothing short of a judge telling them so would make the barristers involved invest more than the standard time and effort into them. The concluding decision was to await the completed psychiatric reports, the one commissioned by the prosecution and the one by the defence.

Meanwhile, in another legal office three hundred yards away, the legal team representing Gavin Malligan were pondering a copy of their own psychiatric assessment of their client. A second opinion has been prepared by a different expert, who was noted in psychiatric circles for expressing some controversial interpretations. The defence had been presented with an unofficial, early copy because the defence team had commissioned it and applied pressure to expedite its completion. The barrister, who, like the prosecution's man had arranged the appointment at 4.30pm in order to avoid any interference to his court commitments and earnings, was airing his thoughts about the case. He considered aloud how a juror may process the information.

"Is it logical," he began, not looking at anyone present, "for a man to actually kill someone in front of a witness, and in full awareness that the police were involved to the extent that they had been remotely listening to the preliminary conversation? And remember also that he was, allegedly, a drug dealer whom the police were desperate to apprehend. How desperate? Desperate enough to take extreme action?" The barrister was performing his oration to an imaginary jury. He continued. "The police indirectly arranged the meeting between Gould and Malligan, the witness Kendal was also there. The recording device having been rendered unserviceable, there is no corroboration of her account of any conversation for the last few minutes of Gould's life. In short, she could have killed Gould."

The solicitor and her junior were stunned by this suggestion, but they knew that such musings were the reason they were present, talking to the advocate who was to present the case in the High Court. The solicitor offered a suggestion of her own.

"As we are considering things from a potential juror's point of view, Candice Kendal has never done anything more violent than push a chap off his motorbike for a prank. It is asking a lot for a jury to see her as a killer, especially of her own boyfriend with whom there is no evidence of any discord."

The Q.C. placed his hands together by only the fingertips.

"Of course, we only have to introduce reasonable doubt. We don't have to prove that she killed him, do we?"

The solicitor, who had not represented Malligan in any previous case and had been chosen and well-paid for her services on the strength of her reputation, silently conceded that point with a curt nod of the head. The Q.C. went on.

"We also have the unnamed individual who, according to the version provided by the girl, sat in the front passenger seat and pointed a gun at the unfortunate pair. What is there to disprove that he killed Gould. Hmm? There is only the girl's evidence and she was a jabbering wreck by all accounts. As for the weapon, is there any evidence that our client had armed himself with it prior to the incident? I think not. Someone else could have introduced the weapon, which would suggest a lack of premeditation on the part of the defendant.

"We have so far considered merely three possible approaches to conducting the defence of this accused. The other I have in mind calls into question the mind of a man who would do what he allegedly did, whilst the police were only seconds behind him. Why did he not try to escape? Why walk into the waiting arms of the police bearing bloodstains from the victim? It is as though his grasp on the gravity of the situation was grossly lacking, which brings me to the report by the defence psychiatrist."

He picked up another document and the solicitor scrambled through her papers to find her copy of it. The Q.C. did not wait for her before pressing on.

"The prosecution is yet to receive a copy of this report and I want the disclosure of it to be kept until the last possible moment. Mr Malligan has been diagnosed after the second examination as suffering from a significant mental disorder. The key word there is 'significant!' Mr Malligan's actions are not those of a rational human being. He has conducted himself as one may without any consideration of the likely consequences. He could not have been in possession of his faculties when he did what he allegedly did and the prosecution will have a devil of a time trying to prove otherwise. His responsibility was diminished by a significant deterioration in his mental health and I therefore suggest that there is a real prospect of a conviction for manslaughter in this case."

*

The trial of Gavin Malligan was, by murder trial standards, short. Following the standard introductory addresses by the respective sides and a potted biography of the late Luke Gould, the forensic and pathological evidence was the first main strand of the prosecution case. Luke's family sat in the public area, occasionally sniffing and sobbing when the loss of their loved one and the austere and unfamiliar courtroom environment combined to be too much for them to take. Candice had never met any of Luke's folks. It was not the time to be doing so. She was emotionally fragile without that added obligation so, although she recognised that it would be polite and that it could help her to come to terms with her own loss, she did not meet any of the Goulds.

When the trial reached the pivotal point of Candice's testimony, it had been agreed that she could give her evidence from the relative anonymity of the other side of a privacy screen. Malligan could not see her, but the judge, barristers and jurors could. She was unable to speak for the first few minutes and the judge was nearing the point of abandoning the process. He reconsidered the case and how it could be progressed without her contribution. The prosecuting barrister appealed for some understanding and patience and reiterated the extent of the trauma this witness had endured. The judge conceded and, after a short adjournment, Candice took to the witness box and spoke of the events leading up to the death of Luke.

She spoke with relative fluency about how they had met at university and had become a close and inter-dependent couple. Questioning of a non-confrontational nature enabled Candice to ease into the role of testifying witness and her clear diction gave the jury the impression of a well brought-up young lady who had no place in such an unpleasant series of circumstances. She evoked sympathy among most of the jurors, although there were some who resented that Candice was from a privileged elite and was therefore too far distant from them to be liked or believed. For them, it was the defence lawyers whose forthcoming questions were to provide the focus of their prejudices and entertainment.

Candice was led with soothing tones through the story of the police operation in which she had accompanied Luke to the rendezvous with Malligan. A transcript of the recorded conversation up to the point where the transmissions were abruptly stopped was read to the court and Candice was asked to confirm its authenticity, which she did, albeit whilst fighting back tears. When asked about the moment when Luke was killed, Candice spoke, quietly but with an intensity which engaged both her supporters and her objectors alike. She said that they had been forced into the back seat of the car at the point of the gun which was being trained on them by the unidentified man in the passenger seat. The machete had been waved in their faces whilst Malligan shouted his anger at them. When the blade flashed across her, she had flinched and turned away. Through her entire body, she had felt the force of the weapon chopping into Luke's body and she knew straight away that he was dead. She had braced herself in expectation that she was going to be next but when she regained her bearings, both Malligan and the passenger had gone. Luke was seated next to her, a statue, lifeless and bleeding. She remembered little of the subsequent events.

When the prosecutor sat down and his learned opponent arose, the jurors took their opinions into the next phase.

"Miss Kendal, are you a drug addict?" The defence barrister wasted no time in cutting the carefully built image of the witness down to size. Candice was taken aback and did not answer the question quickly enough.

"I have asked you if you are a drug addict. Well, are you?"

"Yes!" she conceded.

"And is it not the case that you have recently been convicted of supplying controlled drugs?"

"Yes." she spoke more nervously than before.

"What you have failed to mention in your testimony is that you were, with your full awareness and agreement, sent by the police to entrap the defendant. That is true isn't it?"

"Yes, we were helping the police."

"You were helping yourselves!" The barrister raised his voice in an accusatory manner. His aim was to paint a picture in the minds of the jurors that it was Candice Kendal who was on trial and not Gavin Malligan. Piece by piece, he discredited her evidence, eking out every iota of supposition available to make the jurors hate her. Only when her previously found resolve had disintegrated and she had once again been reduced to mush did the judge put an end to her suffering and rein in the lawyer.

By comparison, the evidence of Russell Warren was of little interest. It had served to support the forensic evidence gathered from the scene by others and he did outline the key features of the police operation that had taken place. With consummate ease, the defence barrister worded all questions in a direction that suggested that Warren was acting without integrity in deploying Luke and Candice as he had done. He insisted that all reasonable measures had been taken in light of the information available. The barrister carefully avoided stating it outright, but his hints were shrewdly placed to create an impression of incompetence, dishonesty or both. Nobody was going to come out of those particular court proceedings with any dignity.

Even the Home Office pathologist with all of his qualifications and experience was not spared the savage words of the defence barrister. The pathology report described the scene and in particular the machete which was still embedded in Luke's clavicle and scapula, causing fatal injury to his windpipe and main artery to the brain. In the course of the examination of the body, the machete could not be pulled out without the application of considerable manual force. This, in the expert's view, probably saved the life of Candice Kendal who would no doubt have suffered the same fate if the machete had not become stuck. The defence barrister made strenuous verbal efforts to devalue this assertion. The judge intervened and ended the dispute by saying that it was a matter for the jury to decide.

It was the introduction of the psychiatric reports which became pivotal as the trial neared its climax. Although the wording differed, the central message was that Malligan did have a mental disorder of some kind. The issue within the issue was whether or not the disorder was treatable.

The jury retired to a private room and took three days to return their verdict. Malligan was convicted of murder. After his previous criminal convictions were read out, the judge passed the inevitable sentence of life imprisonment. His recommendation for a minimum term was not disclosed at the time of announcing the sentence. Later, in a letter to the Home Office, he recommended that

Malligan was to serve a minimum of twenty-five years before parole could be considered.

CHAPTER SIX

"I appreciate that you will have your reservations, but it's the best way forward Candice. I realise it won't be what you've been used to but there a lot of positives here," said Cilla whilst driving her Vauxhall hatchback north along the A road.

Candice gazed out of the side window, lamenting the emptiness of her existence. Luke was dead and she couldn't take anything to deal with how much it had hurt and was still hurting. He was the only person she had ever been close to. It wasn't because he was the love of her life, not like it was in the movies. They were both misfits who had gravitated together. She needed him to get her the drugs she craved, and he needed her to have someone to share the drugs with. Either way, they needed each other, and it had been to their mutual benefit. Candice had recently and belatedly experienced the revelation that she had actually enjoyed being needed. She doubted that she could ever feel that again. Nobody would need her, fully and without reservations as Luke had. Cilla, the well-meaning drugs counsellor who had tried very hard to help her may as well have been invisible. Candice could not muster the manners to show Cilla any respect or appreciation, but she couldn't show herself any either.

Cilla glanced sideways at Candice then looked back at the road ahead. She waited to see if Candice was going to speak but nothing was forthcoming. Cilla could not bear the silence.

"This way it's all done in half the time. You get full-time rehabilitation treatment, residential, no worries about getting there every day and you can make a start on your community service too. I'd say that's the best way of doing both, don't you?"

Candice shrugged without uttering any sound hoping that Cilla would stop trying to conduct this, or any other conversation. Cilla's discomfort with the silence was too strong.

"In a couple of months, you could be clean, drug-free and with no obligations hanging over you. Free to get on with your life, now that's a reason to be positive, eh Candice?"

Candice let out a heavy breath of air and sank lower beneath her seatbelt.

"Well, there's no alternative, unless you want the probation officer to go back to the court and ask that you'd prefer to be in prison." There was a sharper and less tolerant tone to Cilla's voice. Even she had limits to her patience. Candice felt beaten down and she had no choice but to play along.

"So, what's this place called, where we're going now?"

"It's called Heavem Hospital. It has many different departments and you will be meeting people who are a darned sight worse off then you are. It would do you no harm to appreciate that. God knows, you don't appreciate much."

Candice found a small scrap of increased respect for the new, intolerant Cilla. Perhaps she should have been like that from the outset instead of all of that do-gooding, hand-wringing nonsense. Candice was beginning to think like her father, a thought that sent a chill through her.

All subsequent conversation was minimal. They left the A road and passed through some residential areas before the wooded road took them up to the huge gates of Heavem.

"Welcome to Heaven," said Cilla smiling.

"Did you call it Heaven?" asked Candice, doubting her own hearing.

"It's what the locals call it. You can work out for yourself why they do that."

"The gates of Heaven," said Candice with equal degrees of cynicism and irony. "Where the sinners come to be judged."

"You've already been judged," observed Cilla, who was feeling raw about speaking so sharply to Candice. 'It's all about trust,' was the mantra for drugs counsellor training. She had to win some back. "You're not here as a sinner, you're here as a patient who needs some treatment and whatever they have you doing for your community service, it's up to you whether you see it as a punishment or as an opportunity."

Passing through the high gates and up to the grand, foliage-covered, stone building, Candice spared it little more than a glance. The car came to a stop and they walked with Candice's two items of luggage into the main building. Candice was administratively admitted by the staff went slowly but without incident. She watched the movement of people and was able to satisfy herself that she could differentiate between the staff and the patients. She watched the shuffling, grey-eyed, long-term residents passing along the corridors. She heard their mumbling and groaning at no-one in particular and she took in the contrasting smells that came along with that: Disinfectant, body odour, clothes overdue for laundering, damp in the plasterwork of the walls. The combination of smells made her feel sick. How was she expected to suffer two months in this awful place?

*

Malligan was taken by secure transport to Walton Prison in Liverpool where all newly convicted prisoners were admitted for initial assessment and appropriate categorisation. Before he had passed through the gates, he had formed a plan to get out of prison and reclaim his freedom. His legal advisers were privy to the initial stage of it, which was to get him transferred to an institution which had a level of security more suitable for his needs.

The psychiatric reports presented at his trial were ignored. An expert opinion for a trial carried a different purpose from one in a prison. There was, effectively, another assessment carried out by the prison medical experts. It was vital to his scheme that Malligan was documented as being unfit for prison life. He had been coached by another solicitor, one with expertise in representing the mentally ill, as to what he should be doing to achieve the desired result. The assessment was to take place within his first week at Walton. He had no time to waste in creating the effect. Conducting conversations with imaginary people was a part of it, as was the eruption of verbal anger with no provocation. Playing the role of the captain of a ship in a storm whilst bouncing off walls was particularly convincing. Although he harmed himself several times, he was careful to avoid inflicting actual violence on others. That, he was told, may result in a move to somewhere with higher security not lower. By the time of the formal assessment, he had purposefully denied himself sleep, food and drink for several days which gave him the pallor of a zombie.

It was clear to the prison doctors that Malligan did not belong in a mainstream prison. It was, until recently, the standard practice in such cases for the prisoner/patient to be transferred to one of the big hospital facilities for convicted prisoners with diagnosed mental disorders. It was never publicly documented that all mental facilities were full and as a cost implication, it was preferable for prisoners in Malligan's category to be housed in one of the smaller, more cost-effective alternatives. A few were approved for overspill purposes and as a temporary option only. This edict was not adhered to.

The Garrin Unit, where fifteen of the twenty-three inmates being housed and treated for serious mental disorders had been resident there for over ten years, became Malligan's new abode. The most striking difference between him and all of the others was the seventeen million pounds stashed in bank accounts in Switzerland, the Cayman Islands and the British Virgin Islands which awaited him on his return to freedom. He had been incarcerated by the state before and had hated it. What had made it tolerable was his ability to understand how prison functioned and how he could work it to his advantage. There was an unwritten pecking order in prison and Malligan knew how to get himself at the business end of that. The same simple approach had proved universally effective. He had to make a judgement about which of two weaknesses an individual had. It was always either one or the other. Fear or greed.

Whoever commanded the most fear was the emperor of that place, the top of the food chain. Criminal hierarchies on the outside had a lot to do with it but, on the inside, the rules were different. If a man could be made to fear, then he was where he deserved to be – lower in status than whoever it was they were afraid of. If fear did not work, he could be bought. Drugs, contraband, money, favours for family, were all standard currency in the power-framework inside Her Majesty's prisons. Malligan anticipated that the same approach would work in Heavem Hospital. He was wrong.

His cell was referred to as a room even though the furniture was bolted to the floor and walls. All sharp edges had been filed smooth and there was nowhere on which to attach a ligature to attempt suicide. In the solitude of his room, he spent his time planning. Using his brain to work things out, create a structure to achieve what he wanted to achieve, avoiding the urge to fantasise about what he would do when released or who he would get even with first. That would wait. There were seventeen million reasons sitting in overseas accounts that made it all worth waiting for. He was prepared to wait in order to do things properly – but he would not wait a minute longer than was necessary.

One notable difference to life in prison was that there was no formal work detail to break up the daily grind. He had done kitchen and later library duties on his previous spells behind bars. They had been seen as soft options and had been given to him by a prison management who had decided to appease rather than challenge his unofficial authority. It was simply easier that way.

In a hospital for the mentally ill, activity which could be likened to a prison work detail was called therapy and was constantly supervised. This was partly because the patient's progress had to be monitored and partly because they were likely to harm themselves or others at a moment's notice. Although their titles indicated that the staff were nurses, their roles were more like prison officers. It was the presence and activities of psychiatrists and therapists that prevented Heavem from being perceived as a mainstream prison.

Association periods were important in prison, especially if the regime was a twenty-three hour a day bang-up. Deals were done, power exerted, business carried out and the madness of cabin-fever averted to some extent. In the communal activities in Heavem, it was different. Nobody knew where they stood in that place, who was top dog, who could be manipulated. Normal rules were hard to establish where nobody knew why they were there. Malligan thought this through and looked for ways to make life easier for himself - in the short term in any case. Longer term plans were in shape but on hold.

A group therapy session was convened in what was called the Paris Suite. There was no obvious reason why it was called that. It was a square room with nothing in it but a circle of stacking chairs under a skylight window. Seven patients were brought in, each accompanied by male nursing staff and seated three feet apart. Their hospital-issue clothing all had broad yellow strips sewed along the sleeves and legs. Two therapists in white medical tunics joined the circle, one had a notepad and pen and a tape recorder.

The lead therapist was a woman who spoke very good English but with a distinct Dutch 'shhh' on the end of some of her words. She introduced herself as Clara Van Der Brea. She explained the purpose of the assembly and spoke of how she had become a therapist because she wanted to help people to help themselves. Her voice was non-threatening and warm. Her accent was barely noticeable after a minute. There was a set and formatted opening speech about everyone being able to express themselves freely. She appealed for an ethos of mutual respect and support. The truth was always the acceptable approach to group therapy. She talked about some of the things she liked to do and mentioned that she enjoys cheese. Clara appealed for anyone to say who they were and share with the group what they liked.

"Who would like to start us off?" she said spanning her gaze across the group as she did so.

"Arthur Elevand," said a man seated next to Clara. She looked at him with an expression of relief that at least one of the group was prepared to participate.

Elevand was twenty-eight, prematurely middle-aged with a sunken chest and protruding belly. His weak chin and prominent Adam's apple gave him the look of a cartoon reptile.

"Thank you, Arthur. What sort of things do you like?"

"Pictures," answered Arthur Elevand innocently.

"Okay, what sort of pictures, Arthur?"

"Upside down pictures," he answered causing a slight giggle from some of the other members of the group.

"Why are the pictures upside down, Arthur?"

"So that the blood doesn't drip onto the carpet."

Clara chose to steer the conversation onto less macabre images. "Anyone else want to tell the group what they like?"

There was a pause which Arthur tried to fill but he was gently discouraged by a raised hand from Clara. Another person chipped in.

"My name is Jeremy, Jeremy Pilkington. I'll tell you what I don't like, women!"

"Thank you, Jeremy, but this part is about what you do like, we can talk about what we don't like later. What do you like?"

"I like grass, in the summer when they cut it, the smell, I like that."

"Good, thank you Jeremy. Who else will tell us something they like?"

A stone-faced, heavily built man with a double-chin, dark eyebrows and darker eyes sucked air in through his nose then let it out slowly. In a heavy, eastern European accent he said,

"Goulash! It is dish from my home country. I like it."

"What's your name please?" asked Clara, managing to keep the tone of her voice consistently non-confrontational.

"I am Bela Ferenquelar - Doctor Bela Ferenquelar. I am real doctor, a surgeon, not like you. You talk, talk,

talk. I operate. I remove the problem, what you do is . . . not being doctor."

The conversations were not going the way Clara had hoped they would go but she was experienced enough to know that they were unlikely to in such an environment. She called upon the other therapist present to help her by telling of something he liked.

"Andy, what do you like please?"

"Erm Hi! I'm Andy Aberfoyle," he began in a Manchester accent which Malligan was used to hearing, "and I like Rock music."

Malligan was seated next to Aberfoyle. He looked closely at him and tried to work him out. He had a nervous manner which showed itself by constantly clicking the button on his pen and rapidly tapping his foot against the leg of his chair. He had operated the recording device which was on the floor at his feet. He was not writing very much on the notepad. He glanced momentarily sideways at Malligan who saw something in Aberfoyle, something fleeting, something he had been looking for.

It was fear.

Now all that was needed was to work out what he was afraid of and give it to him. There was nothing to be gained by mindless torture of the weak. It was far more productive to exploit that weakness in the cause of profit. To identify what that sad, little man could do for him was the issue. Aberfoyle worked in an environment whereby it was usual to be surrounded by unpredictable and violent people. That alone was not enough to cause fear, there had to be something else. Clara Van Der Brea brought the focus of the session back where she wanted it.

"Thanks for that Andy. Who else wants to have a go at that, hmm?"

She looked around and settled her gaze on a small man with a creased face who looked as though he had been crying since before the session had begun. He was in no mood for taking part. He pressed his hands to the sides of his head and with increasing volume said.

"No, no, no, no!"

Clara picked up on the distress of the man. She had seen him do this before and knew his name already.

"Okay, that's okay Lawrence, it's fine. You don't have to do anything you don't want to."

The session was once again on the brink of descending into farce. Faced with an early return to his secure room, Malligan sought to keep the session going, albeit on his own terms.

"I am Gavin Malligan." All fell silent, including the previously distressed Lawrence. Clara nodded her approval for Malligan to continue. "I like to know things, like what's happening and who's who, you know?"

Clara was happy to let it end there and move onto another contributor but Malligan was not finished.

"Right now, I'd like to know what's going on. I want to know what the fuck we all did to get ourselves locked up in this shit hole. Who else wants to know that, huh?"

Clara was struggling to steer the conversation back to where she had intended it. It was not going to be easy. Malligan took control.

"So, who's going to start us off? What about you Jeremy? Why did they put you in here?"

Clara interjected,

"I really don't think . . ."

"Nobody gives a flying fuck what you think, Sweetheart. You wanted us to speak freely and tell the truth. We want to know what Jeremy here has to say."

Jeremy was eager to tell all.

"Those women, they made me do what I did, with their skin and their shoes and . . .and . . . I had to. I couldn't let any of them live."

Jeremy had begun to rub his groin in evident, sexual arousal. Malligan had the feeling he had read about that guy in the newspapers at the time he had committed multiple killings. He found the sexual activity Jeremy was performing very funny.

"Well, that explains him," he said. "What about you Doc? They don't lock people up for being a doctor."

"Nobody here is doctor, only me," said Bela Ferenquelar with unbridled contempt, "I not explain my work here. Only patients have right to know."

"So, you killed a patient, right?"

"Gavin please, this is – "

"Let the fat bastard speak. Go on goulash man. You killed a patient? They don't send you here for doing that."

Bela turned his head slightly to look at Malligan, then at Clara.

"Better to die knowing than to live in ignorance. All of them knew, I told them."

"How many?"

"Thirteen, they say."

"Fucking priceless, you killed thirteen people?"

"They were sick."

"That's fuckin' rich coming from you," said Malligan who was enjoying the chaos, "look around fatboy, we're all sick!"

Arthur Elevand nervously interrupted Malligan's party and re-entered the arena saying.

"Wh .. what about you? What erm did . . did you do?"

Clara had begun signalling for Andy to summon help.

"You really want to know do you?" asked Malligan. Arthur nodded sheepishly.

"I stuck a blade in a guy's throat and killed him because he'd pissed me off and I'm in here and not jail because I don't give a shit about it. That makes me a fucking loony like all of you! So, go on, who did you bump off?"

The footsteps of the nursing staff could be heard along the corridor. Arthur was keen to explain himself.

"They had to die, I had to stop them, they were going to clone Hitler. Imagine, a whole army of Hitlers. They had to be stopped, don't you see? I knew, I'd found out what they were doing - and they were my . . . "

The keys could be heard rattling on their chains outside the door.

"They were your what?" repeated Malligan. Elevand resumed his earlier calm and said.

"My parents, of course!"

When the door came open and the team of six male nurses entered, everyone in the circle was silent. There was no evident suggestion of any danger of physical harm to anyone. Clara looked perplexed and flustered. Andy had lost some colour in his cheeks and his pen was vibrating in his shaking fingers. Malligan sat impassively, waiting to be escorted back to his locked room. He looked at Andy Aberfoyle and saw lines on the insides of his wrists, old, whitened scars. That was what he wanted to know - that guy from Manchester was afraid of everything.

CHAPTER SEVEN

Russell Warren's first few days at Heavem went without any notable incident. He set out to introduce himself to patients and staff alike, each one making their own unique impression on him. The staff tended to express the same jaded views that Heather Fellhouse had displayed on his first visit. They had been ground down into a 'get through this day' existence rather than exercise a profession, with all of the respect and job satisfaction that comes with that. Staff morale was crumbling at the same rate as the buildings.

The patients imparted their feelings in a variety of ways. Some were child-like in their manner, rushing up to say hello to the policeman. 'The policeman is my friend' was the mantra and whereas it was immeasurably preferable to any confrontation, it did require levels of patience he was not accustomed to employing. Some patients were more cautious, keeping a wary distance from the new cop. They were, in some ways, also child-like but of the 'He'll put me in jail' school of thought. Warren decided not to try to overcome such barriers, partly because he had little idea how to and partly because he was only going to be there for a year. He felt no need to ingratiate himself with everybody.

There were a great many elderly patients, shuffling like the undead of a black and white B movie, through the tall corridors and well-worn footpaths of the complex. Uneven teeth, drawn and darkened eyes and papery skin. A lifetime, in some instances, of experimental medication.

The usual substances prescribed were mentioned so often by the staff that, for the layman, it was like another language to be learned.

Warren's first proper deployment came on a Thursday after sunset. A long-term patient called Phyllis had failed to return from her customary stroll around the grass square. With the help of the night nursing staff on Phyllis' ward, Warren was able to begin a search of the grounds but as the hospital covered seventy-acres, the search had to be specific and needed some help. He phoned the night Inspector at the town police station to ask if any uniformed patrols could be spared to assist in the search. The answer was 'No.'

It crossed Warren's mind that Superintendent Henville had issued a general directive that help should not be made available to him. He dismissed that as irrational. He was not usually prone to such paranoia. The lack of adequate resources which had contributed to the death of Luke Gould was nothing to do with Henville. That was just the way things were and he had to make the best of it.

He took a torch and searched the gardens and out-buildings nearest to Phyllis' ward. Moving in a wider arc, he looked around the garden centre, peering into the long greenhouses which did not conceal any secrets. The temperature steadily dropped making Warren wish he had employed another layer. What effect such a chill would have on a frail old patient was a gloomy prospect.

Warren checked in at the ward again to report that he could not find Phyllis but would keep looking. He asked the staff for suggestions which generated the retelling of unsuccessful endeavours of missing patients of the past.

By midnight, they had all but written Phyllis off and made her bed available for someone new.

He did establish that the last person to see Phyllis was a male patient called William who occupied a bed in the ward next to Phyllis' on the first-floor corridor of the main building. The night nurses woke William and brought him in his pyjamas, dressing gown and slippers to the day room to speak to PC Warren. William was neither one of the ones who were pleased to see him nor one of the cautious ones. He looked about thirty and had a comparatively healthy build when measured against the other patients. His most disturbing feature was the constant trickle of saliva emitting from his permanently open mouth. His tongue lolled out of the corner of his mouth and his jaw moved as though half-heartedly chewing an imaginary object. William's speech was affected by his apparent inability to control his mouth. His words, though delivered slowly, were difficult to comprehend. Warren needed the staff to interpret the elements he could not make sense of.

They did gather that Phyllis had been seen walking along the wooded path toward the old reservoir. Mains water now flowed freely through the pipes of Heavem but it had originally relied on a man-made water source, built on a hill for gravity to do the rest. Warren pictured Phyllis floating face down in the disused pond, a thought he tried to dismiss as he thanked William and set off to find the reservoir.

Limited moonlight peeped through broken black cloud to allow Warren to get some bearings from which to find the path. His torch did the rest and he soon ascended the slope to the steep soil and grass covered walls of the reservoir. He spotted a metal ladder fixed to the wall and rising up to a curled rail over the coving stones at the top. It looked as though nobody had used it for years, Moss, twigs and rust combined to make the climb precarious. At the top he saw the full magnitude of the structure. He could see an expanse of stagnant water the size of a football pitch with enough spare capacity for the water level to rise another forty feet. How deep the black water actually was could only be estimated. He scanned the surface of the water with his torch, occasionally helped by the moonlight when the clouds parted. There was no sign of Phyllis.

Warren clambered gingerly back down the ladder and walked around the far side of the reservoir. At the point where the ground was lowest, and the wall was highest, there were some ancient brass valves over broad cast-iron pipes. The pipes sprang from a concrete platform which was wildly overgrown with vegetation. Warren moved lower down the hill and saw that there was an opening beneath the brass valves, a man-made cave constructed to facilitate the egress of the stored water. A negligible trickle ran out of the abyss and down the hill. Warren shone his torch into the void.

"Hello?"

His voice echoed back to him. He could have left it and carried on with the search and a loud part of his brain was saying that he should but, despite the damp and neglect of the opening he was crouching down to enter, he shuffled sideways as though to brace himself from a frontal assault. The water on the inside of the walls dripped and more fell on him from the concrete top. The ground beneath him felt like a soaked sponge and then his boots were in water up to the laces. He judged that the walls of the reservoir must be near and should indicate the end of the cave. He moved a foot forward into the black water, half expecting to step into some deeper water and lose all traction. What he did step into did make him fall forward dipping his right knee into the cold water. He cursed at his own clumsiness and held the torch away to keep it from the water. An unserviceable torch was the last thing he needed. When he regained his footing he scanned the scene with the beam. At his feet was the back of a head with a mass of wet and thinning grey hair. Warren pulled at the clothing as a reaction to what he had seen. The wizened form turned over, its eyes fixed open and all life extinguished. Warren caught his breath on the intake. He settled in a few seconds and solely to appease himself he said.

"Oh Phyllis, what on earth made you come down here?"

*

The alcohol and drugs rehabilitation unit in Heavem Hospital was call The Bowers. It accommodated up to eighteen people and had the atmosphere of a poorly funded seaside hotel. The lounge was a large rectangle with windows on three sides and high-backed upholstered chairs lining the walls, each chair of a different design, age and state of wear. A kitchen which allowed residents to prepare their own meals took up a similar floor space to the lounge. It had an alcove with two washing machines and two tumble dryers, also past their best. The whole building was amateurishly decorated and some of the curtains were too short or too long for the windows that they hung over. Cracks in the plasterwork and pieces of coving missing from the top of the walls together with threadbare carpets and rugs bearing insufficient numbers of tassels added to the sadness of the facility.

Candice's first emotion was to feel her heart sinking. However, the mood she had arrived in had not allowed much depth for her heart to sink lower than it already was. Forgetting the deportment tuition and ballet lessons which had taken up so much of her early development, she sauntered, round-shouldered up the creaking staircase to the room she was to occupy during her recovery. The room was the same as the rest of the house but there were two beds. She was not enthused by the idea of sharing with a stranger. She pictured some noisy, aggressive alcoholic spewing forth their venom at whoever happened to be near. Closer inspection showed that the second bed was not presently occupied which afforded her a modicum of relief. She placed her case on her new bed for the staff to search it and her. Both searches were intrusive and invasive. There was no way any illicit substance would get through to undermine their good work. The member of staff who was admitting her wrote Candice's name in thick, red, marker pen on a small, white card. He slid it into a frame on the outside of the bedroom door.

When she returned to the admissions desk at the bottom of the stairs, Candice was asked to sit whilst the paperwork was completed. The staff wore non-nursing clothes but did wear identity badges to eliminate any doubt as to who was who. As Candice sat on the only chair, she listened to the low and tinny sound of a radio-set fixed to the desk and connected by wire to a socket on the wall behind. A piece of orchestral music predominantly played on harps emanated from the single speaker. When the music stopped, a velvet-smooth male voice said.

"*The day is getting brighter here in Heaven.*" It was the first confirmation of what Cilla had told her about the local interpretation of the hospital's title. The voice continued,

"A big welcome to any new arrivals, we hope you feel the warmth and fellowship that can only happen in a place where nobody really wants to be. It says a lot about the power of the human spirit that people can find loveliness in their surroundings. It's all up and away from here on in. Heaven Radio wishes you every happiness on your personal journey, pilgrim. Good luck!"

By the time the music resumed, Candice was almost convinced that the radio presenter had been talking directly to her and her alone.

After a dinner of pasta and a shape of reconstituted chicken in breadcrumbs which Candice prodded with her fork more than she ate, she took a tablet prescribed by an unseen doctor and retired to bed. The medication worked its magic and she knew nothing more until she was awoken by a male and female nurse to help to prepare breakfast, which, in The Bowers, meant 6.30am.

Breakfast around the long kitchen table involved sixteen people. Some looked like hospital patients whilst some appeared fully fit and healthy. They were mostly men, but Candice spotted at least four women. She managed to avoid making eye contact with anyone and therefore achieved the degree of invisibility she desired.

The day unfolded to reveal what Candice was expected to do. Cooking, vacuuming, washing-up and laundry routines were displayed on replaceable wall-charts in the kitchen. Her name was added in several vacant spaces which meant little to her as she had never been required to perform such tasks before. As the gloom was about to descend on her again, she recalled Cilla's advice the day before, 'It's up to you whether you see it as a punishment or as an opportunity.' Realising that her time there would drag unmercifully without some activity, she made a conscious decision to participate in the daily functions of The Bowers.

A mid-morning assembly took place in the lounge. She was introduced to the rest of the gathering which made her cringe with embarrassment. When invited to do so by the chairing therapist, Candice gave her name and said hello. That was enough to begin with. She heard the others speak about how they were feeling that day. There was a supportive atmosphere which was actively encouraged by the group leader. When she was invited to express how her day was going, she uttered minimal words without really saying anything, giving them what they asked for, not what they wanted.

The afternoon took Candice to the main building where the wards housed long-term residents. Entering the high-ceilinged wards, so formal when compared to her surroundings in The Bowers, she felt as though she was a reluctant relative visiting a patient in an austere and outdated hospital in an old movie. The smell was dank and the air stagnant. Even the disinfectant smelled old.

The nursing staff had no time to waste in familiarising the new helper in the ways of the wards. They had been given ex-cons on community sentences before and had frequently been disappointed with their contribution. Several patients had been selected to go to the day room along the corridor for some activities aimed at keeping their limbs working. Candice was told to walk with an evidently handicapped male patient called Harry. He was virtually toothless and breathed loudly and heavily. He walked slowly and hunched forward, his grey trousers of man-made fibres trailing in the floor behind him and his yellowed shirt hanging out at the front like a comic schoolboy. Candice looked away in involuntary repulsion at the hopeless specimen she was expected to escort. Harry beamed a gummy grin at her, but she did not return that sentiment. Had she eaten more she could have vomited at that moment. She moved slowly along the corridor with Harry holding her arm. The full picture reminded her of a dystopian apocalypse-scape, the medicated mass of barely human shapes rocking from side to side as they tried to walk stiff-legged across the linoleum-covered floor. As they passed through a pair of tall cream-painted doors, Harry began a coughing fit of deafening proportions. Candice shrank into her clothes. She couldn't let go of him for fear of him falling over. They reached the day room, and everyone sat down to recover from the walk before embarking on the exercise regime.

There were ten patients, three nurses or therapists, it was hard to differentiate, and Candice was the only lay volunteer. Activities included throwing small, coloured beanbags to each other and catching them. Very few of the patients' throws resulted in catches. The names of the other patients were revealed as the activities progressed. There was a man with both arms twisted inwards and an owl-like ability to turn his head around. His name was Wesley, he could not catch anything as his hands were permanently inverted and he invariably looked the other way at the optimum moment. Candice soon tired of reaching down to pick up the beanbags from Wesley's feet. When he reached out and ruffled her hair she recoiled in abject disgust. Her expression made no secret of this.

Another patient was called Mike. He brayed like an asthmatic donkey and Candice could not tell if he was happy or suffering. Mike's noises did make it difficult for anyone to hear the instructions being issued. Having not experienced this session before, Candice found herself at a distinct disadvantage to the others. Mike's hand-to-eye coordination was little better than Harry's which meant more things to pick up off the floor for Candice.

Another patient, a woman called Brenda, found a distraction in Candice which made her lose interest in the bean-bag activity. She tried to engage Candice in friendly conversation, but her pronunciation made it a challenge to understand her.

"Et moo me, et moo me!" she said pulling at Candice's sleeve. Candice looked at her, then at the main therapist for some help in understanding. Inside, she simply wished that Brenda would stop and leave her alone. The therapist, who was used to Brenda and her habits, came to her aid.

"Brenda is saying 'excuse me.' She wants to talk to you," he said.

"Erm hello?" tried Candice, hoping that would satisfy Brenda's desire to communicate. It didn't.

"Ooo me my fen," said Brenda.

"What?" said Candice giving away her distaste as well as her frustration.

The therapist who was too busy running the session to dedicate too much time to interpreting explained in brief.

"Brenda wants you to be her friend. That's right isn't it, Brenda?"

"Ha yeah, ha yeah," confirmed Brenda in her own way.

"Sure," said Candice, "I'm your friend, okay?" hoping that she would finally be placated. It appeared to work, at least it did until a red beanbag landed on the floor in front of Brenda. As Candice dipped down for the thirtieth time, Brenda's excitement at the expansion of her social circle became too much for her to contain. She threw up all over the back of Candice's hair, neck and shoulders.

"Oh for fuck's sake!" erupted Candice, frozen to the spot in abject disgust. As she slowly raised herself upright, dripping foul-smelling matter onto her jeans, she expected that someone would come to her aid and do something to help her.

"There there. It's alright. No harm done. Nothing to worry about," said the therapist, who by then had been named as Nigel. "Worse things happen at sea and all that."

Candice found a crumb of comfort in hearing those words, delivered in such a calm manner. It came as a further shock when she realised that the comforting gestures were for the benefit of Brenda and had no purpose in affording her, the actual victim of the vomiting patient, any assistance at all. She had to make her own way to the toilet to get cleaned up whilst Brenda was reassured that everything was going to be fine. When she came back, still showing the rancid stains of the wet onslaught and smelling like a pig sty, Nigel spoke to her away from the hearing of the patients.

"Candice, it's best not to swear in front of the patients. It tends to upset them."

Candice shook with rage but did not speak. She knew that there was nothing she could do. It was an alternative to being in prison after all. Nigel spoke about how sensitive Brenda was and how she was keen to be Candice's friend.

"Maybe she should try not puking on people then."

Candice was aware that someone was standing next to her. She turned to see William standing tall over her, his head tipped forward shyly and still dribbling saliva onto his shirt. In his outstretched hand and out of the range of the dribble, he held a faded, red T shirt. Nigel sought an explanation.

"What is it William?"

"A shirt for her," he said, affected by his disability but with significantly clearer speech than Brenda. "It clean one, from my bedroom."

"Have you been to get a clean shirt for Candice, William?" asked Nigel.

"Yeah, Ca'ice need clean one."

Nigel left to continue with the group exercise session. Candice was genuinely moved by William's gesture. With the exception of Cilla, whose job it was to support her, nobody had shown her any kindness for such a long time, not since Luke died. It overwhelmed her and she burst into tears. William stood motionless with the clean shirt in his hand. Candice composed herself to take it and thanked him.

"You sad?" he said.

"A bit sad," she sobbed, "but I feel better now. That was kind and I appreciate it. William, right?"

"Yeah." He touched her on the back of her hand, just for a second then turned to join in the group session again. As he was one of the more capable patients, they welcomed him back to the game.

Candice went back to the toilet and returned wearing William's T shirt. It was too big for her, but it was much better than the soiled one which she balled up for laundry later.

As the session ended, all of the patients shuffled, ambled and held onto carers back to their wards. Candice again supported Harry with her arm finding more patience than she had managed to muster earlier in the afternoon. William waited for Candice and Harry to exit.

She looked at him and saw that he had a pleased-with-himself look on his face. She smiled at him.

"Thanks again William, I will have it washed and -" she checked herself before continuing, "I will wash it and get it back to you."

"S' okay," he answered, then he went along the corridor in the direction Candice had not been to before.

*

The instruction was clear and unequivocal. It was to be a message to the criminal element of Manchester and beyond. It must not be mistaken for suicide or accident. It must reinforce the message that although Gavin Malligan was being detained at Her Majesty's Pleasure and officially a mental case, he was still very much in control of his empire.

On a Sunday night in Manchester city centre, Mark Masood was in a bar in the Printworks, trying to earn himself a living, or a fix, selling a product cut down to the point where it was almost legal to possess it. Since Malligan's arrest, he had been laying low on the Isle of Man where he believed that he was out of reach of the others in the pay of Gavin Malligan. Only when he had heard that Malligan had been convicted of murder and sentenced to life imprisonment did he venture to return to his home town. Masood wanted to bring his talents to a new employer, and it was necessary for him to find out who the new broom was and then inveigle his way into that network, preferably at a higher level than before. In the meantime, he had to operate on a solo basis, unsupported and living off his wits.

He had endured an unproductive evening, which had resulted in the indignity of being thrown out of the bar by the door-staff following some customers reporting his attempts to deal drugs to them. Lucky not to have been reported to the police, Masood headed off through the back streets toward Canal Street where he had hoped his efforts would prove more successful. He did not reach Canal Street. Passing under a metal walkway, he was confronted by a large and menacing figure, his face unseen in the shadow of the distant streetlamps behind him.

Masood knew instantly that this encounter was no happy accident. He turned and darted back through the alley away from the spectre blocking his egress toward the light. With his breathing on hold and his skin temperature dropping rapidly, Mark Masood sprinted to the turn in the back street, forgetting where he had come from and giving little thought about where he was going. He spotted the lights of another street and he headed for it, there may be people, cops, anyone. He didn't reach the light.

Another figure, leaner and less imposing, stepped out from a position of invisibility and clothes-lined him with a straight arm across his face. Falling to the rough, gravel ground, Masood had no time to react. His assailant grabbed him by the hair and held a fisherman's knife to his throat. As the giant he had seen first jogged laboriously up to join in the one-sided exchange, the man put his face to Masood's and said.

"You thought you could get away with what you did, didn't you?" Masood was barely able to speak but he knew that he was going to die if he did not. He could not see his face, but he recognised the voice as that of Dermott Conlon, which meant that he was acting on the orders of Mally.

"Ah, please! I fucked up, I know, please, I can make it right, I can, please!"

"You were off your face on gear. Mally was cleaning up your mess when he got nicked, that's down to you, you little shit!"

"I'm sorry, really, so sorry. I'll do anything, please, no more gear, no more, I swear."

"He's in that fucking hole because of you."

"I know, I'm sorry, I'll do anything to put it right!" Masood was crying and offering no physical resistance.

"Too right you will. You are going to take a message from Mally."

"Sure, okay. I will, message, yeah." There was a note of hope in his voice. A task, something for him to do, something to begin the climb back to the position of trust he had enjoyed before. "What's the message, who's it for?"

Conlon maintained the grip on his hair and pressed the edge of the blade against the skin on the side of Masood's neck.

"You will deliver this message. Listen carefully, 'Mally is still in charge. Anyone who lets him down will pay for his mistakes!' You get that?"

"Okay, okay, I get it. Mally still in charge, yeah, I get it!" Conlon reminded him of the full message.

"And anyone who lets him down . . ."

"Yeah, yeah, pay for his mistakes, yeah I get it." Masood's ability to breath came back at a rapid rate. Panting like a dog in a heatwave he said,

"I won't let you down, I won't fuck up."

"Say it back to me, all of it." Conlon spoke calmly and with unquestionable power over Masood.

"Okay, okay. Mally is in charge –"

"Still in charge," he corrected him.

"Yeah, still in charge, still in charge, and, anyone who lets him down . . ."

"Go on."

"Anyone who lets him down will pay . . . for his mistakes."

"Good boy."

"Who, who is the message for?" asked Mark Masood, showing signs of relief at having been entrusted with a task. There was a way back for him after all.

Conlon turned the blade so that the razor-sharp edge was forming a deep crease in Masood's neck. He thrust it in through the flesh and swept the blade across the front of his throat making a deep incision from ear to ear and severing his windpipe and main artery. The last words Mark Masood heard in his life were,

"The message is for everyone!"

CHAPTER EIGHT

"Tell me about what goes on behind the big fences, Heather." asked Warren as they shared mugs of coffee in the staff room near to her office in the main operating centre.

"Ah, of course, you have yet to have the pleasure of The Garrin Unit, have you?" She said extinguishing another cigarette and contemplating how long was a respectable period before igniting another one. Warren saw no need to answer. Heather continued, "Think prison then think mental hospital, times it all by ten and there you are!"

"Is it really that grim?" he asked, still thinking about finding the unfortunate Phyllis in the reservoir culvert. At least that was unlikely to happen in a prison environment. Drains had grids welded over them in prisons.

"Oh, it's probably no worse than in this side," she conceded, "just with dangerous criminals with mental disorders."

"How dangerous are we talking here?"

"The ones that get into the papers, the mass murderers, they get sent to jail for life, right?" she began. Warren nodded and sipped his coffee. "If they find them insane at their trial, they get sent to Rampton or Broadmoor or Ashworth, you get the picture. Well, this place is right up there with them. There are some total psychos beyond that fence. I've never set foot in there and I don't want to. The ones on this side are weird enough for me, thank you very much!"

It was time to light another cigarette.

"There's a chap you must meet, he's the director of The Garrin, name's Ron Jeaver."

Russell Warren's police radio sparked into life. It had become a rarity to receive any communication from the town police station. It was usually Warren who was the one to initiate any contact, often to ask for help which was invariably refused. He had adapted his approach to only making contact when it was unavoidable. It wasn't as though he was going to get transferred for not appearing to be conscientious after all. The dispatcher informed Warren that a patrol van had picked up a man in the town who appeared to the officers to be a mental case. The custody officer had refused to accept him at the police cells, and he was being brought up to Heaven. Warren found amusement in hearing that even the officers of the local constabulary called the place Heaven. The request was for him to lend assistance as the man was being violent. He acknowledged the message and confirmed that he would assist.

He walked over to the assessment unit where all new patients are brought. Inside were two male nurses in high-buttoned, white tunics bearing embroidered Heavem Hospital lettering. They were larger than average men who looked in good shape, the sort of people who could look after themselves in a confrontation. After ten minutes, the police van arrived outside. The welcoming party heard the account of the incident in the town from the van driver. He related how some shop staff in the pedestrianised shopping area had been threatened by the man who had been shouting in the street and scaring their potential customers away. He repeated phrases such as 'evil from under the ground' and 'fires of hell will come to kill us.' He had been screeching until his voice had gone but he continued to lash out at anyone near to him. The nurses explained that they could find a safe room for him where a psychiatrist could conduct a formal assessment. He could be detained under the Mental Health Act but that would depend on the results of the assessment. Warren could hear the muffled rants of the new arrival who was rocking the police van from side to side.

The two patrol cops, the two male nurses and Warren surrounded the van.

"Ready?" said the driver. All nodded and braced themselves for a physical attack.

The back doors of the van were pulled open and the sole occupant sprang forth, diving at the five men standing there. His arms spread like wings, part trying to fly and part trying to reach all five men at the same time. An unspoken and involuntary move aside by cops and nurses alike resulted in the man falling directly to the ground, an impact which may have caused some injury to anyone who was in full control of their faculties. It did bring a hiatus to his high-energy activities, a gap long enough for his arms to be held in place and handcuffs to be applied behind his back. The other police patrol explained that he had initially got into the van without physical resistance, so they had not needed to put cuffs on him. His reaction to being placed in a van had since escalated.

The man was about forty with greying ginger hair and was wearing a dirty white T shirt and saggy, black jeans. He was barefoot and had grazed his hands and feet on the ground. He was sweating and panting for breath. His voice was still hoarse from shouting, but he continued to try.

"Do you know who he is?" asked Warren.

"Nope, no idea. I've not come across him before," answered the driver.

"Nor me," agreed his mate.

The nurses also shook their heads in concurrence.

"We could take his fingerprints and check them against records," suggested Warren.

"We can't do that," said the driver, "the custody sergeant made it quite clear that if he's a mental case and hasn't committed any actual offence, we can't take his prints. He's not done anything serious enough to get arrested. That's why we had to bring him here."

The restrained man was raised to his feet, grinding his teeth and emitting spittle from the corners of his mouth. He made no eye-contact with either of the five men he was trying to fight with. He had the manner of a man who was fighting with the world.

He was taken to a part of the hospital which Warren had not seen before. Although the nursing staff had the more euphemistic title of 'maximum safety room,' Warren would have used the term 'padded cell.' It contained nothing but a low bed, fixed to the floor and a space in the corner where the padding was cut away and a drain was available. The smell told a wordless story of the previous occupants of that cube.

"Leave him with us," assured the ward nurse. "We'll give you a ring when the duty psychiatrist has had a look at him."

The police patrols returned to their van and headed back to town. Warren returned to the main building and made a note on his desk to contact Ron Jeaver at the secure unit. The piped music from the radio on the desk was producing an Ike and Tina Turner number as Warren scribbled a summary of his activities. The velvet-voiced presenter seamlessly followed the tune by saying.

"Another classic for you from Heaven Radio, connecting everyone across our little world of joy. A big welcome to the boys in blue who put in an appearance today. Always good to see the county's finest, keeping us all safe. This afternoon they have brought someone new to appreciate Heaven's unique brand of homeliness. Ahhh, Heaven, where we put the 'hospital' into 'hospitality.' Coming up next, Johnny Cash."

Warren had again been surprised by the radio announcer's up-to-the -minute knowledge. His perceptive delivery suggested that the radio station was an all-seeing eye, something which made Warren curious. He should find out more about the radio station. It may prove useful to him.

*

Gavin Malligan did not have any visits from his family. He had no family. He had people who he used in order to further his interests. In the course of his drugs empire he had amassed a considerable amount of money and had the foresight to have it stashed offshore. For this he needed accountants who could be coerced into breaking the laws governing the housing of funds obtained from questionable sources. He also had to have some accessible money in order to pay the people who were making arrangements on his behalf. These people also had to be trustworthy, which in a criminal sense meant that they also had a lot to lose if the wheel fell off and the money was seized by the authorities.

Even though many of the accounts generated interest on the initial deposits, Malligan insisted on knowing how much money he was worth at any time he wished. The clever balance was to keep the helpers both well paid and in fear at the same time. This would ensure that his decisions were carried out promptly and nobody dipped their fingers in the till.

At the time he was admitted to Heavem Hospital he had over seventeen million pounds in accounts in other countries. To coordinate operations, he relied on two men: to ensure that everyone was paid. There was his solicitor, Robin Purcell and to instil fear where it was required, he needed Dermott Conlon.

Purcell was a fully qualified solicitor who had been a sole operator for twenty-seven years. He had narrowly avoided prison and being struck off by the Law Society following a police investigation into the use of client account funds to participate in a speculative property venture. The strain of the overworked, solo, legal practitioner and sloppy administrative methods was the line of defence he utilised, although he had to hire a more reputable lawyer to conduct his defence. Realising that he had had a narrow escape, Purcell had resolved to sharpen his skills and steer his little legal ship away from the jagged rocks of criminal malpractice. With what was left of his reputation in tatters, he eked out a crust doing legal aid work and as the duty solicitor turning out at all hours to police stations to advise clients and accompany them during police interviews.

Barely making enough to support even a modest lifestyle, Purcell's lucky break came when he was summoned late at night to represent a drugs suspect at a police station in Bolton. The mule produced a small package from inside his underwear which had been missed by the police officers who had initially searched him. He told Purcell to take it to a particular address. There was to be £100 in it for him. Despite the evident ethical and professional considerations, Purcell did as he was told and collected the cash.

The suspect had been dealing for Malligan who later paid Purcell a visit. He recognised the lawyer's vulnerabilities and calculated how useful it would be to have a qualified solicitor on his payroll. Purcell provided a façade of respectability to the business dealings of Manchester's most productive and profitable drugs baron. Purcell had amassed more connections in the criminal underworld than he had ever done in legal circles. The standards of his suits went up as did his social stock. He moved to the Cheshire champagne belt and bought the status and influence which had previously eluded him.

Purcell's experiences enabled him to recognise the factors which can lead to professionals operating on the fringes of the law. Financial people who had earned well, could find themselves unable to support their lifestyles. People who could move dodgy money around and get away with it became of use to Purcell who was answerable directly to Malligan. Profits, in abundance, were surreptitiously placed in legitimate businesses then transferred to offshore holdings in countries without strict financial regulation. The U.K. authorities and financial investigators were powerless to act without specific evidence and details of the account codes. That information was held only by those holding all the aces. Malligan had allowed his acolytes to know enough to be able to put money in and move certain small amounts for running costs where necessary. Only he knew the codes for large amounts to be moved. Without him, nobody could get to the mother lode.

Dermott Conlon was an active and accomplished criminal operator where he had grown up in Sydney, Australia. Born in Dublin, his family had emigrated in the 1960s as 'ten quid poms.' Having dual nationality, he was able to relocate back to Ireland where he was unknown to the authorities and able to operate under the radar. That valuable attribute was the basis for his quest to be as anonymous as possible for nefarious purposes. His value to Malligan was immediately recognised and once trust had been established, he soon became Malligan's right hand man.

During Malligan's incarceration, Conlon had taken over the day-to-day running of his business interests. With Purcell as the messenger, Malligan continued to pull the strings from inside his hospital wing. Sticking to his practices formed by knowing how to gain compliance from people, Malligan knew Conlon well enough to realise that he was not likely to be controlled through fear. Conlon was paid well enough, but he also revelled in knowing the real magnitude of the profits. Conlon was fully aware of the seventeen million and more and he knew where it was stashed. However, only Malligan had the account details and passwords for those accounts. Conlon was a patient man, but he was not willing to wait for his share. The longer Malligan remained incommunicado, the less patient Conlon became. The plan was to spring Malligan and get access to the offshore money. Malligan was willing to cut in Conlon in return for getting him out. Conlon's willingness to accept what Malligan might see as his fair share was less clear. In his lifetime, Conlon had killed seven men and two women. It meant nothing to him to kill again.

Conlon had spoken with Purcell by phone after each of the lawyer's visits to Heavem. Purcell imparted Malligan's wishes and Conlon delegated any necessary actions to selected individuals, who carried out any directives issued. Conlon was Malligan's enforcer and business associate, although there was no doubt that Malligan was the senior partner. It went without saying that Conlon did not initiate any direct contact with Malligan and his meetings with Purcell were cloaked in subterfuge. This involved Purcell falsifying his records to the effect that he had been providing initial consultations with potential new clients, all with different names and legal needs and all subject to lawyer/client confidentiality.

Each communication from Purcell generated some form of action to be carried out by Conlon or his nominated team, selected for specific purposes according to their skills. Within days of Malligan's conviction, he issued the order for Mark Masood to be killed and for it to serve as a warning for others. It was an order which, throughout his period on remand, he had desperately wanted to carry out personally. After hoping that the trial would collapse and that he would be free to administer the

114

brand of justice he had engineered over several years, he had to accept that his incarceration meant that other people had to do those things instead of him.

CHAPTER NINE

Russell Warren was in his tiny office in the main building of Heavem Hospital. He had spent the morning tapping disjointedly on an old Olivetti typewriter using only his two forefingers. The missive he was working on was his report to the Coroner about the death of Phyllis Joan Hardling, long-term resident of Heavem. Patients and staff moved around the grounds outside his window. The cacophony of different noises made concentration difficult so, with evident impatience, Warren closed the office window and continued typing. The hospital records department had furnished Warren with the full file on the late Phyllis, which he paused his typing to read. The file was a collection of papers, some formally prepared by more skilled typists than himself and some were handwritten scraps of paper, the content of which were occasionally unreadable. The documents dated back to the 1930s and when placed in order, told the story of Phyllis' life as a patient, although that story was told by everyone except Phyllis herself.

Every significant assessment of Phyllis was recorded, some took just two lines of writing and some merely repeated verbatim what someone else had written earlier. The oldest documents told of a headstrong and rebellious girl who, as a teenager had become a worry to her family. She had run away from home and her parents had struggled to control her. When she fell pregnant, she was committed to the Heavem Lunatic Asylum, as it was then known. This was because, reading between the lines, it was less shameful to the family than to admit to their social world what the truth about Phyllis was.

It was probably due to the circumstances whereby Warren had come into contact with Phyllis, but he felt a certain affiliation with her. A sympathy, an obligation toward the memory of one unable to speak for herself. He considered how different life could have been for Phyllis had she been born thirty years later than she was. Headstrong young women were now accepted and to a degree, celebrated by society, not locked away for the rest of their lives. Getting pregnant wasn't such a shameful event anymore.

Warren closed the file, placed it carefully, as one might lay down the head of a person one cares about, on the desk next to his typewriter and sat back in his seat. A noise outside brought him back into the here-and-now. He looked out to see a huddle of four or five patients being taken from the wards to the garden centre, each making their own noises and performing their erratic and bizarre hand gestures.

There was Leo, who seemed to be troubled by an imaginary flying insect, flapping his hands around his head and cursing under his breath. Kathleen, who laughed like a whinnying horse and tapped the backs of her hands together as she edged forward with short, tentative steps. Douglas was always mute in Warren's experience of him. Overweight and extensively freckled, he gave no indication of what he was thinking but he was living his silent life in Heavem without complaint. Finally, there was the ever-trustworthy William, pushing an empty wheelchair along and seeming to be waiting to serve the needs of any of the others who may need the use of it.

Each one different, each one vulnerable and each one unable to function in the outside world.

Warren felt like a fool, a selfish and small-minded fool. He had categorised all patients into one and dismissed them all as unimportant. They were people, each one as important as any other person, inside or outside that strange place. They deserved to be treated as human beings and he resolved to do so. He reopened the window to let in the din, the colours and the life that prevailed at Heavem. He sat back down to continue typing and absent-mindedly said aloud,

"Thank you, Phyllis."

*

Malligan spent days and nights silently going through his plans as to how to get out of Heavem. During periods where patients could meet and converse with others, he revelled in the unspoken status he felt that he had. He was the only one there who wasn't crazy.

Could any of them have commanded the fear and respect he had - and continued to have? Did any of them have a large fortune stashed away for when they got out? Would any of them have the imagination and brain power to picture themselves existing on the outside? No, he wasn't crazy, he had played the system, steering a wide arc from the mainstream prison system and the mainstream mental hospital system simultaneously. They may call this high security, he thought, but that description is as good as a challenge. He was not going to spend twenty-five years in that place.

What had become a project for him, in the short term, was to explore how those nutters could be of use to him. He was willing to adapt some of his practices and he was certain that some of the hierarchy which existed in a prison could work in this place too. He felt it right for him to apply the same rules, with some flexibility in their execution. He set about engaging in conversation with the patients he had met in the first ill-fated group therapy session and sought to find out more about each of them. The more he knew about them, the more he could exploit them to his own ends.

He started with Jeremy Pilkington, who he had since remembered from the television news several years ago. His reign of terror throughout his six-month campaign of effecting retribution against an entire gender had made the national television news. Committing his crimes in the leafy residential areas of the Home Counties had earned him the questionable appellation '*The Suburban Murderer*' by the popular press, although this title had failed to permeate the collective psyche of all of the tabloid reading masses. His malice far outstripped his criminal mastery. He was caught and convicted on a wealth of physical and witness evidence linking all scenes. He even gave a lengthy and almost frenzied anti-female oratory from the dock during his trial, whilst still maintaining that the case against him was fabricated – by all of the women in the world.

Knowing that Pilkington held a hatred of women, Malligan offered some empathy in order to win his confidence. Pilkington did not hesitate to unleash a verbal barrage of anti-female vitriol, pledging his continued will to possess them, detest them, adore them and punish them in no particular order of preference. Malligan knew he was

119

making progress when Pilkington began to retell his nefarious activities; how he had selected his victims, studied them and planned his moment to kidnap, torture and murder them. Pilkington was evidently enjoying reliving his past, often getting over-excited and visually aroused. Malligan managed to be absent when the staff had to deal with Pilkington's excitement.

Bela Ferenquelar was a hard nut to crack. He conducted himself in the firm belief that everyone was his intellectual inferior. Malligan found that calling him Doctor often enabled a conversation to start. Ferenquelar was profoundly susceptible to flattery and the more Malligan played on that, the more Ferenquelar spoke to him. His crimes had been committed across several countries because he had been working in a multi-national medical organisation under the auspices of the United Nations. There had been no proper checks and balances on the work of the medical staff and as a surgeon, Ferenquelar had been considered to be beyond reproach. The fact that his mental health had deteriorated to the point where he insisted on carrying out complex surgery on patients who were still awake took far too long to be challenged. His reasoning for such a method was that he insisted on the rights of the patients to know what was happening to them. The suffering and unnecessary deaths of at least thirteen healthy people was an abomination worthy of wide news coverage, but the geographic scale of the crimes made it somewhat watered-down as a news item.

Malligan tested Ferenquelar by probing what he would do if he was not incarcerated in Heavem Hospital. Ferenquelar obliged him by giving detailed diagnoses of some of the people he came into contact with, some patients and some members of staff. He would make deep incisions to get to the rotten core that was making these fools behave the way they did. He was their saviour, the one – the only one – who could help these unfortunate people and cure them of their complicated illnesses.

Malligan tried to elicit similar levels of candour from his other fellow patients. Some did not speak at all whilst some uttered incomprehensible passages at him and heard nothing of what he asked. The man called Lawrence was completely incapable of conducting any semblance of conversation. He wailed and screeched when spoken to and effectively rejected all verbal interaction from staff and patients alike.

Malligan was careful not to appear too inquisitive. To arouse suspicions amongst the staff ran the risk of him being reassessed and that might not go his way as it had before. A shift back to a Category A mainstream prison was an undesirable possibility and one that must be avoided. The occasional outburst during communal activities, the upending of a meal tray and a show of aggression was enough to maintain the status quo.

When circumstances allowed, he engineered a conversation with Arthur Elevand. Remembering the group therapy session when he had first come into contact with Malligan and the others, Elevand began by imparting a conspiracy theory about the staff keeping them all there to thwart a plan to overthrow the government. He believed they were about to replicate the policies of Nazi Germany in the 1930s. Elevand took the bait and spoke animatedly about his mission to stop the gathering storm of extreme right-wing militia, government sponsored and hell-bent on the destruction of civilisation as we knew it. Elevand confided that he had been granted authority, but he did not say by whom, to administer the ultimate sanction on anyone he believed to be a part of the worldwide conspiracy of the Nazis. Malligan managed to win Elevand's confidence simply by agreeing with him in his damning appraisal of the prospects for global war.

Andy Aberfoyle was the main prize. Malligan had assessed him as the one member of staff he could establish and maintain some control over. The tell-tale signs of self-harm gave Malligan the notion that he was a vulnerable soul and that his vulnerabilities, once identified, could be used against him to gain some degree of compliance. He was to be the main target.

*

The troubled soul who had been brought to Heavem by the town's police and detained under the provisions of the Mental Health Act 1976 had, once a change in his demeanour allowed it, been assessed by the psychiatric consultants at Heavem. Although there was no instantly recognised condition forthcoming from the tests, he was in no state of mind and body to be allowed back into the community. He spoke of harming himself and others which was the key phrase when considering keeping someone away from the general public under such circumstances. The compromise was that he would remain on a ward at Heavem for a month as a voluntary patient, free to leave at any time but treated as a sufferer of a non-specific, mental condition. He had regained sufficient communication to be able to say that his name was Roger Reid and he had served in some military capacity in the past. This was found to help the assessing psychiatric team. Active service in the armed forces was a recognised cause of mental ill-health in some people and it was decided that Reid was an obvious case, once his past had come to light.

Roger had not nominated any family to be informed of his stay at Heavem, nor had he alluded to any person or body who might have taken an interest. The mention of the Royal British Legion as a possible source of support for him resulted in an angry outburst and the suggestions stopped at that point. PC Russell Warren saw Roger in the hospital grounds. He was dressed in clothes left behind by patients of the past and seemed subdued and alone with his thoughts. Warren made a comparison in his mind to the fiery eruption of energy Roger had displayed on his arrival. He put it down to the medication he must have been given by the clinical staff. All Roger had been given was a pill to help him sleep each night. Otherwise his medication was minimal. After a few days, Warren dismissed Roger from his thoughts. He was just another of the challenged branch of humanity who occupied Heavem and spared the rest of society the inconvenience of seeing them in their day-to-day lives.

Warren's opportunity to visit the secure part of Heavem came on a rainy Thursday morning. He received a call from the secretary of Ron Jeaver at The Garrin Unit. It was a complaint of assault. A patient had allegedly assaulted another patient. Warren phoned it in to the main police station who were happy to record his deployment but offered no other assistance.

Warren presented himself at the main gates of The Garrin Unit. He explained to the stone-faced guard at the gate who he was and that he had been summoned by Ron Jeaver. A call was made to confirm this, and Warren was allowed entry. The smooth progress so far was a stark contrast to the confrontation he encountered once inside.

Whilst standing in the gatehouse, he was asked to hand over his truncheon, handcuffs and the contents of his pockets which included his pocket-notebook and pens. He was also told that he was to be searched thoroughly before being allowed to proceed. He refused to accede to any of this on the grounds that he was there in his capacity as a police officer and he could not function as one without his formally issued appointments. His pocket-notebook contained confidential and sensitive information recorded during earlier incidents which have had a duty to preserve. A stand-off ensued, which resulted in the director, Ron Jeaver, arriving at the gatehouse to mediate.

Jeaver was an overweight, balding man in his fifties. His round face and ill-fitting grey suit gave an initial impression of a man who took little pride in his appearance. However, in conversation he was erudite, softly spoken and engaging. He was the voice of reason and without detracting from the rigidity in which his security staff had operated, he managed to broker an exemption to the rules to allow Warren to enter with his equipment still in his possession.

"Sorry about that old chap," said Jeaver as they walked from the gatehouse and across an open area toward the main building. "I'm sure you can appreciate the need for not cutting any corners."

"I do appreciate that Mr Jeaver, I also hope that your people appreciate that I can't just hand over these items on request," explained Warren.

"Quite so, quite so." said Jeaver, "All's well now I think, yes. No damage done."

Warren followed him through the security gates pausing to look up at the CCTV cameras placed high on the uprights of the gates and trained on the opening parts. Once the manual operator was satisfied that it was Jeaver and a policeman entering the gate clicked open and they were allowed to progress toward the building.

The Garrin Unit was a mix of the same old and weathered stone of the main hospital building but with flat pebble-dashed grey walls added on decades later. There were no accessible windows on the ground floor, only some horizontal, narrow strips of glass to allow only light to pass through, and those higher up on the upper floor were kept behind wire cages riveted to the walls.

Once inside, by use of his own set of keys chained to his belt, Jeaver escorted Warren to his own office which was minimally furnished but the room smelled considerably nicer than the rest of The Garrin Unit and the rest of Heavem. Tinkling away on the desk was a radio speaker, identical to the one in Warren's own office. Turned down low, it gave out a Shirley Bassey number Warren had not heard for a while. Jeaver made some introductory conversation effectively welcoming Warren and wishing him well in his new post.

Jeaver brought the conversation around to the assault. He explained that a long-term patient called Bartholomew Lerry had taken objection to a relatively new arrival called Anthony Sherratt. Sherratt had said or done something that was not to Lerry's liking and Lerry had demonstrated his displeasure by driving his knee into the side of Sherratt's head as he held it against a radiator. The staff had been sufficiently alert to prevent any serious injury but Sherratt had sustained visible bruising and complained of severe pain to the head and neck. The medical staff had treated

Sherratt and had therefore alleviated the need to take him to the casualty dept of the town's hospital. Such deployments were hugely problematic and tended to occupy several members of staff that Jeaver could not afford to do without, especially at short notice.

"Nothing is straight-forward in Heavem, Mr Warren," he began. "The functions of life outside are all different in here. Even though Anthony Sherratt's previous activities may be abhorrent to any civilised human being, he is still entitled to have his say when it comes to being a victim of a violent crime."

"What did he do? I mean to get sent here," asked Warren in compelled curiosity as well as in the course of gathering information about a crime.

"It would be easier if you had a read of his file and that of Barty Lerry." Jeaver moved to the side of the wall and unlocked a filing cabinet with a key from his pocket. He slid open the middle of three drawers and flicked through with his fingertips until he came across the file marked 'Lerry, Bartholomew' in faded handwriting.

"They are in alphabetical order. You'll find Sherratt's file easily enough when you are ready."

"Thanks," said Warren, pleasantly surprised that the access to what were effectively the hospital records of patients was so readily granted to him. Jeaver left the office, closing the door behind him but not locking it. Warren sat at Jeaver's desk and opened the file.

Shirley Bassey belted out her concluding big note and was replaced by the velvet-voiced man who had already evoked Warren's curiosity.

"*That's our girl, Shirl, what a voice. Good for the soul. Let's hope the unfortunate souls here in Heaven can get a lift out of that tune. Might make people less tense, don't you think? There's always room for a bit more of that around here. A bit less for our PC Warren to do? Let's hope so. We don't want him overworked now, do we? We know what happens if we allow that. This will cheer him up, a bit of Englebert Humperdinck, enjoy!*"

As '*The Last Waltz*' sailed over the airwave, Warren again felt that the presenter was speaking directly to him and nobody else. He had forgotten his decision to find out the source of these cryptic radio links. He shook his head and resolved to press on with the matter in hand.

Lerry had been a resident at Heavem since it was designated as a high-security facility over ten years earlier. He had been transferred from a maximum-security hospital in the south of England, one which Warren had heard of and he had always though that its name represented all that was grim about the incarceration of human beings. Lerry had initially been committed to hospital after attacking a queue of shoppers in a supermarket with a meat cleaver. He had caused grievous bodily harm to seven people and was convicted of seven counts of attempted murder. It was mentioned in the summary that he only failed to kill anybody because of his haste to attack more people rather finish anyone off with additional strikes. His stay in custody was no less violent. With little provocation he had attacked patients and staff over twenty times. Warren was unable to find any indication as to how these assaults had been dealt with by the hospital and the police. He wanted to know if Lerry was capable of being interviewed, charged and tried in court or was it a foregone conclusion that the law did not stretch to applying justice to such people.

Warren decided to ask Ron Jeaver on his return. Jeaver had been more than helpful so far. He stood up and closed Lerry's file. The cabinet drawer remained open and Warren flicked through the personal files until he reached the name Lamb. He pulled it forward and was about to insert Lerry's file back in its ordered place when he caught sight of the name of the next patient in the alphabetical scheme of filing.

He should have been pleased. He should have been reassured that the man who he had tried to put behind bars was exactly where he should be, but he experienced feelings that were far from at one with the situation before him. Gavin Malligan was without doubt a dangerous and extremely violent criminal. Anyone who could stick a machete in the neck of an unarmed kid like Luke Gould deserved to spend the rest of his existence in jail, but there he was, officially mentally deficient and being treated as a patient and not as an offender. Even the pieces of paper bearing his name brought back all of the chilling and empty sensations he had felt on finding Luke dead in Malligan's car. The subsequent organisational pillory he had been through added to his discomfort as he stood still at the filing cabinet in Jeaver's office. Forgetting that he was supposed to be looking at the personal file of one Anthony Sherratt, victim of assault, he was unable to resist drawing Malligan's file from the cabinet and opening it.

CHAPTER TEN

Robin Purcell arrived at the twenty-foot high gates of Heavem Hospital feeling taller than the gates. He stepped out of his limited-edition Range Rover and steered his £300 Churchill brogues across the lightly gravelled forecourt and through the extensive security processes as though he had ordered them to be carried out.

He was only allowed into the consulting room with his client once both had been searched and cleared for contact. He had handed over the contents of his pockets and was only in possession of a notepad. Even the pen he was intending to use was issued to him by the staff. This was because the pen was flexible and was less likely to be used as a weapon. The staff had learned from the mistakes of the past, mentally ill they undoubtedly were but, in the main, they were not stupid.

The consulting room was also fashioned with the unpredictable in mind. A single four-person table sat centrally and was bolted to the floor. Two seats on either side of it were also immovable. High on the wall above the door was a CCTV camera, set to enable staff to see but not hear, and high on the back wall was a shallow, horizontal window of opaque glass behind a mesh frame. Purcell sat in one of the chairs nearest the door. The nurse-guards brought in Gavin Malligan and seated him in a chair opposite Purcell. Warnings were issued about how the two participants were obliged to conduct themselves. No movement of seats, nor any passing of items between them. The door closed and the room fell silent.

Malligan looked up at the CCTV camera knowing that their every gesture was being watched and probably recorded. There were topics for discussion which he did not wish to share with his captors, and he could not be too careful. Lip-reading was a risk and he took measures to prevent any leaking of information.

Purcell began to speak then Malligan interrupted him. Seated at the table with his elbows resting on it and his hands joined in front of his mouth and nose, he explained to Purcell how the meeting was going to be.

"Hello Robin, nice suit."

He stared at his solicitor who glanced at the yellow-striped, hospital-issue garments Malligan was wearing. The Saville Row suit and every other trappings of affluence had been paid for through his work for Malligan.

"Erm, yes. Thank you. Shall we crack on, so to speak?" he said, abandoning his earlier swagger and adopting the contrastingly sheepish air of a man who was intimidated by the surroundings and more so by his client.

"Our last conversation raised certain matters with which I can update you. Firstly, the investment programme is gathering speed. I haven't brought documented figures with me for obvious reasons, but I can tell you that I have secured the services of two investment bankers in London and another in the Cayman Islands."

"Where's that?"

"Erm, Caribbean, I think. Anyway, your portfolio is steadily prospering through the cautious placement of funds in, shall we say – more traditional business pursuits. The account details are as we have previously discussed and the passwords remain fragmented and, as a result, can only be accessed, for making deposits and running-cost withdrawals only of course, by the combined input of the trustees, myself being one of them."

Purcell continued with his financial report. Malligan sat in silence, thinking what he would do to Purcell if he ever chose to dip into the coffers. Purcell concluded with some figures which had been complicated until he made them simple and understandable.

"Of course, all of this financial business has little value to you in here, does it?" he said in a more relaxed manner, "Which brings me to other matters."

Malligan stared impassively as Purcell continued, albeit at a quieter volume.

"News from the other side of the fence first; our source is able to gain access to the low-security hospital areas which border this facility. I know from what you said last time what your intentions are, and this is an important step in that direction. I don't know how you intend to do it and frankly I'd be better off not knowing. In this respect I am a messenger only, of course."

Malligan stared at him silently for a few seconds. Without blinking, and without any evident reason, he said.

"I hear noises from over there . . . voices." He nodded to his right.

At first Purcell thought that Malligan was referring to voices in his head, a sign that he really was crazy or that he was playing the part even when not being heard by the staff of The Garrin Unit.

"Voices, Mr Malligan? What erm, voices?"

"Kid's voices. I hear them shouting, you know, how kids do that when they're out of doors. What's that?"

"Ah, I can answer that for you. There is a children's home in one of the hospital buildings nearby. I haven't been to it personally, but I am aware, through legal circles, of its existence."

The casual, almost, relaxed way that Purcell relayed that snippet of information brought on an acute and physical tension in Malligan's gut. It flashed the worst of his childhood memories back to the forefront of his mind whilst his face gave away nothing. With the composure of a man who was used to showing no weakness he said,

"Okay, that's fine. Now what else have you got to tell me."

"I do have some news to impart which I know you will be interested in. The girl who gave witness evidence against you in court, Candice Kendal? She is here in this hospital."

Malligan's eyebrows were raised for a half a second, the only notable facial expression he had demonstrated since their conversation began. His mind was working at a rapid rate.

"What's that slag doing here?" he spat out from behind his hands.

"Our source says that she is serving her community sentence whilst undergoing drugs counselling."

"Rehab? She's doing fucking rehab here?"

"It would appear so, yes," replied Purcell quite unnecessarily. "There is erm, another erm development of a similar nature."

"Go on," ordered Malligan impatiently.

"Detective Constable Russell Warren, formerly with the Drugs Squad is now in uniform and patrolling Heavem Hospital.

"Warren!" Malligan's fingers turned white at the knuckles. The people who had set him up, still living that is, the reason he was in that place. It brought on a maniacal wave of hatred in him. Whilst he had always found sport and amusement in exercising power over others, the prospect of gaining revenge on those who had wronged him made his heart race.

"Erm, does this change any of your plans Mr Malligan?"

"No, but if I can deal with the girl, it would be a loose-end tidied up, it would. Warren is nothing, I'm not bothered about him or any like him."

Purcell was trying hard to avoid thinking about what Malligan may have meant. It was undoubtedly going to be something he had to distance himself from. To round up the meeting he asked what instructions he was to take action on. Malligan spelled out his wishes.

"There's a man who works here, name of Andy Aberfoyle. I need to know everything about him. Where he lives, who with, his weaknesses, what he has to lose, dirty secrets, maybe. I'm going to need him to do some things to help me. I need to make it so that he has no choice. You get that, Robin?"

"I understand," said Purcell who would not be doing such a task himself, but he knew where he had to go in order to fulfil his obligations.

*

Candice Kendal had been in The Bowers for a week before she met PC Russell Warren. It happened on a Tuesday morning in light rain. Warren was emerging from a doorway at the back of the main building when a party of shuffling patients descended on the doorway. Warren stood aside and waited for them to pass. He found that he was able to put names to most of them, having encountered several patients in a variety of situations. Walter was the guy with only one tooth and hair that stood up to attention on the top of his head, Geraldine heaved asthmatically and looked down at the floor and Brenda was the one who got very excited at just about anything. There were some patients that Warren had seen but did not know the names of.

One was a middle-aged man of middle eastern appearance who made rapid and erratic hand movements across his chest and in front of his face like a racecourse bookie. Perhaps he was flicking away some of those wasps Warren had been warned about. Another was a fat woman with snow white hair plaited in two lines down to her waist. Bringing up the rear was a younger man with a saliva-soaked T shirt, who Warren recalled was named William, and next to him was the responsible member of staff who must be escorting the group. She was young and shy-looking with long blonde hair, a baggy white shirt with blue buttons and loose-fitting blue jeans with designer faded patches on them. She looked familiar but somehow, she wasn't. The last time he had seen her she had looked ten years older and had the pallor of the

134

heavily medicated. Since then, in the enforced but ultimately healthier regime of The Bowers, she had regained some of her body attributes which had been suspended through her narcotically-induced suspension from normal life. Her appetite was better, and she was no longer painfully thin. Her menstrual cycle had restarted, and her complexion was a healthier shade of pink than it had been.

She ushered the patients through the door toward the dining room. Although she noticed that a uniformed policeman was holding open the heavy oak door, she did not look at him with sufficient attention to be able to recognise who it was. On the previous times she had been in Warren's presence, he had dressed in the scruffy and unkempt manner which suited the work he was doing. A haircut, a shave and a military-style cap with a chequered band together with the healthier lifestyle he was also enjoying had made him appear taller. It all contributed to the lack of recognition. Candice had passed by him and entered the corridor when the realisation hit him.

"Candice?" he exclaimed, expressing his disbelief.

She stopped and turned to see who had spoken to her. The patients invariably could not speak very clearly and her initial thought was that it was a member of hospital staff, probably from The Bowers. The drooling young man called William stopped too and turned to see who was speaking. Candice focussed on the policeman who was still holding open the door. Since leaving the family home in North Yorkshire, her only contact with uniformed police officers had left her with a deep distrust. What did this one want and how did he know her? Warren realised that he was unrecognisable to anyone who had known him in his Drugs Squad role. He let go of the door letting it close slowly, everything seemed to be happening in slow-motion. He stepped forward and removed his hat. Something set off a spark in Candice. She resisted it because it was going to be painful although she did not know what or why. The final invisible barrier came down when Warren said.

"Russell Warren? You can't have forgotten me so soon, can you?" His tone was light-hearted, but he had not given a thought to the painful memories he could be evoking in Candice.

She responded fearfully with trembling hands and cracked voice.

"No, no! Leave me alone, I can't believe you have come here to torture me again, just leave . . . me . . . alone!"

"Hey, there's no need for that, I'm just saying . . ."

William stepped forward and positioned himself just in front of Candice. Although his expression did not change, there was a purpose in his voice, an edge which made his stunted speech emit an unequivocal message.

"Ooo leave Ca'ice alone, Ooo P'liceman."

Warren reluctantly accepted that his initiation of that conversation had turned out to be ill-thought. He had brought back the trauma of her recent past and with hindsight he realised the insensitivity of his actions. He was unable to see a way of healing that rift at that moment, so he apologised and swiftly left.

William turned to look at Candice.

"Ooo okay Ca'ice?"

She took deep breaths and regained some composure. "Yes, I'm okay William."

"Dat p'liceman, he made ooo sad," said William in profound concern. "Ee bad p'liceman."

Candice settled and resumed her normal breathing rate.

"Honestly, I'm fine, I know that policeman. Seeing him just brought back something horrible that happened to me. I'm sure he didn't mean to, but it did. He isn't a bad policeman, not really. I don't know why he is here, though."

"I know," said William. "Ee foun' Phyllis, Phyllis wa' dead."

It dawned on Candice that Warren's presence at Heavem was not connected to her and he was probably speaking to her out of concern rather than to persecute her. Was she so paranoid? The drugs counsellors kept saying that paranoia was a likely consequence of drug abuse although she never accepted that it could apply to her personally.

*

Purcell had travelled on the train from Cheshire to Manchester on a Saturday morning. He was accompanied by his wife who was intent on shopping for clothes and make-up. She gave no thought about what he was intending to do whilst she was occupied with retail therapy. As long as she had the requisite credit card, she was quite content. Without any unnecessary show of affection, he parted from her at Piccadilly after agreeing to meet later at her preferred restaurant off Deansgate. In stark contrast, Robin Purcell headed across town and into a neighbourhood at polar opposites in sartorial elegance. Neglected buildings housing underinvested business premises, rough ground between dilapidated structures and a criss-cross of wrought-iron canal bridges told a grim story of a part of the city that the shoppers and revellers were never supposed to see. Tucked away under a railway arch and set in shadow from the road was a plain stone-fronted edifice which, on close inspection, was still functioning as a pub. The crumbling sign was set at a tangent on a metal bracket and could only be seen when standing at the door.

The Lord Derby was every bit as dour on the inside as it was on the outside. Dirty windows allowed limited light and the fug of tobacco and other smoked substances permeated the fixtures and fittings. The carpet and curtains had not been cleaned for an eternity and the glasses which hung from rails and sat in narrow shelves about the bar were far from see-through. Twelve to fifteen men were drinking pints of beer, some had whisky chasers with theirs. Purcell's presence was no surprise to some of them, but the uninitiated looked with ill-concealed contempt at his Harris Tweed jacket, beige jumbo cord trousers and deck loafers. Purcell would not have chosen to attend such an establishment, but he was there on business.

He caught the eye of two men at the bar. They were brothers, Kenny and Dean Rogerson. With a sideways movement of the head, Kenny signalled toward a booth on the side wall in the least frequented part of the pub. Purcell slipped into the booth and the Rogerson brothers brought their drinks over and stood by it.

"You want a drink?" asked the younger brother, Dean.

Purcell felt that he would rather imbibe arsenic than take a drink in such a health hazard of a place.

"I'm fine, thank you. This won't take long," he said nodding to them to be seated. Once comfortable, Kenny asked.

"Have you seen Mally? Is he alright?"

"He is his usual self," said Purcell subtly alluding to the questionable nature of Gavin Malligan's character and mental health. "He has sent instructions which I understand Mr Conlon to have selected you to follow, so please listen carefully. There is a member of staff at Heavem Hospital who Mr Malligan has identified as being capable of affording him some assistance, although he doesn't know it yet. He is a therapist called Andy Aberfoyle. You are directed to ensure that this Mr Aberfoyle is forced to take certain actions to Mr Malligan's advantage. This will, I understand enable an early departure for him from the establishment. Do I make myself understood?"

Although his educated manner and use of flowery language could be difficult to digest by those across the social divide, the Rogerson brothers had spent enough time in the company of solicitors for them to be able to absorb their meaning without any misinterpretation, at least Kenny did.

"Yeah, we get it, mate." said Kenny. "We have to make this bloke do what Mally wants, help get him out, right?"

"That is correct. Aberfoyle has a troubled past, self-harm I believe. It could be that he has undergone some therapy himself, at some time. He is from here in Manchester so it shouldn't be a problem finding out about him. Try and find out what the nature of his anguish was and identify ways to exploit it. Once we have his compliance, he can be expected to bypass whatever security arrangements are in place at the hospital."

The brothers looked at each other and nodded. Dean had understood that part for himself.

"Okay, we're on that," said Kenny.

"What about Conlon? He's chosen us for this, you said that, right?" asked Dean.

"I understand so, yes. I have conveyed some instructions from Mr Malligan and Mr Conlon has acted upon them. He chose you for this task. There are several different arrangements in place. You just concentrate on your own."

Purcell left the Lord Derby and headed back across the canal bridge, through a narrow alley and onto a main road where he waited at a bus stop and observed the alley. Once he was sure that he had not been followed, he left the bus stop and walked back toward Castlefield. He entered a classy but overpriced coffee shop and ordered an espresso. After allowing himself a few minutes to clear his head, he headed up Deansgate to re-join his wife and her designer shopping bags, for a lunch of seafood, green salad, artisan focaccia bread and Chablis.

*

A council flat on the eighteenth floor of a Swinton tower block was home to the Rogerson family, or what remained of it. Their father had left when they were very young and they were brought up by their mother, whom they had consistently disappointed all through their lives. Only upon her death at the age of forty-one from cirrhosis of the liver did she bestow on them an equivalent degree of disappointment.

Kenny was two years older than Dean and had spent his life looking after him. Dean had been different from other kids. He took a little longer to understand some things and there was some suggestion that he should be schooled in an institution away from the norm. It did not really matter because their attendance in any description of school had been minimal. All of the petty criminal acts they had committed had been carried out as a pair and their subsequent imprisonment in Youth Offender Institutions in Littledale, Hindley and Yarm had been spent sharing a cell.

Dean had long held a desire to be an elite soldier. Fuelled by countless movies, comics and his own imagination, he saw himself as the highly trained commando, capable of being dropped behind enemy lines and pulling off the missions nobody else could have done. Kenny had been unable to deny Dean his fantasy. To gain his compliance, usually when he needed his cooperation to perform some menial task, Kenny reinforced Dean's belief. 'Come on Bro' we're the fucking S.A.S.' and similar mantras were enough to get Dean to do practically anything. Kenny too got some air of superiority over this practice. He always got Dean to do the driving which gave Kenny the status of being chauffeured. It was his ambition, and by comparison a realistic one, to make the

Rogerson brothers a useful addition to any criminal enterprise. This did earn them a living, of sorts. They could be trusted to steal vans, alter their identifying features and drive them between sites of criminality. They were little more than removals men for stolen goods, but they generally performed such duties to good effect. They were occasionally called upon to apply some corrective force to non-payers in the narcotics trade, strictly low-level and heavily reliant on Kenny's experiences of rising to the defence of his brother whilst in custody.

In Malligan's absence, it had fallen to Conlon to make the selections. Purcell's announcement that Conlon had nominated them to do a job on this Aberfoyle bloke represented a step up in their perception of their own status as a two-man criminal asset. They were going up in the world, at least in what they believed the world to be.

CHAPTER ELEVEN

Warren was in his office on the Wednesday after breakfast. He was reading over his 'No Further Action' report on the assault allegation against Barty Lerry whilst listening to the hospital radio with the sound turned down low. An old Matt Munro song was struggling to get out of the tinny mono-speaker. An unplanned early call out over the absence of one of the residents of the children's unit had resulted in the voluntary return of the errant youngster, once he had realised that he was hungry. Warren made a report of the missing person and noted the conversation he had tried to carry out. The child said virtually nothing. Satisfied that the child's safe return was sufficient reward for his efforts he was about to go off duty in order to return later for his prescribed shift. There was a light tap on the office door.

"Come in please, it's not locked," he called.

The door opened and Candice Kendal sheepishly entered the room.

"Hello Candice," he said quietly, trying to avoid a repeat of the distress he had caused the day before. "Come in and take a seat." He indicated the empty chair next to the wall by his desk. Candice sat down and looked anywhere but at Warren.

"I've come here to apologise," she said in little more than a whisper. "I should not have reacted like that and I am sorry."

"I'm sorry too," he said, "I was so surprised to see you I didn't consider what bad memories my presence might bring back." He let out a sigh and slapped both hands on the desk. "Can I get you a cup of tea?"

"No, thank you. I have things to do," she said.

"What are you doing here?"

Candice summarised the court order compelling her to perform her current duties and added that she was undergoing addiction treatment at The Bowers. Warren then filled her in on his removal from Drugs Squad duties and subsequent posting to the least desirable beat in the county. She was about to leave when he stopped her to add something.

"Candice."

"Yes."

"I'm not trying to alarm you and there's no reason to be so, but I found out something which made my heart stop and I think you ought to know."

"What is it?"

"It's about Gavin Malligan." He saw her visibly tense her shoulders and a look of dread came over her face.

"What about him?" she said with trepidation.

"He was declared mentally unfit for a mainstream prison. He's in The Garrin Unit within this hospital. It's a high security facility, you'll have seen the high fences, I'm sure. He can't get out, so he doesn't pose any threat to you, or to me for that matter."

More unpleasant memories returned to her mind. The blade of the machete flashed through night-lights across her face on its way to Luke's neck. Her brain had removed any visible images of Malligan as a self-preservation measure. The panic passed swiftly, and she resumed normality.

"Thank you for telling me that. Does he know that either of us are here?"

"I can't see how he could. I know this will sound unconvincing to you when you think of how I failed to keep Luke alive, but you are safe here, well, safe from him anyway."

She left the room and closed the door. Matt Munro was long gone from the radio set and the velvet-smooth voice was there instead. Warren picked up his pen and continued with the missing person report.

"Things are getting interesting here in Heaven. All those lost souls seeking redemption but is that for everyone? Sometimes we just have to accept our lot in life. So many unhappy people, so little time. Ah well, it could be worse. Try being the lone police officer here, that's a job you wouldn't want. Beware of Greeks bearing gifts, PC Warren and stay safe. Here's a lovely number from Carole King."

Warren stopped writing and tried to comprehend what the radio presenter was saying. It was not the first time something cryptic had emerged from the omnipresent radio announcer. Warren decided, when commitments allowed, to find out who the mystery voice belonged to and what he might be hinting at in his radio links. An intermittent buzzing sound could also be heard. It was not coming from the radio set. Warren looked around at the window and saw a wasp, flying slowly up the inside of the pane, its wings touching the glass to make the sound. Opening the sash window to usher the unwelcome creature out, he remembered Sergeant Vinnie Davies' warning about wasps at Heavem. He hoped that Davies had meant what he had said literally.

*

Candice was supposed to commit four hours a day in her role as hospital helper. Without neglecting her counselling sessions and obligatory contributions to the domestic functions of The Bowers, she made it her default position, often returning to the wards in the evenings to help out. Her earlier experiences, including getting vomited on by Brenda, had left no trace of disillusionment and her enthusiasm to help had gathered momentum. She found herself coming to the defence of any patient who had been spoken to harshly by a stressed member of staff. All the time she was with the patients, William was at her side, eager to help in any way he could.

As the Spring evenings became longer and warmer, Candice organised walks in the grounds for those capable of doing so. By borrowing wheelchairs and co-opting those capable of pushing them, Candice was able to include patients who would ordinarily be left behind and effectively prohibited from such activities.

The paths through the hospital grounds beyond the garden centre and its long greenhouses had been cleared of creeping weeds and were accessible to both walkers and wheelchairs. The evening sun warmed the faces of the seven patients who were enjoying the sights, smells and birdsong of the season. Candice effortlessly steered the easily distracted few back onto the path when they strayed. At a mature willow tree, somebody went under the hanging branches and emerged again to raucous laughter. It was the funniest thing ever and all present had a go at entering and leaving the willow cave to the high amusement of the others. The child-like manner of most of the patients and the resultant innocent laughter was infectious to Candice who was encouraged to duck under the branches and emerge as the others had done to great elation.

As Candice dipped to enter the hidden chamber of branches and leaves, William too darted forward to join her. As Candice stood up straight inside the confines of the ancient tree, William was standing next to her. She thought nothing of it until she felt his hand on her breast, cupping her nervously but with clear deliberate intent.

She was shocked and did not move for a second. She calmly took William's hand from her breast and acted as though nothing had happened. She emerged from the willow tree to the now-customary mirth of the assembled party. The practice continued, albeit with Candice remaining on the outside of the hanging tree. The party headed back to the wards with some reluctance evident from some participants. William walked alongside Candice, pushing a wheelchair-bound patient along the gravel path. The breast touching incident was not mentioned but it was on the mind of Candice and probably on William's mind too. Candice had decided not to report the incident, better leaving it as not ever having happened.

She considered how William would have felt. Had he developed a crush on her? He certainly never missed the chance to be near her and he had picked a moment of relative privacy to make his move. Candice had not until then considered that patients could have sexual urges, assuming that was what William was having. She had grown fond of William and was mortified to think that she may have caused him offence or any lasting animosity toward her. She couldn't have done anything else under the circumstances. Her decision to do nothing may have been interpreted as encouragement and making a big issue of it was not a good idea either. It made her smile at the irony of it all.

She had not been in any situation of intimacy since before Luke had died and those times were usually fuelled or inhibited by chemical accompaniments. William had paid her a compliment and she was unused to such things. It was not a bad thing. It was a nice thing. She put it out of her thoughts, other than to use the experience to enable her to understand the patients better. She was only meant to be there for a few weeks, and she should use that as a starting point for getting on with her life. What was becoming clear in her mind was that she was getting more out of Heavem than Heavem was getting out of her.

CHAPTER TWELVE

In the weeks since the last time any other police officer had been to Heavem, Warren had formed the view that he was wholly unsupported in his role as the Heavem Hospital policeman. His phone calls were accepted and the information and reports that he submitted were recorded and filed. He could have been forgiven for thinking that he was a law unto himself, free to do whatever he wanted and largely unaccountable for his actions. However, he knew the police force well enough to know better. His place in the police pecking order was somewhat adrift from the bottom of the pile. He had no status, no reason to have his opinions respected and no friends within the force. His former colleagues in the Drugs Squad had made no contact nor had they returned the calls he had made to them. What was also abundantly clear was that Superintendent Henville would not hesitate to pull the rug from under him should the opportunity arise. It was up to Warren to ensure that it didn't.

On occasional Weekend nights at Heavem, the staff social club burst forth into life, albeit on a modest scale compared to past years. Warren had called there for a drink a couple of times and had been able to socialise sufficiently to avoid spending the evening standing alone at the bar. Those conversations had helped him realise the affection in which the Heavem staff had held the late PC Bob Tasker. His predecessor had cultivated good relations with most of the staff and Warren felt the benefit of that with some unspoken gratitude.

Most of the social club crowd conducted themselves with reasonable decorum. Some elevated pitches and increased volume passed along the pathways and into the distant corners of the grounds without incident of action necessary from Warren. Occasionally, some workplace stress could result in a flash of temper and the possibility of a punch being thrown. These altercations were invariably low-level and called for low-level responses. The usual route to a restoration of peace was provided by the friends and colleagues of those involved. After all, to get arrested or charged with assault or threatening behaviour could result in a dismissal, and everyone knew it.

Warren observed such an exchange on the car park outside the club. As was usual, he had no involvement other than to show a presence and prevent the heated conversation from escalating into something more serious. When all had passed from earshot, he turned and headed back toward the main building. He spotted a dark figure move against the backdrop of the ground-floor mullioned windows. It was only for a second, but he was sure that it was a person, a person who did not wish to be spotted.

Warren approached the building and silently looked for the figure again. There were bushes in the garden lining the walls and blending in with the ivy. Whoever it was must be concealed within them. He took out his torch and trained the beam on the bushes. He stopped five yards from the bushes and waited. Nothing moved for thirty seconds.

"Come out here please, let me have a look at you," he said with authority. Nothing happened. He stepped forward and peered between the bushes and the building wall. There was a figure huddled in a ball hiding his face.

"Step out and I will try to help you," said Warren in a less austere manner. The man stayed where he was.

"There's nothing to worry about," said Warren, who was by then convinced that it was a confused patient out of bed and in need of some help to get back to his ward. "You can't spend the night there."

The shape slowly moved and emerged from the bush. Warren stepped back to allow him to return to the open space of the grass. Warren's torch revealed that it was Roger Reid, the former soldier who had been brought in a police van and had remained as a voluntary patient. As there was no legal order in place to compel Reid to remain in the hospital, his movements were of his own choosing and he could not be compelled to be anywhere or do anything. All Warren could do was to encourage Reid to return to the ward with him which he wordlessly agreed to by following Warren to the door.

"What were you outside for?" asked Warren in a less accusatory tone than he would normally adopt.

"Fresh air," said Reid in an accent which seemed to be a mix of many places. Warren had met many former service personnel and he knew that their accents could become tempered and non-descript due to a number of factors.

"There's a time and a place for such things. Maybe you could ask for a window to be opened on your ward. Either way, wandering the grounds in the dark is not a good idea." Warren was thinking about the late Phyllis as he said that. Reid did not respond. He returned to the ward and was accepted back by the night staff who had been unaware that he was missing.

The Rogerson brothers had no difficulty tracing the back story of the hospital therapist Andy Aberfoyle. The rarity of his name and an illicit connection to the staff records of Manchester hospitals revealed that he was recently qualified, having started the training on the back of his participation in therapeutic sessions as a volunteer. Although he had family in Manchester, he was estranged from them. A conversation in a pub near to the Aberfoyle family home revealed that the family had disowned Andy when he was in his early twenties. There was a suggestion that he had developed a drug habit and his folks had been unable to deal with that. He had since cleaned up his life and was drug free. He had moved away from the city to get a new start.

Kenny and Dean retired to the Lord Derby to review what they had discovered and plan what to do next. Getting some useable dirt on Aberfoyle was the aim but there was no firm information available yet. If his current employers knew or were tolerant of his shady past, there was nothing to exert any leverage on him. The next aim was to find a current weakness, something in his life which could be placed under threat of harm or unwelcome exposure. They agreed to raise their game and examine Aberfoyle's current life more closely.

From reading the telephone directory for the area which included Heaven Hospital, the only 'Aberfoyle, A.' it contained gave them his current address and by observing the house from a non-descript grey van they quickly identified the man himself. Armed with a flask, sandwiches and a camera, their moving stake-out went on for several uninspiring days and nights. Pictures were taken, not because they revealed anything of use, but to show Purcell that they were at least trying to carry out Mally's instructions.

Several of Aberfoyle's journeys to work at Heavem were accompanied, three of four vehicles behind, by the grey van, always stopping short of the hospital where the Rogerson brothers knew CCTV cameras to be in operation. The same happened on Tuesday and Thursday evenings when Aberfoyle went to do extra work at a Local Authority home for troubled children. The day room of the children's home overlooked a sunken garden which had once housed a tennis court, now partly concealed by overhanging tree branches. Beyond that was a grassy slope up to a canal towpath. Whilst Dean took a nap in the van, Kenny walked along the canal to where he could see across the garden and into the day room of the children's home. He saw five or six teenagers, boys and girls, all sitting on settees and beanbags and two adults, one of whom was Aberfoyle. Conversations were taking place without movement from the chairs. Kenny took some zoom pictures of the session. All seemed to be civilised and productive in a therapeutic way, but as Kenny prepared to give up and return to the van, something changed the mood in the discussion group.

A girl who looked about thirteen or fourteen jumped to her feet suddenly and leaned over the face of another person who had their back to where Kenny was. He heard her shout angrily, but it was too far away for Kenny to hear what her indignation was about. The girl dashed out of the circle of people, pushed open the French windows and ran out into the sunken garden. Kenny formed the view that the girl had a short fuse and had taken objection to something said by someone in the group. As the girl crossed the old tennis court, Andy Aberfoyle emerged onto the grass in casual pursuit of the runaway girl. She stopped by a sycamore tree where she could not be seen by her housemates in the day room.

Aberfoyle found her standing next to the tree. He looked back at the house and stepped forward toward her. The girl jumped up at him wrapping her legs around his waist and her arms around his neck. He too embraced her with vigour, kissing her passionately, heads to the left then heads to the right. They were squeezing in as much physical contact as they could in those secret seconds before they had to return to what their world expected of them. Aberfoyle put her back down on the grass, still kissing her lips with reckless abandon. She released her arms from his neck and slipped them both down the front of his trousers.

Kenny snapped away furiously, crouching on the canal towpath to minimise his presence. He saw the other adult walk across the grass toward the sycamore tree.

"Andy, is Beverley with you?" called out the man. Aberfoyle extracted his lips from the girl and turned his head toward the voice.

"Yes, it's fine. She's okay," he called back before he whispered something to Beverley who instantly let go of him and sat on the ground. Aberfoyle sat down six feet from her.

"Ah! there you are," said the other member of staff. A minute later they all walked back to the building.

The final picture Kenny took was of Beverley touching Andy Aberfoyle's hand as they walked behind the other man.

The following afternoon saw Aberfoyle leave Heavem at 3.15pm and arrive home at 3.35pm. At 3.50pm Beverley arrived, in her school uniform. He answered the door and she went inside. Kenny managed to take another twelve photographs before the door closed and a further three of Aberfoyle closing the bedroom curtains.

CHAPTER THIRTEEN

Warren's day had been spent searching for another child who had absconded from the Children's Unit. The kid was only eleven and tiny in build, he had been reported missing numerous times. With predictable method, Warren carried out a search which started at the bed of the absentee and spread in circles away from that point through the building and then the surrounding area of the hospital. He had called in the job over his radio but, although he was thanked by the dispatcher, no offer of help was forthcoming. Again, he had to search that huge, sprawling hospital site on his own. He recalled his time on the Drug Squad when he had searched for, and found, very small things. Why then did it take so long to find something a large as a child?

He found the boy standing by a vast metal container which was down some steps from the garden centre's expansive stretch of greenhouses. The green-painted cube was an industrial sized and fully functional incinerator and, thankfully, the boy was merely standing by it throwing sticks and anything else he could find into its aperture, a gravity-feed hopper chute high up the side and out of reach.

Upon seeing the uniform, the kid took flight as a reaction driven by his nature rather than a process of logic. Warren caught him with minimal effort and when a token struggle had abated, he sat the boy down and asked him what was bothering him. The boy's name was Christian, and he had been living in the Children's Unit since he was eight. His response to anything he didn't like was to run away, although he had lacked the imagination or staying power to be able to do this for any significant length of time.

Christian was skinny and pale-skinned with a circular face and mousey hair cut like a wartime evacuee. He spoke with a local accent but with a permanently blocked nose. There was no school uniform at the unit, so he wore whatever was available. Whereas most kids had some say in what they wore, Christian appeared to be wearing whatever was there that nobody wanted. It was an out-of-date polyester tracksuit, albeit with a red top and green trousers of a different cloth. It was all too big for him.

"What has caused you to run off today then?" he asked in the personal awkwardness of an adult who knows he is not good at talking to children.

"Nothin'!" he snapped, looking away.

"I can't do anything about it if you don't tell me." Warren attempted to reason with the boy. "If you can explain it I might be able to help."

Christian looked down at the grass beneath his feet.

"They're always picking on me."

"Who's picking on you?"

"Them big kids, they hit me for nothin'."

"Have you told the staff?"

"They don't want to know."

"Who's your friend in the Unit?"

157

"'Got no friends, 'cept Sal, sometimes."

"Sal? Sal's your friend, you say?"

Christian said nothing. He looked down and shuffled his feet in turn, half-heartedly kicking an imaginary pebble along the ground. Warren was regretting embarking on this conversation. He was further out of his depth than the kid was, but he had started it and he couldn't think of a way out.

"It's nearly lunchtime, you are going to miss your grub if we hang around here much longer."

The boy remained staring forlornly at the ground.

"Come on, I'll speak to the staff, it'll be alright."

Christian rose to his feet with low energy and sauntered along with Warren. They reached the Children's Unit and the carer on duty accepted Christian back into the fold with the manner of a firm but concerned parent. He was sent straight into the dining room where the smell indicated that lunch was near to being served. Warren spoke to the carer who confirmed what Christian had said. He was one on the smallest kids and there was a pecking order in which he was positioned unfavourably. They had tried to find a hobby or interest for him which could set off some spark of interest in him, but they were still looking for that.

Warren thought about Christian's bedroom which he had searched earlier that morning. In his wardrobe were several toy police cars and some children's books about the police.

"Is he interested in the police?" he asked.

"He is actually, now that you mention it," replied the carer.

Warren left with the beginnings of an idea.

*

The hospital incinerator was activated on most weekdays. It was perfectly safe and functional and operated by the maintenance staff with admirable efficiency. Its purpose was to dispose of waste from Heavem but it also served to generate revenue from outside users including other hospitals and health providers in the county. Vans arrived with yellow plastic sacks of clinical waste, marked with skull-and-crossbones warnings of the potential dangers to health contained within. On the days that the incinerator was working, there was an unmistakably unpleasant aroma permeating from its vents. The smell often blew away across the surrounding woodland and toward the old reservoir which did not really affect anyone, but, when the wind changed direction, it could take the foul air toward other parts of the hospital.

Gavin Malligan was in his secure room in The Garrin Unit. The staff tended to avoid calling them cells. The high window, which was impossible to open, had a ventilator slot in it to allow some fresh air in at the will of the occupant. Malligan became aware of the pungency of the air outside. At the next period of association therapy, he asked the nurse where the smell was coming from. The nurse explained that the hospital had an incinerator which could on occasion produce that unpleasant small he had mentioned. Nothing could be done about it. It was just something else that they all had to put up with.

CHAPTER FOURTEEN

Warren's police radio sprang into life.

"Patrol to attend The Bowers at Heavem Hospital, report of a man threatening one of the residents."

Warren thought it silly that the dispatcher was asking for a police patrol to go to deal with that job when it was patently obvious who was going to go. They could have nominated him personally.

"I'll attend that," he said. "Is there anyone to back me up?" He knew what the answer to that was likely to be.

"We will get back to you on that," said the charmless radio operator. Warren knew that it meant 'Not if we can possibly avoid it.'

He hurried to The Bowers where he could hear raised voices before he entered the building. In the hallway was Candice Kendal, white as a ghost with her mouth hanging open and her eyes widened in a state of shock.

"Up . . . stairs," she uttered through trembling lips.

Warren leapt up the stairs two at a time and heard screaming from one of the first-floor rooms. The screaming stopped abruptly. He opened bedroom and bathroom doors until he found the one he was looking for. Inside a twin bedroom was a man kneeling over another man and punching him viciously in the back of his head.

The man beneath him offered no resistance but the punches kept on coming at a rapid pace.

"Stop!" shouted Warren, his heart thumping at a frantic rate. "Get off him!"

The attacker did not acknowledge him. He punched the lifeless individual again.

Warren ran at him and grabbed his raised arm. With another hand around his chest, he pulled him off and onto his back in the worn carpet. The punches were then aimed upward at Warren who leaned back out of range and took out his truncheon. He struck the man's arm causing sufficient pain to inhibit his attack. A further blow with the wooden baton made the man curl his arms across himself in a defensive pose. Warren dropped the baton and pulled his handcuffs from his belt. He grabbed the man's hand and placed one cuff on his wrist. Getting to his feet, Warren exerted pressure on the man to turn onto his front then he pulled his free hand clear and snapped both together behind the man's back. It wasn't a text-book arrest, but it was effective. Warren leaned his body in his prisoner. They both wheezed and heaved to regain a normal rate of breathing.

Warren looked at the other man lying prone on the floor. He seemed to be disturbingly still.

"Can somebody get in here now please?" he called out between laboured breaths.

Candice and another man timidly entered the room.

"Check him, see if he's breathing," he ordered as he leaned on the manacled man beneath him.

The pair went to the man and referring to him as Ralph, tried to revive him.

"He's breathing, he's breathing," repeated Candice.

"If he's unconscious he'll need an ambulance," said Warren who was thinking that it should be obvious but temporarily overlooking how people rarely think clearly when placed in such situations. The man with Candice was about to go and call 999 but Warren stopped him and instead used his police radio to arrange the ambulance.

"What's this all about?" He asked everyone in the room. Nobody answered so he made it specific. He pulled the head of the prisoner around and said to his face.

"What is this about? Why were you beating that guy?" The attacker said nothing.

"Does he belong here?" he asked Candice, who was the only person present who he knew really did belong there.

"No, he just came in and when he found Ralph, he just went mad and attacked him," she explained.

"So, Ralph is a resident, right?" he asked. Candice nodded.

Warren looked at the unknown assailant. He was scruffy and unkempt with several day's growth of stubble. His cheeks were gaunt and colourless, his teeth broken and blackened and when Warren pulled up his sleeves there were recent tracks of needle marks. Putting that together with the plain fact that they were in a treatment centre for drug and alcohol addictions, Warren worked out what the altercation had been about.

"Is it fair to assume that Ralph owes money, drugs debts?"

"Probably," said the man who had entered the room with Candice, who Warren had by then identified from his badge as a member of staff at The Bowers. "A lot of people owe money from before they came here. Being in Rehab doesn't cancel the debts."

Warren had a great deal of experience of the drugs world, but he had not come across this aspect of it. He remained restraining the man and waited until a police van arrived from the town. Meanwhile, an ambulance crew collected the still unconscious Ralph and headed off the Casualty Department of another hospital

The period of waiting allowed Warren to be able to take in what had happened in more depth. What struck him was the inability of the people in The Bowers to step up and come to the aid of one of their own who was being attacked. Had they lost any sense of common decency or comradeship along with their self-respect? Drug abusers were vulnerable people. He knew that well enough. What he had just learned was that they remained vulnerable, long after they had managed to distance themselves from drugs. His thoughts were brought back to the present when the police van pulled up outside.

It had been so long since he had seen another police officer, he could not find sufficient common ground to be able to conduct a conversation with them other than to summarise what had happened. The two constables took the prisoner away and Warren assured them that he would complete a statement and forward it to the custody office at the main station. Before they departed, one young constable turned to Warren and said.

163

"It's not us, you know. We don't like this."

"What do you mean?" asked Warren.

"We've been told not to come here, unless it's an emergency, like this," said the young cop. "Normally, we are to leave it all to you, any jobs here. It wasn't like that when Bob was here. We could come and give him a hand when he needed it." The other constable looked disapprovingly at his younger colleague. Warren ignored him and continued to speak to him.

"Who has told you not to not to give me any help?"

"It's from the top. Henville said so himself. He didn't say why, he just ordered us all not to come."

"Thanks for telling me anyway," said Warren, preoccupied by the small-mindedness of the Superintendent. At least he knew a bit more about what he was up against. He established that the young constable was called Charlie Cannon. He thanked him for his honesty and, before leaving, Charlie told him to call on him personally if he needed anything.

Warren later phoned the Casualty to be told that Ralph was awake and had sustained a fractured skull during the attack. Warren went to the Casualty and took a statement from Ralph. In a Geordie accent, Ralph told him that he was in debt to a drug dealer in Newcastle who had found where he was and sent an enforcer, who was himself an addict, to collect on the debt. Warren was unable to suggest any fool-proof way of preventing further attacks. If they could find him this far away from Newcastle, there is nowhere which could be considered as safe.

He returned to Heavem and took witness statements off the male nurse at The Bowers, whose name was Martin, and from Candice. He sent them and the statement from Ralph through by fax to the main station and he returned to his own office and sat looking at the bare walls and featureless fittings. His feelings of isolation, it seemed, had been facilitated by Superintendent Henville.

*

Malligan spoke to one of the guard-nurses on his way back to his room following an association therapy session. Adopting an unfamiliarly nervous manner, he confided in the member of staff about a concern he had for his own safety.

"It's about that Bela bloke, I think he's got it in for me, he has," he said in apparent anticipation of something dreadful. Malligan's uncharacteristic display of vulnerability understandably evoked some cynicism.

"What do you mean, got it in for you? Has he said anything?" asked the nurse, who was less than convinced but knew such things could not be overlooked.

"Yeah, he said he's going to do me in. He didn't say how or when, but he did say how he was going to dispose of my body."

"Did he now? And what did he say about that?"

"Well, you know that incinerator next door? He wants to kill me and put my dead body in it so I won't be found," said Malligan in a secretive manner, although it was clear that they were not being overheard.

The guard-nurse was used to variations in the confidence levels of the inmates of The Garrin Unit. Even the most extreme and dangerous offenders could become like timid mice and with little or no reasoning behind it. He put that down to something in their brains that worked differently than normal, healthy people.

"So, he didn't tell you how he was going to kill you or why he wanted to kill you or how he was going to get out of The Garrin and up to the incinerator to pop you in it, is that right?"

"Yeah, but I think he means it. Maybe he has a way in mind, you never know with these psychopaths."

The guard-nurse stifled a smirk at the irony, one homicidal psychopath distancing himself from another.

"All I'm saying is, you write that down somewhere, because if I'm snatched from my bed in the night, it will be that nutter who's done it and my remains won't be found. You'll need to know all that, if it happens, when it happens."

Normal procedure at The Garrin Unit was to record any incidents or conversations which could, however unlikely they may seem, cause a risk to an inmate or staff. They also had a duty to record any change of mood or demeanour of the residents. Malligan knew the drill. He knew that the staff were obliged to make a written record of it. He had seen them doing it many times as he had observed the incidents which had led to such written reports. He needed there to be a findable and properly documented record of his suggestion because, when the time came and a burned body was found in that incinerator, he needed the authorities to believe that it was his. To succeed, that plan required a body. He already had in mind who it was he was going to sacrifice.

CHAPTER FIFTEEN

The road to recovery from substance dependency is often a rocky one. It was so for Candice Kendal. On some days she could be quite optimistic, all high-energy and bright-eyed. However, on other days, she felt empty, lifeless and like she wanted to throw it all in and accept the inadequacies she clearly had. On the good days she went to great lengths to help the patients of Heavem who she was deployed to care for. On her own initiative, she had arranged activities for them to participate in, such as fashioning pottery and she provided the materials to make greetings cards. She organised games and group activities out on the grass and played music for them to sing along to, albeit in their own limited styles. On the bad days, she was surly and withdrawn, even the most fundamental task seemed too much for her. Her basic hygiene suffered, her teeth went uncleaned, her hair unbrushed.

At the afternoon meeting of the residents and staff of The Bowers in the big lounge, Candice did not attend. A delegation went to her room to request that she came to the meeting and participate in its deliberations. They found her concealed beneath the covers, fully clothed except for shoes. With some persuasion followed by the removal of the bedding, Candice had to accept the inevitable and drag herself down the stairs. Her appearance made the others uncomfortable, partly out of pity and partly out of a sense of superiority. For those with low self-esteem, it was a godsend.

The meeting could not progress until Candice's evident fall from grace had been discussed. She made minimal contributions to the debate and, despite the best efforts of the staff at The Bowers, it rapidly descended into a parental rant about her getting a grip of herself.

Candice felt a wave of anger brewing inside her. What right had these people to criticise her, especially as she was determined to inflict considerably greater punishment on herself. Nobody had asked her what it was she needed. Instead, they were lecturing her, telling her what she was supposed to be whilst nobody was listening to what she was unable to verbalise. Her behaviour should have made the message loud and clear. She was not a project, she was not a case, she was a person, a person with needs, a person who had not managed to come to terms with the shocking death of her boyfriend and the subsequent bereavement with all of its erratic surges of grief.

The coldness and remoteness of her father and the suffocation imposed by her mother had not prepared her for the challenges of adult life. She simply did not know how to deal with such challenges. What she did know was that she felt at her happiest when she had been with Luke, not because it was the big love story, but because she had someone who needed her – she needed to be needed.

The tension welling inside her reached its peak when a fellow resident, who had been screaming at the staff only two days before, suggested that she was getting The Bowers a bad name and it would reflect badly on all of them.

"Fuck off! Just fuck off all of you. Leave me alone. You don't know anything about me."

Candice ran from the room and out of the building. No protest was forthcoming from anyone. She ran across the grass and into the wooded area. She sat on the ground and wrapped her arms around her knees. She wept uncontrollably.

Eventually, a calmer demeanour returned to her, regaining some composure but still sobbing and trembling with her intake of breath erratic and laboured. Her forehead remained fixed on her knees and her eyes were closed. She felt a presence near her, silent but benign. She opened her eyes and looked up toward the stippled light through the trees. A shape was standing over her. She could not adjust her eyes to the light straight away.

"Who is it, who's there?" she mumbled.

"Ca'ice, it's me, William. Are you okay, Ca'ice?"

The irony brought her some perspective. It helped her to regain some calm. There she was, an emotional wreck being comforted by one of the patients she was supposed to be caring for, although she had perceived William to be the most capable of the patients at Heavem.

"I will be William. What are you doing here?"

"I saw you run. You crying. I help," he said in a soft and concerned tone which hit the spot for Candice with far more accuracy than the people at The Bowers had done. William sat down on the ground next to Candice.

"I should be helping you, not you helping me William."

"We 'elp each uvver," he said making more and more sense as he spoke.

"I just need a hug please," said Candice descending into tears once again and forgetting the earlier time when William had touched her breast under the willow tree.

William wrapped his arms around Candice. It was not sexual. It was a gesture borne of genuine concern and an attempt to alleviate the unhappiness of another human being. It was exactly what Candice needed. She had not had any such contact for so long. William had forged a bond with her and he, in his own disjointed way, needed her too. He craved physical contact, her approval and her company. It was mutual.

Neither moved nor spoke for five minutes. Only their breathing made any movement or sound. When they got up, Candice saw that William had made her shirt wet with saliva. She decided that it was time to clean herself up. She held many complaints and resentments about her upbringing but knowing how to keep clean was not one of them.

"Thank you, William. You have helped me a lot," she said.

"I 'elp you. You my best frien' Ca'ice."

They walked back to the open grass and William left her at the door of The Bowers. He went back toward the main building as she slipped in through the door.

*

Warren had been reading the Missing Person reports dating back several years, copied and filed by Bob Tasker. Noting the places and circumstances of the resolution of these old cases, he tried to build a picture of the actions of the runaways in the hope that he could predict their future movements and find them more quickly. The finding of Phyllis had preyed on his mind and the thought that finding someone else too late was disturbing him. He thought how small Christian was when compared to the vastness of the Heavem grounds. He was a particularly small needle in a very large haystack. He could have climbed into the incinerator he had been using for target practice and never be found. Something had to be put into place to prevent that from happening and it would be a good start if the kid stopped running off at the drop of a hat.

Warren looked at his police hat on the coat hook behind the office door and an idea came to him. He picked up the phone and called the main police station to ask if Charlie Cannon was on duty. He was told that Cannon was at a job but could call him back when he was free to do so. Ten minutes later Charlie Cannon called him.

"Hello Charlie, thank for calling back so soon."

"That's okay. How are things in Heaven?"

Warren was amused to know that the local constabulary were also in on the 'Heaven' joke.

"Exactly as you would think it is. I'm going to be a patient here before the year is out. Anyway, I need a little favour Charlie if you could."

"Go on, what have you got in mind?"

"There's a police cadet scheme in place isn't there?" asked Warren who had already confirmed that there was.

"There is, I help out with it, two evenings a week. We get kids between eleven and sixteen and give them police-related activities to do: crime prevention campaigns, leafleting, that sort of thing. They have a uniform, of sorts: a cap and a T shirt with the crest on it. They love it."

"Are there any kids from the Children's Unit at Heaven?" asked Warren, joining in with the running joke.

"No, come to think of it, there aren't, but there's no reason why not."

"There's this kid who keeps running off. I think it might do him some good, be a part of something, give him something to keep him from going AWOL all the time. I'll take responsibility for him, getting there and back. What do you think, Charlie?"

"Sure. The staff at the Children's Unit will have to sign the form but it should be fine. I'll send you the stuff he will need. I'll put a cap and T shirt in a bag and leave it for you. What size is the lad?"

"Small, the smallest you've got."

*

Andy Aberfoyle was at home on a Saturday reading a psychotherapy textbook as a part of the Master's degree he was studying for by a correspondence course. The phone rang and he reached for it with the confidence that he knew who was calling. He received very few calls and the usual caller was Beverley.

"Hello Beautiful!" he said presumptively. The voice at the other end was far from that of the teenager Beverley.

"Aberfoyle, we need to have a little chat about your love life."

"Who . . . who is this?"

"I'm the bloke who has your future in his hands mate. Be at the café next to the lake in Hodge Park in half an hour. Don't pull any stunts and come alone, understand?"

"But, what for? Why should I go anywhere you say? I don't even know who you are."

"Shut up Aberfoyle. Be at the café in half an hour or your dirty secret will no longer be a secret."

The caller hung up and Aberfoyle felt the blood run cold through his body. Until then his liaison with the underage Beverley had gone unacknowledged by anyone other than the two of them. Now, some gruff-sounding stranger was using it to work him like a puppet. He couldn't contact Beverley to ask who she had told because the staff at the Children's home she lived in would become suspicious. How far the caller would go to expose him could only be guessed at but there was no doubt about the confidence behind his demand. The caller had demonstrated that he was in a position of strength over him. Thankfully, he had called him and not his employers or worse still the police. He had no choice but to go where he had been sent and to try some damage limitation. The man might not have any evidence anyway, but he had to find out. He put away the book, put on his jacket and shoes and headed off to Hodge Park.

He only just made it in the allotted half hour, hurrying to almost a jog as he entered the ornate Edwardian park. He had not needed to hurry because Kenny and Dean Rogerson were waiting to see if he had really come on his own. Kenny was occupying a bench across the lake. He was sitting near an old couple and appeared to be in their party. Dean was positioned in the van across the road from the park entrance. Aberfoyle waited for a further half hour before giving it up as a sick joke and heading back toward the entrance.

Dean saw him approach the road. He also saw Kenny following him. Dean started the engine and moved the van to the kerb near to where Aberfoyle was to emerge. Kenny picked up speed and got to within five yards of their man. Dean leaned over the seats and opened the sliding nearside door. As Aberfoyle reached it, Kenny stepped forward and pushed him into the open rear of the van then he climbed in after him and slid the door shut. Aberfoyle was taken completely by surprise. He could neither breathe nor speak. He rolled on his back on the floor of the van as Kenny leaned over him and held him by the lapels of his jacket.

"Go!"

He indicated to Dean who pulled out into the sparse traffic and drove sedately away. Kenny turned to Aberfoyle.

"Listen to me, you little shit. We've seen you and your child girlfriend so there's no point in denying it. We've even taken pictures of you two together and they're enough to put you away on the 'pervs' wing of Strangeways for ten years, and that's what will happen if you don't do exactly what we tell you to do. Nod if you are following all this so far."

Aberfoyle nodded vigorously, his eyes were set unblinkingly wide. His limbs had frozen and his heart was frantically beating its way out of his chest.

"Good boy," said Kenny, patting Aberfoyle on the cheek.

Dean glanced at his mirror, adjusting it downwards to be able to see what was happening on the floor of the back of the van. This was real S.A.S. stuff and Dean was loving it. Kenny pulled Aberfoyle upright and sat him against the side behind Dean.

"Now, just to make sure you know what's going to happen," said Kenny reaching up to be handed an envelope from the front passenger seat by Dean. "This is a taster for what will be given to the cops if you do or say anything that pisses us off."

Kenny pulled the print photographs out and showed Aberfoyle. They showed him and Beverley kissing by the sycamore tree at her children's home. Her hands and legs were all over him and his arms were holding her up to be able to do so. The photo scene changed to Beverley entering Aberfoyle's home in school uniform. She could even be seen in the room as he drew the curtain.

"Look," he burbled, trying to appeal for reason when it was clearly futile, "it's not some sordid affair. We love each other. We are going to get married when –"

"When she's left school?" interrupted Kenny. "We don't give a toss, mate. You are looking at jail and that's that."

Aberfoyle fell silent. His will, his resolve at being able to deal with this situation, for all it was worth, was broken. He knew the risks, but he had chosen to take them anyway. She was worth it, they were going to be together but if he was going to prison for ten years, would she wait for him? Visit him inside?

"Okay, okay. What do you want? I can pay but I'm not a rich man."

"You are a prick, you know that?" said Kenny. "It's not about what we want you to pay, it's more about what you are going to do to avoid spending ten years getting the shit kicked out of you inside."

The van stopped in the loading area of a disused warehouse. Kenny slid open the side door and stepped out gesturing to Aberfoyle to do the same.

"You are going to go about your business nice and normal. We will tell you what we want you to do and when and you are going to do it."

"And if I do, I mean, when I do what you want, this will be over, right? No police or anything?"

Kenny stepped forward and grabbed Aberfoyle by the genitals, applying adequate pressure to ensure complete compliance. Personally, Kenny would have taken great pleasure in stamping on the head of any nonce. However, he knew that this guy had a job to do and he couldn't do that if he thought it was all pointless and he took the coward's way out. He had to give him something to keep him alive, at least long enough to do as he was told. After that, he didn't care either way.

"You do as we say, and you'll get all the prints and the negatives. You'll never hear from us again."

He climbed into the passenger side of the van and Dean drove away leaving the psychotherapist unable to process his own thoughts for a change. He staggered forward and leaned against the loading platform. His breathing was still uneven. He leaned forward, vomited and started to cry.

*

Christian jumped at the chance to become a police cadet. Warren got the consent forms signed and issued him with his T shirt and cap. Within a week he had asked for another T shirt as the boy insisted on wearing it every day. The deal, as Warren had laid down to him, was that any running off would result in a suspension or dismissal from the police cadet group. Christian accepted without question. He was always ready early, and he came to Warren's office to help with other duties too. He tidied the papers on the desk, took responsibility for recharging the radio batteries and answered the phone to take messages if Warren was out, efficiently greeting callers with 'Police Cadet Christian Wood, can I take a message?' He took huge pride in his role, even though Warren made most of it up for him as he went along. Despite his reading and writing challenges, Christian always wrote down the name and number of the caller satisfactorily. His run of going missing from home ceased instantly.

One message recorded by Christian was a request for Warren to call Charlie Cannon at the main police station. Warren returned to the office and made the call.

"Hi Russell, thanks for calling back."

"No problem Charlie, what can I do for you?"

"I thought you should know that the bloke, Paul Joseph Rand, the one you nicked for assaulting Ralph

178

Tranter at The Bowers? He has been charged and released on bail. There's a possibility that he might go back and have another go at Ralph."

"Okay. I'll go and see Ralph and warn him. Can you send me up a copy of Rand's custody photograph so I can forewarn the staff?"

"Good idea Russell, will do."

Warren hung up and went straight to The Bowers. He found Ralph in the kitchen washing up. He explained the development regarding Ralph's attacker and Ralph acknowledged this with little more than a shrug. Whilst Warren was not looking for any grand gestures of gratitude, he was surprised that Ralph had nothing to say to the guy who had saved him from a beating, or worse. Even cops don't like being taken for granted.

He compared the levels of approval and appreciation he had experienced from the patients who had severe impairments. At that moment he saw William sitting on the grass near the door of The Bowers with a large book on his lap. William was usually civil to him but he had proved himself capable of challenging him when he felt it appropriate. Warren admired that about William who he saw as the most rational and capable of the hospital's disabled patients. He reached the main building and turned to see Candice emerge from the front door of The Bowers.

Upon seeing her, William got up and approached her, thrusting out his book for her to see something in it. Warren watched Candice interact with William. Remembering the drug-addled mess she had been when he had first met her, Warren found it uplifting to see what she had become. She appeared healthier, taller, more purposeful. She even smiled now. He was unable to recall a more dramatic recovery from drug addiction. That could only have happened at Heavem Hospital. Amidst all of the human misery and suffering in that place, there was hope – lots of it.

CHAPTER SIXTEEN

Malligan continued to sow the seeds for his future beyond the high fences of The Garrin Unit. Periods of isolation were spent meticulously thinking through the possibilities, chewing over ways of achieving each strategic element of his plans. He was constantly identifying an aim then working out how to make it a reality.

Periods of association were convened in order to minimise the risks to the mental stability of the inmates, which Malligan found amusing. They provided him with opportunities to probe his fellow patients to establish if they could be of use to him in his endeavours. Barty Lerry was capable of conducting a conversation only when he was not in the vicinity of Anthony Sherratt. The two of them were often exercised individually to avoid the bickering and violence they seemed incapable of resisting. Lerry had been the sole aggressor but Sherratt had had enough of it and had resorted to fighting back, often pre-emptively. Malligan used this division to engage both of them in dialogue separately. These peaceful interludes were welcomed by the nursing staff, who were content to leave Malligan to talk quietly without impediment.

Malligan was satisfied that Ferenquelar was right for what he had in mind, but he needed more helpers, willing or otherwise. The main quality that Ferenquelar had demonstrated was that he could be steered and directed toward a particular purpose. His arrogance and disdain for all others made him susceptible to flattery and Malligan preyed on this weakness without compromise. After all, Ferenquelar had shown no mercy toward his victims, all thirteen of them, and all children. In the prison hierarchy that Malligan had experienced, there had always existed unwritten strata of acceptability. He had found himself at or near the top, commanding respect and fear from the many. Anyone who had harmed kids was invariably consigned to occupying the bottom level. Killing thirteen of them was possibly the only level lower than that. Ferenquelar's importance was not related to his earlier crimes. The fact that he was of use to Malligan had elevated him to the only status, of the captive kind, that he may ever enjoy. It was bestowed upon him by Malligan, who he saw as an inferior as he did with everyone. What Ferenquelar was too self-absorbed to realise was that his use was to be short-lived. He was Malligan's whipping boy and he didn't even realise it.

Ferenquelar was only one part of the plan. Malligan needed another stooge. He probed his fellow inmates for the qualities he required from them. Anthony Sherratt could not be engaged in any form of conversation without erupting in anger. He was more heavily medicated than anyone else as a result. Barty Lerry interested Malligan only because he had a propensity for using a weapon which was similar to his own preferred machete. Lerry had been in The Garrin Unit for so long there was nothing in him that recognised that there was any world beyond it. Malligan probed Lerry and Sherratt for evidence of their value to him. He finally formed the opinion that they were too unpredictable to be of any use. What Malligan needed was someone who could be persuaded or would be otherwise motivated to leave their room and wreak havoc when allowed to.

Arthur Elevand was clearly deluded to his core. His constant mentioning of an army of Hitler clones threatening the stability of the civilised world was boring to hear but anyone who could execute his own parents was not a man to turn one's back on. Elevand's bizarre obsession precluded him from the plan. He was simply too strange and hard to read to be able to behave in any manner which could be of use. The next recruit had to be Jeremy Pilkington.

Pilkington was round in body and face. His bald patch had developed to resemble that of a monk and his habit of joining his hands as though in prayer added to that image. His other habit of rubbing his hands up and down his thighs in sexual arousal was not monk-like at all.

When distracted, Pilkington was capable of conducting a conversation of a harmless nature. He aired views on politics and literature and gave the impression that he was of good education. However, it was never long before his favoured subject of his hatred of all women came onto the agenda. Malligan played on this to further his own ends, telling Pilkington about what lay beyond the high fences of The Garrin Unit.

In the shower block whilst being supervised by staff at the end of the room where the only door was situated, Malligan chose his moment to engage in conversation with Pilkington. The sound of the falling water and the resultant steam made it impossible for the staff to overhear what they were saying. Initial pleasantries over, Malligan wasted no more time.

"Fifty yards from where you are standing now is a place full of women," he told Jeremy Pilkington knowing it would drive him crazy. "Lots of them; tall, short, thin, fat, young, old. What would you do to them if I could get you out of here?"

Pilkington began rubbing his thighs again. His breathing deepened and his eyes widened with desire.

"I would, I would, I would make those bitches pay for what they did to me, to every man!"

His body began to tremble, spit gathered and flew from the corners of his mouth. Malligan went into the shower and left him to be placated and controlled by the guard-nurses, who were unaware of what had triggered this behaviour. Pilkington ranted his abject hatred of all things feminine and pledged to humiliate, mutilate and annihilate without compromise. That was precisely what Malligan wanted to hear.

The next step was to see who else was going to participate. The one which had fascinated him the most was the Hungarian doctor of death, Bela Ferenquelar, who remained unaware that Malligan had registered a fictitious complaint about him. He found the former surgeon standing alone in the corner of the association room. Harmless conversations between patients were encouraged by The Garrin staff but any talk of their crimes or any other homicidal thoughts they may have been experiencing, had to be monitored and controlled by the therapists. It therefore proved difficult for Malligan to learn about the inner workings of Bela Ferenquelar, which carried its own irony as it had been the doctor who had taken an unwholesome interest in the inner working of his thirteen victims.

It had been decided that Lerry and Sharratt could co-exist, albeit at opposite ends, in the Paris Suite during periods of association therapy. Malligan had already dismissed them from his deliberations. They could, however, facilitate another idea he had since formed. He needed to have an uninterrupted conversation away from the hearing of the staff and other inmates. Having spoken to both Lerry and Sharratt individually before, it was not seen as inappropriate for him to do it again. He chose Lerry because the aggression between the two of them had more frequently emanated from him. Standing next to where Lerry was seated by the wall, Malligan opened with,

"Hey, Barty, how's it going?"

"S'alright, n'you?" answered Lerry, slightly surprised at Malligan's amiable manner.

"Yeah, fine mate. I heard about what happened. No ill effects then?" said Malligan, wielding an imaginary fishing rod over his companion.

"What are you talking about?" asked the bewildered Lerry.

"Oh!" said Malligan. "Maybe it's not true then." Lerry was beginning to sour in his expression. His shoulders rose and an intense expression of confusion came over him.

"What's not true? What have you heard?"

"Okay, promise you won't get mad. I'm only the messenger, right?" Malligan effortlessly teased the worst out of Lerry and could have kept it going all day if he had wished to.

"Tell me, out with it, man!" demanded Lerry, showing exactly why he was a long-term resident of The Garrin Unit.

"That fellow, Anthony?" began Malligan. Lerry's hands became fists and his knuckles turned white.

"What about him?" he growled.

"Well, it can't be true then?" said Malligan.

"What? What can't be true? What's has that lying bastard been saying about me?" Lerry was reaching boiling point, which was where Malligan had intended him to be.

"Well," said Malligan in a conspiratorially quiet voice, "he said that you tried to kiss him."

"What?" Lerry shook all over, his nostrils flared like a prize bull.

"According to him, you are a closet puffter and you fancy him. That's what he said." Malligan held out his opened hands in a gesture of innocence.

Lerry sprang from the chair which flew sideways across the floor, alerting all present to a sudden change of mood in the room. Malligan stepped aside to let him do what he did best, or at least most often. Lerry sprinted across the carpet and launched himself at the unsuspecting Sherratt, who was sitting with his back to the open space. Lerry dived headlong at him, knocking Sherratt off his chair and onto the floor. Others not directly involved moved away, leaving the now-familiar war to play out its present scene of battle. Sherratt was taken by surprise and was unable to offer any resistance to the onslaught. He curled into a ball and took the furious punching and kicking inflicted on him until the staff managed to gain sufficient control to be able to restrain Lerry.

As the chaos was being played out and during the subsequent transportation of the individuals involved to their respective rooms, Malligan spotted a chance to interview Ferenquelar without interruption.

"Alright Doc?" he said, knowing Ferenquelar's propensity to have his status confirmed in every exchange with any person.

"Hmmm!" he shrugged, dismissing Malligan as having inferior status whilst accepting that he had spoken to him.

"You are the main guy in here, aren't you?" Malligan used flattery that he knew Ferenquelar could not resist.

"What is this to you? What you mean?"

"Well let's look at the fact, Doc. I'm in here for killing one bloke, that's fair enough, but you - you topped thirteen – thirteen!"

Malligan's voice went up an octave and was then virtually silent at the repetition of the death toll of the doctor's past patients. It had the desired effect.

"I don't kill, I cure. I cut out disease. I tell patients what is happening to them. They have right to know, even children."

"Wait a minute Doc, are you telling me that the patients you bumped off, some of them were children?"

Malligan already knew this but chose to allow Ferenquelar to enlighten him anyway.

"All of them children, is why they sick. Only children have this sickness. I cure them."

"By killing them, that's what you're talking about isn't it?"

Ferenquelar looked at Malligan anticipating some objection to his version of medicinal intervention. Sensing this Malligan sought to keep him on board.

"Hey, I'm not judging you Doc, oh no, not me. Like I said, you're the main guy around here, I've gotta respect that."

Ferenquelar seemed to accept Malligan's non-judgemental monologue. He acceded to the point of allowing himself to make eye contact with his new biggest fan.

"Hmmm!" he grunted.

"So how does this go? Are you saying that all kids are sick, and you have to 'cure' them?"

"Yes!" said Ferenquelar who had not, until then been able to find any party open-minded enough to engage in conversation with him about it.

"And you would keep them awake whilst you are operating on them, just to be able to tell them what's happening, is that right?"

"Yes, is right."

"So, if you were to get out of this place, what would you do?"

"I continue my work," said Ferenquelar, resuming his naturally self-righteous air.

"You know there's a children's home right next to this place, don't you?"

"I have heard them, over fence," he said without looking at his interviewer.

"It's a hospital and it's full of kids, all sick. They must be sick, they're in a hospital. They're in need of your help, Doc. If I can get you out of here, you could cure them, couldn't you?"

"It is my duty, as doctor!"

"Good for you Doc . . . good for you!"

*

"But I just don't understand it, we've been so careful Andy," said Beverley, sitting on the sofa in Andy Aberfoyle's flat behind closed curtains in the late afternoon. Her thirty-two-year-old boyfriend was pacing up and down in front of the dormant television screen.

"I know, we couldn't have been more careful, but someone has found out. They have photos of us kissing and of you coming here."

"They took pictures of me? Here?" She found it hard to comprehend that anyone would go to such lengths to torture them in this way. "Why would anyone do that? Why do they hate us? We've done nothing to anybody."

She descended into tears. Her face dipped into her upturned hands and her shoulders shook tremulously. Aberfoyle sat next to her and wrapped both arms around her. He kissed the back of her head.

"There are some nasty people around. That's all. Nasty people who can't let someone else be happy without trying to spoil it, but we won't let them. I promise, I won't let them or anyone else hurt us."

"Oh Andy, I do love you so much. They can't keep us apart. I couldn't bear it."

"Shhh now! I love you too, with all of my heart. We will be together for ever. We've just got to be more careful than we have been."

Beverley sat upright as though a new wave of shock had arisen in her brain.

"Photographs! What are they going to do with those photographs?"

"Don't worry about that. I've got that in hand, it's going to be fine."

"How? What do they want? Who are they anyway?"

"Just a pair of idiots, chancers, they're not clever people. I just have to do something for them, something that's no trouble at all and they'll give me the photos and all negatives. It will all be over in a few days, I'm sure of it."

"Do you have to, like, give them money or something?" she asked through trembling lips.

"No, no, nothing like that. It's all under control." He took both of her hands in his and looked into her tear-filled eyes. "Trust me Bev, I will sort it out. It's going to be okay. Just you and me, together."

"I don't want to let you down," she said in a pained voice. "You're the only person who has ever loved me. You mean the world to me."

"And you mean the world to me too. This situation, it won't last for long. Pretty soon, you'll have left school and we can be a proper couple, not hiding from the world, not worried about getting caught."

"I want that, more than anything," she said, smiling for the first time during that visit.

"You can trust me Bev. I won't let you down."

CHAPTER SEVENTEEN

The group activities for the long-term patients at Heavem were as varied as the staff's imagination allowed. A demotivated and disillusioned workforce proved to be less and less imaginative as their years of service went on. Every now and then, a new person managed to inject some energy into the place, give them some life and optimism to be able to get through the day and try to achieve something – anything.

Candice's arrival had brought some of that spark. She had quickly overcome the inauspicious beginnings of her stay and, apart from the few days of depressive behaviour in which she could barely get out of bed, she had committed considerable efforts to the benefit of the people she was looking after. She introduced a wider range of music to the sessions and encouraged singing, of sorts. The piano lessons she had been obliged to attend as a child had given her sufficient skill to be able to operate an old teak upright piano with broken keys. A request for the musical relic to be professionally tuned had been rejected by the hospital management on the grounds of expense but Candice was not put off. It was still more in tune than the singing of the patients. She also expanded the range of garden centre activities, trusting the few with sharp objects and monitoring those who were moved to eat the soil.

Candice asked the nursing staff if any of the patients could read. It was universally accepted that none of the long-term patients could do. Some liked to peruse magazines and look at the pictures whilst most were unable to do that with any purpose. She wanted to know if anyone had tried to teach them. This generated a great deal of sighing but no offers to try. She resolved to ask the patients if anyone wanted to try reading. Only William volunteered to learn.

William volunteered for anything that Candice was involved with. She felt some relief that at least one person had risen to her idea, but she was realistic enough to know that William would have joined her in any activity regardless of his suitability for it.

After fulfilling her designated duties, Candice sat with William and went through the basics of letters and numbers. He was able to recite them back to her then identify them without prompting. This she found encouraging. She knew that William had displayed the capability to perceive the changing feelings of others, to step in and offer comfort to those who may need or want it at any given time or circumstances. In that respect he conducted himself as an adult. The same was true of his listening skills and, to a lesser extent, his spoken communication. To Candice, it seems strangely juxtaposed to be treating him like a small child when it came to reading.

William showed an unequivocal enthusiasm to learn to read, a will which went beyond his desire to sit next to Candice. He was soon able to read short passages of one or two syllable words and comprehend their meaning by describing it in his own words too. Even the jaded older members of the nursing staff had to grudgingly concede that Candice's initiative had resulted in reading skills in William that nobody had previously thought worth pursuing.

On a Wednesday evening in light summer rain and the closed-in atmosphere that comes with it, Candice was preparing to leave The Bowers to cross to the day room in the main building to give William his reading lesson. She was wearing a blue denim skirt and plain T shirt of a dull orange. As she went up the stairs to her bedroom to get a coat to keep off the rain, she was called back by a member of staff who explained that a parcel addressed to her was in the kitchen. She came back down the stairs and collected the parcel, which was two feet long, one-foot wide and nine inches deep. It was wrapped in brown paper and secured with packing tape. The label taped to it gave away nothing of its origins. She picked it up, with some difficulty, and took it up to her bedroom.

She sat on her bed with the parcel beside her and peeled off the wrapping. It was a cardboard box which had originally been intended for the transport of apples. She pulled up the flaps of card to reveal its contents: some cotton cloth which unfolded into a shirt; a cigarette lighter which smelled of petrol; some magazines; a radio alarm clock; a small picture frame with a face in it, a girl's face. The face was proud and demanding, superior, scornful. It was her own face, taken only one year before but she could barely recognise herself. The box contained the contents of the tiny studio flat she had shared with Luke and it had been sent either by the landlord or the police after Luke's murder.

The box and its contents brought back bitter and painful memories to her. Primarily, the night Luke had been killed and the subsequent hollow loss that comes with bereavement and subsequently, the absence of anyone who really understood her, someone who she could allow to know her well enough to understand her. It all came back at once, how she had needed him because he needed her. The flood of emotion made her shrink into a ball on her side on the bed. She curled her fingers into fists and clutched the shirt to her body, his shirt. A sob and an intake of breath came in and out sharply. It brought her back to the here-and-now.

She sat up and took a huge breath, enough to make her light-headed in normal circumstances. She wiped her eyes and stood by the bed. This box, this stuff in it, it was just stuff. She had a life to get on with, to rebuild. She put on her coat and headed down the stairs to go to the main building. The drizzle made the summer air fresher. She needed that to clear her mind, get on with what she had set out to do, don't let some old box of crap derail her plans. Inside the main building she paused by a large old mirror in the entrance hall. She made a token gesture of wiping her eyes and sweeping her hair from her face before entering the patients' day room where William was already sitting on the sofa. He was alone and had a large book open on his lap.

"Hi Ca'ice!"

He looked very happy to see her. She went to sit with him and made a determined effort to put her distractions aside. William did not deserve to endure the awkwardness of her emotional instabilities. He had enough troubles of his own, which he handled far better than she could have done.

"Hi William, sorry I'm late." She bustled her way across to him slipping her wet coat off and shaking it before putting it on the back of a nearby dining chair. "But I'm here now, so, what is that book you've got there?"

"A 'cycapeedier. It ha' evrythin' in the world in it."

"Am I in it?" she said smiling.

"Ha! Nearly evrythin'." William made himself laugh, which in turn made Candice laugh.

"Go on then William. Find something in the encyclopaedia and read it to me."

"You 'elp with long words please, Ca'ice?"

"Of course."

She sat next to him on the settee and looked at the page. William pressed on with the narrative about the kings and queens of England. He mentioned the monarchs of the Tudor period and how Henry the Eighth had had six wives. He struggled with the word 'Eighth' and Candice assured him that everyone struggles with that word because it does not sound like it looks. William accepted this and continued.

As he read with fewer and fewer interjections required from her, her mind strayed to the box of things from her previous life. Coming out of a traumatic time and dumping all of its memories on her without warning or waiting to be invited, that box had no right to dominate her thoughts as it was doing. She was powerless to avoid the hanging cloud that it put her under. The thoughts of feeling close to Luke, the only person she had ever felt close to, and the reality of losing that. She was stronger now, more aware, more capable, better equipped to make her own decisions and her own way in life. Why then was she silently crying as she went through the motions of listening to William reading his book?

William saw a teardrop fall from the end of Candice's nose and drip onto her denim skirt. He turned to look at her and saw that her face was screwed up with the futile resistance against unstoppable forces emanating from within.

"Ca'ice? You crying? Why you sad?" said William, still holding the book with one hand and pointing a finger of the other hand at the word he was about to read next. "I 'ave made you cry?"

"No William," she sobbed, "you haven't made me cry. I was thinking about someone who made me happy, but he died. That's why I'm sad."

"How he made you happy, Ca'ice?"

"He held me and made me feel safe, I suppose," she said without rationalising too much.

"I 'old you, make ooo safe, if you like," offered William. Candice felt another surge of sobbing sweep over her. William put down his book on the floor and wrapped both arms around her shoulders. She buried her head into his chest and felt that instant sensation of safety, as though she had stepped off a ship in a storm and onto dry land.

Her sobbing abated. William loyally and stoically protected her from further attacks of high emotion. She closed her eyes and allowed his presence to comfort her. She felt hugely grateful to him. His affection and care were freely given and without any complicated agenda. She had witnessed William stepping up to help anyone he saw who might need some. It was in his nature. He was a kind and caring person and she felt lucky to have him there, being that pillar of strength she craved.

Did he want more from her? He had touched her breast under the willow tree. Had it been curiosity or sexual desire? She could only apply her own rationale and personal code of conduct to that episode. She had no way of telling what he was thinking at that time. It had been the only intimate contact she had experienced for too long and she had accepted it as a compliment, however clumsily it had been offered. Candice moved her body back from William's chest. He loosened his hold on her. She took his hand and placed it on her breast. William froze, a statue holding the breast of a woman, a woman he felt strongly attracted to. Slowly he caressed her with such gentleness. Candice was moved and turned on by it. She saw that William was also in a state of heightened intensity. All logic and consideration for the consequences of what she was thinking was bypassed. She was all-consumed by the feeling that she was, once again, a woman. A fully-functioning, sexually desirable woman and the man she was now in an intimate embrace with was the reason she felt that way. Steered by her, they slipped, in full embrace, off the seat and onto the carpeted floor. As she took control, a surge of energy and life raced through both of them. It was reckless, passionate and intense whilst also being beautiful, close and affectionate.

No words were needed.

CHAPTER EIGHTEEN

Only under the strictest conditions were inmates of
The Garrin Unit allowed out into the open space of the
secure facility. When that did happen, there were double
staffing details on hand, and everything was tightened up
to suffocation levels. Only the staff could pass through the
grounds and this took place mainly during times when the
inmates were safely incarcerated in their individual locked
rooms.

The grassed area was surrounded by a twenty-foot
high fence which was topped with rolls of barbed wire. A
fifteen-yard corridor ran between the first fence and an
identical one which bordered the wider hospital grounds.
Mounted on steel posts supporting the outer fence were
CCTV cameras, monitoring all movement and recording it
on videotape in the control centre of The Garrin Unit. To
the collective memory of the staff, no legal representative
of an inmate had ever asked to inspect the outdoor
recreational area. Not all legal representatives were as
thorough as Robin Purcell.

Purcell was undoubtedly the keenest legal
representative of all of those serving the needs of clients
inside The Garrin Unit of Heavem Hospital. His visits
were prompt and regular and he became familiar with
many of the gate staff and guard nurses deployed to escort
Gavin Malligan to and from his meetings with Purcell.
The staff were, of course, unaware that Purcell's client
was sitting on a large fortune in offshore bank accounts.

Once inside the consulting room, the usual positions were adopted with Malligan facing the camera and covering his mouth to speak. Purcell commenced by reporting on progress with the instructions he had been given on his last visit. The activities of the Rogerson brothers were a particular field of interest for his client, who had become used to Purcell's euphemistic language when describing any activity which he knew to be unlawful and unethical for a lawyer to involve himself in.

"The two gentlemen you have identified have carried the work they were asked to do and the additional 'team member' is now fully participating. It seems that he has a romantic interest of a somewhat youthful nature, dangerously so in his profession. He will do what is required of him, no doubt."

"I knew it," said Malligan, making a fist yet still concealing his mouth from the camera. "I knew that guy had something to fear. He's a fuckin' nonce!"

"Erm, quite!" Acceded Purcell who was reluctant to agree too enthusiastically. "He is awaiting further instructions. Meanwhile, our source on the other side of the fence reports that the power supply can be accessed without too much difficulty and the hospital incinerator you asked about does not rely on electricity. It is oil fired, apparently. It can be operated without power."

"Good. Now, there's something else I want," said Malligan, "and this is how I'm going to get it."

At the conclusion of the consultation, Purcell asked the staff to show him the outdoor recreational facilities of The Garrin Unit. He was asked to explain why he needed to inspect that part of the site because all unusual activities were subject to being challenged as a matter of course. He assured the staff that he was ensuring that his client's welfare was being addressed and that meant he was able to breathe fresh air regularly. Satisfied that Purcell's request was reasonable, he was taken to the grassed area at the back of the building. He saw the wide green expanse which led up to the inner perimeter fence, beyond which he saw the outer fence and the tops of some of the taller buildings of Heavem. Purcell made a mental note of the positions of the CCTV cameras. He spotted that the cameras were fixed and not oscillating, affording the viewer a picture of the corridor of land between the fences but not on either side. He drew the visit to a close and left in his four-by-four. Three hundred yards beyond the hospital gates, Purcell stopped the car at the side of the road under the canopy of overhanging trees. He got out and opened the bonnet of the giant car. Going through the motions of checking the functions of the engine, he waited for three minutes until he heard a voice from inside the wooded area. Purcell did not look up.

"How's our friend?" said the unseen man.

"In a positive frame of mind, I would say. He has asked me to pass on some additional instructions for you."

"I'm listening."

*

PC Russell Warren was standing at the entrance to the garden centre talking to the supervisor, Albert O'Neill, and writing in his notebook.

"He was here one minute and gone the next," said O'Neill who was in enormous beige overalls over his heavy build. He was well passed retirement age but had a ruddy complexion of the well-fed, outdoor type.

"Is he a long-term patient?" asked Warren who was reciting standard mantras.

"No, he's only been here a few weeks."

"Is he subject to any court orders then?" he probed.

"No, he's a voluntary, can go anytime, but I'm still supposed to report him missing in case any harm comes to him."

"That's fine, you do the right thing. I'll make a start looking for him. If you can just give me his name and a description, I can -"

"I'll do better than that, he's here now," interrupted O'Neill.

He pointed at a man who was approaching with no urgency or apparent preoccupation in mind. He ambled through the trolleys full of young plants, stopping to inspect and sniff some of them as he went along.

"His name's Patrick Miller," said O'Neill to Warren. "He's odd, even by Heaven's standards."

Miller reached them and finally acknowledged with a smile that there was anyone else there.

"Where have you been Patrick?" said O'Neill in a combination of frustration and concern.

"Oh, I just wanted a walk around," said Miller apparently under the influence of calming medication.

He was about fifty, thin and pale, as many of the patients tended to be at Heavem Hospital. His tattooed forearms suggested prison rather than the military, but the faded ink showed that they had probably been applied decades before.

O'Neill calmed down sufficiently to appeal to Miller not to absent himself without telling a member of staff and he went on to list the unpleasant possibilities which could occur if he did. Warren put away his notebook and left O'Neill to it.

*

Two days later, Andy Aberfoyle left the back door of The Garrin Unit and walked across the grass. He did so at 9.58am by his watch, which he had set to the radio news bulletin time at 8.00am that day. He crossed the grass toward the inner fence, positioning himself in line with the central CCTV camera between the fences. At exactly 10.00am, a dark green missile was thrown over both fences. It landed twenty feet from him, making him jump nervously but he managed to avoid showing it. He slowly walked toward where the package had landed. He was unable to find it.

Aberfoyle shuffled along the grass, sliding his feet through the trimmed blades trying to find what it was he had been told to recover. Panic was getting close to the surface with him. Soon his presence there would be perceived as suspicious and, as he knew very well, anything odd would be challenged.

His left foot struck something solid, something that moved. He glanced down and saw nothing. He dipped down onto one knee to pretend to retie a shoelace and he saw that there was an item concealed in a wrapping fashioned from long grass and bound with green garden string. It was flat and measured eighteen inches by three inches and it was narrower at one end. He picked up the thing, which was unexpectedly heavy, and eased it inside his jacket keeping his back to the building throughout. Pressing the item against his body with his arm, he headed back to the doorway he had emerged from.

Once back inside the building, Aberfoyle was clear to move around without being searched or otherwise questioned, unlike at the main gate. He went to the residential wing and asked to be able to speak to Gavin Malligan. Aberfoyle told the head guard-nurse that he was concerned that Malligan was displaying the symptoms of depression and that he wanted to speak to him in his room rather than in the goldfish bowl of the association or group therapy sessions. His request was granted, and he was taken to Malligan's room and allowed in by the nurse.

Malligan was lying on his bed waiting for Aberfoyle. When the door opened and Aberfoyle entered, the guard-nurse was asked to allow them some time to consult in private for professional confidentiality. Once alone with Malligan, Aberfoyle produced the grass-wrapped object and placed it in Malligan's outstretched hand. Aberfoyle had eliminated from his mind any logical thought about what the item actually was. Malligan thought about little else. Aberfoyle turned to leave but Malligan stopped him.

"Wait!"

Aberfoyle's froze. He could not explain his presence there for any length of time and he was keen to get away from this killer. He felt exposed and his churning stomach reminded him of it.

"Tell me about the night staff here. How many are there of them?"

"Erm, four, normally, I think," said Aberfoyle, who rarely stayed late.

"You think?" Malligan turned the screw with alarming ease and Aberfoyle reacted accordingly.

"Yes, it's four, inside that is. From nine at night to seven in the morning."

"Where?"

"In the control centre, the other end of the main corridor from here."

Malligan recalled seeing the corridor, albeit through a heavy barred gate, on his way to the outdoor exercise area and under guard. He pictured the door at the end, although he had not seen it open nor anyone come in or out of it.

"What's in there?" he demanded.

Aberfoyle was in denial that he was helping with something which was abhorrent to him, there was clearly a plan in progress, a plan to either escape or cause significant harm to someone. He had to shut those thoughts from his mind. The alternative was that he was going to prison and he would never see his underage girlfriend again.

"CCTV screens, you've seen the cameras?"

"What else?"

"A small kitchen with a dining table, four chairs, they play cards all night. There's a microwave oven and an urn for hot water. They drink a lot of tea, I suppose."

"And the master key fits this door and the control room does it?"

"All outer doors, it's for all the outer doors in The Garrin."

"And what about the internal doors?" asked Malligan in a lower whisper.

"The nursing staff have to let me through, I don't have a key for internal doors – like for here."

Aberfoyle jabbered nervously about the guards who patrolled the perimeter. Malligan cut him short because he already knew about them.

"That will do," said Malligan, who was also keen to avoid casting suspicion on Aberfoyle, at least for the time being. "You will be told what to do next. Now fuck off!"

Aberfoyle left the room which was swiftly locked. He went about his duties hoping that his ordeal was over, that he had complied with the demands of his blackmailers and that they would leave him alone. His naivety was boundless. Malligan looked at the object and thought that Aberfoyle could have removed the grass from it before giving it to him - a pervert and an idiot. He would have to dispose of that without raising suspicion. Distasteful as it seemed, he formed a plan to eat the grass and the string in order to dispose of it. Meanwhile, he unravelled the string and grass to reveal what he had wanted, exactly as it should be. He held it in his hand, stroking the blade and feeling the destructive power one just like it had brought to him years ago. It was the first time had felt that since he had ended the life of Luke Gould. It felt good, very good.

CHAPTER NINETEEN

Heavem's patients were admitted and discharged at a rate which Russell Warren could not keep abreast with. There were so many informal or voluntary admissions that he could not begin to monitor the movements of them. No sooner would he become aware that a patient had arrived and was being treated than he would see the same troubled soul being re-admitted, unaware that they had left in the interim period. He took more notice of the patients who were there under formal arrangements such as those who were subject to a court order or a clinical decision made under the Mental Health Act. Unfortunately, it was the less secure patients which caused him more work. They were not locked in their respective wards and were allowed to roam free and many of them took that to extremes. The memory of finding the late Phyllis was never far from his mind.

It was on a Thursday morning at ten-thirty that this predictability of the movements of the people of Heavem was turned upside down. Warren received a phone call at home in his flat. It was from a frantic nurse stating that a long-term patient was on the roof of the main building and threatening to jump off.

Warren grabbed his radio and pulled on his uniform coat over his civilian clothes. He went up to the main building and saw that a crowd had gathered on the grass beneath the tall bell tower capping the apex of the old stone building. Standing on what appeared to be the guttering running along the edge of the slates was a ghostly figure in a pale green nightgown, wavy grey hair blowing in the breeze. The figure was gripping the police radio booster aerial and it momentarily crossed Warren's mind that his radio would not work without it and he hoped that the figure didn't break the thing. He spotted Heather Fellhouse on the grass talking to some of the nursing staff.

"Heather, what's going on? Who is that?" he asked.

"It's Brenda."

Warren knew Brenda, but he knew her as the excitable soul with speech difficulties who just wanted to be everybody's friend. He did not know her as the heroine of a desperate and suicidal tragedy being played out in full view of the staff and patients she had existed alongside for so many years.

"I can't imagine what's brought this on," said Heather, "she's usually compliant and no trouble at all."

"How did she get up there?" asked Warren, trying to rationalise rather than come up with a solution.

"There's a metal ladder, I'll show you." Heather explained on the way that the ladder was only used for maintaining the chimney pots and the radio aerial She took Warren up the main staircase as far as he thought it went. At the top of the stairs there was a wall panel without any handles or hinges visible on the outside. The panel was open, revealing a four-foot square space lit by daylight from above. The metal ladder Heather had spoken of was fixed to the back wall. Spider's webs and dust hung around it in the damp space.

"Has anyone been up to try and speak to her?" asked Warren.

Heather gave a wry smile. "Now who do you think would do that Russell?"

"Oh, I get it." The penny dropped.

He wondered if he was the right man for this particular task, surely the nursing staff would be better qualified and experienced to be talking a suicidal mental patient down off a roof? In the absence of any other willing volunteers, he began climbing the ladder to an opened trapdoor and out onto the exposed and windy expanse of the highest point of the hospital. He saw Brenda, standing on the precipice as though on the prow of an ocean liner, looking out at the sky as the wind ruffled her hair and her nightgown. She must have been freezing.

With one hand on the sloping slates, Warren edged along the ten-inch wide strip of old and crumbling concrete, beyond which was a sheer drop of four floors to the gravel edged grass below. His toes curled inside his trainers in a vain and futile attempt to grip the surface. The moss on the slates made it all precariously slippery. Brenda was turned away from him, seeming not to notice him approaching. He was worried about startling her, but he had, at some point, to engage her in some dialogue. He got within ten yards of her when the wind dropped and a moment of relative quiet ensued.

"Hi Brenda!" he said with a tone of light-hearted friendliness which did not befit the circumstances.

She did not acknowledge him.

"Brenda, Hi! It's me PC Warren, Russell Warren. Remember? I'm your friend."

Brenda turned her head to look at him. She was sobbing and miserable, there was none of the enthusiasm she habitually displayed with everyone she met, excitement at being with people she saw as her friends. Her eyes were blank, resigned and empty. She looked alone in life, abandoned, with nothing to live for.

"Brenda, what are you doing out here, love? It's a bit chilly, don't you think?"

"Brenda turned her head back and lowered her face. She began wailing with heightened distress. Warren was having the opposite effect than the one he was aiming for. He had to try something else.

"Brenda!" He edged a yard nearer. "Brenda, how did you get up here? Did someone help you?"

Brenda stopped crying enough to say something but with her communication difficulties it was impossible for him to making out what it was she was trying to say.

At that moment, a roof slate which had been in that position for many decades, moved under the faintest pressure from the touch of Warren's hand. The slate careered down the slope, across the ledge and out into the open air.

"Look out!" called Warren to the onlookers below. Many of them scurried backwards as the slate hurtled to the ground. It missed the assembled people and smashed into pieces on the gravel. Gasps of shock and relief emitted from the crowd. Warren also felt relief, it was only a slate. It could have been Brenda or himself or both. He regained the thread of the conversation he was trying to conduct with her.

"Say that again please Brenda," he appealed, trying hard to appear calm when he was far from it.

"Ee no ma fen!" she virtually shouted. Warren got the gist of it.

"Who, Brenda, who isn't your friend?"

"Da ma' ee no ma fen, ee ba' ma'!"

"Who is this man, Brenda? Who is this bad man? Because, he's not my friend either if he has upset you." He chanced a couple of steps. He was within five yards of her. He darted a quick glance over the edge then quickly looked back regretting having done so.

"Ee no' dow' there," she said.

Warren looked down at the assembled crowd. The experience made him feel queasy. There were about forty people standing in several groups. Brenda seemed to be saying that whoever it was who had upset her or caused her to be on the roof was not amongst the onlookers.

"Brenda, come with me please. I will look after you, I'm here, I'm your friend."

"I' true?" Brenda finally showed some acceptance that his presence was a good thing.

"Yes Brenda, it's true." He held out his hand. Brenda let go of the metal aerial and stepped forward to take his hand. She smiled and sobbed simultaneously.

"Steady now," he said, "one step at a time, let's go and have a cup of tea where it's warm."

They edged to the open skylight where Heather was standing on the higher rungs of the ladder with her head and shoulders visible. She dipped down and allowed Warren to ease Brenda onto the ladder, placing her hands on the sides and keeping hold of her wrists until she was well inside the building.

A round of applause rose from the crowd below. Warren felt it inappropriate to acknowledge it. He prepared to climb inside the square hole but stopped to examine the broken hasp which had held the padlock sealing the hatch. It had been forced with some tool leaving recently made grooves in the wooden frame. He was sure that Brenda had not done this alone.

Once back in the warmth of the ward, Brenda was dressed and treated for exposure to the cold. Hot, sweet tea and woollen clothing were all it took to address her physical needs but her emotional state continued to be of concern. She was unable or unwilling to speak about what had made her go up onto the roof. Warren sat with the staff as they gently and caringly questioned her about it. When the issue arose about who the bad man was, she became upset and the question did not get answered.

A phone call was taken by the ward clerk. It was for Warren. He went into the office and answered it. It was Heather asking him to come to the Operating Centre. Leaving the ward staff with a request to let him know if Brenda said anything of interest, he set off to see what Heather wanted. She met him in the corridor and turned him around to walk outside, explaining as they walked.

"The electricity sub-station has been broken into. You'd think all of those 'Danger, high voltage' signs would mean something, wouldn't you?"

"Why would anyone want to break into that?" he asked.

"Beats me," mused Heather. "It must have happened whilst Brenda was up on the roof this morning. So, I guess we can rule out Brenda as a suspect!" she joked.

Warren had a loosely formed idea that Brenda's presence on that roof and the break-in may, in some way, be connected, although, he was unable to come up with a reason for it.

*

Kenny and Dean Rogerson met Aberfoyle in different places and at different times. There was no pattern to it. They were cautious to the point of obsessive about police surveillance activity. They need not have been so. The police had no such covert operation in place. Nevertheless, the duo operated as though there might be. This added to the satisfaction for Dean and fuelled his imaginary role as a military spy. Kenny was somewhat more focussed and practical in his perception of their activities.

In a ten-pin bowling alley a mile from Aberfoyle's flat, they sat in the 'Burger 'n Fries' café around a white, plastic table. Kenny sat next to Aberfoyle and Dean sat opposite him. Surrounded, dominated and intimidated, Aberfoyle had by then fully accepted his place in the grand scheme. Kenny placed a newspaper on the table and appeared to any observer, of which there were none, to be studying the racing form. Inside the newspaper were photographs of the inside machinery of the electric sub-station at Heavem Hospital.

"This," said Kenny, pointing to the large switchgear unit in the picture, "is the main power unit for the hospital. Someone else is going to knock that out so you don't need to worry about that. But this," he pointed to a smaller version of the machine against the side wall, "is an emergency generator. There's another one of those inside The Garrin Unit and you are going to disable it."

"I, I don't know anything about generators," said Aberfoyle, half anticipating the response.

"Well you'd better listen carefully, mate," said Kenny through gritted teeth. "You remember why, don't you?"

Aberfoyle nodded and looked at the photographs. Kenny explained what Aberfoyle was to do with the generator. Aberfoyle momentarily allowed himself to digest the facts and take in the magnitude of the plan he was to play his part in, albeit reluctantly. He was readying himself to go when he was told by Kenny to stay where he was. There was another task for him to do.

Dean took out a spectacles case. It was quite old and was of a rigid structure. It bore the name of an optician Aberfoyle had not heard of.

"Take this," said Dean.

"But I don't wear specs," protested Aberfoyle half-heartedly.

"You do now!" asserted Kenny, staring at him. Dean explained.

"Inside this case is a space for a pair of glasses. Under that are two plasticine moulds. You have a key for the outer doors with you in The Garrin Unit all day long. You will put the key in there and press the pads together to make a perfect mould of the key before giving it back when you leave as usual. Clear?"

A shiver ran through Aberfoyle's body. What if he got caught? What if his luck ran out? He had got away with taking the grass-covered thing into Malligan's room but was this pushing things too far? They were about to be pushed further.

"One last thing, mate," said Kenny, being anything but amiable. Aberfoyle felt that he had been given quite enough to remember and carry out.

"What?" He showed some impatience which the Rogersons chose to ignore.

Dean took out a stack of square teabags from his pocket and gave them to Aberfoyle. They were the type sold at every supermarket across the nation. The difference was that each one had been cut with a razor blade, about a centimetre in length and several powdered tablets had been poured into the hole using a drinking straw. The tablets contained a strong sedative, normally used for anaesthetising a patient before surgery. They had been stolen from a hospital store in the centre of Manchester. The hole in each teabag was then sewn up with white cotton and virtually invisible to the eye.

"When we tell you to, you are going to swap these for the ones the night staff will be using," He handed over a small jar of coffee of another popular make, "and the same with the coffee."

216

Aberfoyle looked at the harmless-looking items. A spectacles case, some teabags and a jar of coffee. He thought how innocuous they looked then about the harm they could cause.

"These won't kill anyone, will they?" he said, uncomfortably loudly for Kenny's liking.

"Shhh! Keep your voice down. They will make them sleep, that's all."

Aberfoyle found a crumb of comfort in hearing this, a moment's respite from the horror of the situation he was in – up to his neck.

CHAPTER TWENTY

Warren was getting used to the functions of Heavem, its standard practices, the habits of its residents. He followed many of the protocols put in place by his predecessor and, with the help of the ever-reliable Heather, introduced a few ideas of his own. One such initiative was a time-saving measure for when the kids in the children's home went missing.

Previously, the taking of a vulnerable missing person report meant starting from scratch; Filling in the details of the child: description, past-history, preferences, then acquiring a recent photograph if one was available. That all took time and had proved to be necessary but largely inefficient. As many of the runaways headed straight down the only road in and out toward the town, time could be of the essence. A lot of work could be avoided, both for Warren and his colleagues in town, if the system could be streamlined.

The first change he made was to ask the reception of new children to include the taking of an instant photograph of the child. That could be attached to an information sheet which could be faxed to the main police station along with the details of the child which did not vary in time. Updates could be added later. All that Warren needed to establish each time a new report came in was when the child was last seen and any new indication as to where they might have gone.

The first time he utilised this new approach was following a call he received from the children's unit informing him that a twelve-year-old girl called Sally had gone missing following an argument with the staff. Having not encountered Sally before, he said that he would call at the children's home to look at the picture before staring the process of tracking her down and returning her.

Whilst he was still speaking on the phone, Police Cadet Christian Wood came in the office, resplendent in his official cap and T shirt with embroidered badge on the left breast. He heard Warren concluding the telephone conversation.

"Okay then, just confirm for me, Sally Imsworth, twelve years old, four-feet-seven. Maroon jacket and black leggings, tennis shoes. Okay, thanks." He put down the receiver and looked at Christian.

"Alright Cadet?"

"Fine," said Christian who had become quite at home as the office deputy. "Has Sally run off again?"

"Again?" I haven't had any previous report of that name."

"Well, they don't always tell you straight away," said Christian imparting the wisdom of his experiences. "They often come back before anyone has missed them." Warren did not doubt that Christian could be considered an authority on the subject.

"You know this Sally then?"

"Yeah, she's my friend. She's twelve but she's very small." Warren found amusement in hearing the diminutive Christian call another person small. He asked him,

"Does she get a hard time there, for being so small I mean?" Christian screwed up his face in the effort of trying to explain.

"Nah, not really. She's too small for most people to notice her."

"But you've noticed her, haven't you?" Warren was teasing Christian. "Is she your girlfriend?"

"No! She's just my friend, not my girlfriend!" Warren left the ribbing at that and concentrated on the matter in hand.

"I don't suppose you know where your friend might have gone, do you?"

"Oh yeah," said Christian as though everyone knew the answer to that one.

"Well? Where is she?"

"Down the old lane. Do you want me to show you, or is it best if I go and look for her? She might be scared of you," said Christian without a hint of superiority. Warren stood up and slipped on his jacket and cap.

"Come on, you can show me where it is and be ready to do the talking if she won't speak to me."

They set out across the grass and past the long nursery greenhouses of the garden centre. When the established path appeared to end and overgrown bushes prevented further access, Christian pushed hanging branches aside and passed through ten yards of bushes and onto an old farm track with knee high grass along the edges and up the centre. It had not seen a vehicle in some considerable time. The path stretched out for a hundred yards then curved to the left as the hill fell away. Through the uneven hedges lining the path, Warren could see across fields for miles.

"I didn't know this was here. Where does it come out?"

"Don't know," said Christian, "never been that far down here. Sally will be somewhere around."

They continued down the path which allowed access to several fields in active agricultural use. Warren surmised that it was used for tractor access and missing kids only. Two hundred yards along the path, it widened to a double gateway next to a concrete block of the sort intended to house old milk churns. Instead it was being used as a raised bench for a girl of tiny frame and features, wearing a maroon jacket, black leggings and tennis shoes. Upon seeing Christian, she smiled, but on seeing PC Warren she let out a heavy sigh and made a 'tutting' sound of disapproval.

"Come on Sal," appealed Christian, "you can't stay out here for ever. You've missed dinner and it's going to be teatime soon."

"Oh, I suppose so," she said, clambering down from the cube of concrete. She wiped the light grey stone dust from her clothes and set off to walk with Christian back along the rough path. Warren decided to let them go alone.

He would go to the children's home later to finalise the 'returned unharmed' paperwork. He watched them disappear around a curve in the rising path then he climbed onto Sally's concrete platform to see over the hedges and get his bearings. The view was quite expansive and uplifting. He had not considered that side of Heavem before. Despite, or possibly because of, the overgrown and unpeopled nature of the old lane, Warren found it to be a place of beauty and spiritual refreshment, so close to a place of human sadness and torment. Perhaps this was the bit that made those who knew it call the place Heaven.

*

Andy Aberfoyle's fingers were still shaking when he handed back the spectacles case to Kenny Rogerson. The latest meeting place was in the Fried Chicken restaurant in a large shopping complex. The twin pads of plasticine had successfully assumed the exact shape of the master key which was accounted for with strict and military rigour at the beginning and end of every day he went into The Garrin Unit. Aberfoyle resisted the urge to ask what was going to be done with the replica key, although he craved knowing when so that he could get on with his life.

Kenny questioned him about the back-up generator and Aberfoyle told them that he had found where it was and could gain access to it without difficulty. As before, Dean made Aberfoyle repeat what he had been told about what to do with the generator. It involved the removal of several replaceable fuses and the destruction of them and any other spares that might be stored nearby. Aberfoyle was able to satisfy his tormentors that he was capable of carrying out these tasks. On his way home, he allowed himself the brief sensation that his troubles would soon be over. He could resume his life as before only with a greater degree of secrecy until Beverley was old enough for them to be a couple for real, not living in fear all the time. The Rogerson brothers held different views on the outcome for Aberfoyle. Theirs were, perhaps, somewhat more realistic.

*

Warren was leaving his office in the main building of Heavem Hospital. He was on his way to collect his protégée Christian Wood to take him into town to join the other police cadets for the evening. Warren passed an alcove off the corridor which housed two payphones which he had, until then, not seen anyone use. He would have passed the alcove without noticing but for hearing the word 'Fuck!' exclaimed in anger. Warren stopped to see a figure of a man with his back to him. He was leaning on the wall and was holding the telephone receiver to his ear. Apart from the expletive, the conversation was taking place in hushed tones, so hushed there may not have been any words at all. Warren's initial thought was to avoid prying into another person's private conversation and to continue on his way. It was the anger in that one word which made him stop and at least find out who it was.

He stepped forward and coughed to announce his presence. The man stood up instantly and moved from the wall. He turned to see Warren who immediately recognised him as Patrick Miller, the voluntary patient who had wandered off from the garden centre a few days before.

"Is everything alright, Patrick?" he asked, inadvertently sounding like a housemaster in a boarding school. Miller said nothing. He stood motionless for a few seconds then he dropped the phone receiver and left it swinging. He walked past Warren and along the corridor toward the wards.

Warren picked up the receiver and listened. There was only the dialling tone. There was no way of telling what Miller was trying to do or who, if anyone, he was swearing at. In that place it could have any number of possible explanations. He wasn't going to look into it further. As Albert O'Neill at the garden centre had commented, Miller's behaviour was odd, but Warren found it no more so than many of his fellow residents. Miller was there on a voluntary basis and could leave whenever he wanted, which applied to dozens of others. He would probably be gone soon anyway. Warren replaced the receiver and went out to the Children's Unit.

CHAPTER TWENTY-ONE

On the Friday, Andy Aberfoyle arrived at work at Heavem, trying hard to appear normal and to not give away that he was about to commit a crime which could either cost him his job and his liberty or could free him from the invisible thousand-ton weight he had been carrying for weeks. He was, by his nature and past habits, nervous in his everyday manner. He hoped that he was not going to be seen differently that day. One suspicious moment and everything could collapse around him. It was vital that he remained calm enough to do what he had to do. He passed through the routine search carried out by the now familiar colleagues staffing the main gate of The Garrin Unit. There was nothing unusual in a member of staff bringing in coffee and teabags, it happened all the time. A cursory glance at the contents of the pockets and bags of staff members was all that was required, and Aberfoyle passed through without a hitch.

His duties went as the usual routine dictated, although the group session which included Gavin Malligan made him sweat and feel sick. He heard and digested little of the words spoken by Clara, whose speeches all too frequently became sermons. That session was about empathy and was lost on everyone present. Arthur Elevand was humming an unidentifiable tune, Lawrence was picking at the skin around his fingernails, Bela Ferenquelar had his eyes closed and Jeremy Pilkington had resorted to rubbing his thighs again with no explicable reason. Barty Lerry and Anthony Sharatt silently resumed their ongoing hatred of each other, the earlier altercation having fallen away to nothing as was usual, in the manner predicted by The Garrin's director Ron Jeaver, although their feuding was restricted to malicious staring during Clara's deliberations. Malligan looked at Aberfoyle without expression and any discomfort or other silent communication went unnoticed by anyone else. To Aberfoyle, Malligan's eyes were saying to him 'Have you done it yet?' and 'You had better get it right or your life won't be worth living!'

Aberfoyle's palms were hot and clammy. He dropped his pen several times and had to reach down to pick it up, each time fumbling to grip the pen on the floor. Malligan just looked right through him, giving nothing away. At the close of the session, Malligan gave him one final glance as he shuffled out of the room. Both men hoping that they would never set eyes on each other again.

Meal times were a clinically efficient process at The Garrin Unit as they were in the rest of Heavem. Aberfoyle knew that time-honoured pattern and because his role was not as a guard or a nurse, he was usually free to eat or to catch up on his admin whilst the rest of the place took a meal. The nurses served the meals to the inmates and dealt with the outbursts of disapproval as and when they came. Aberfoyle had intended to make the switch of tea and coffee during the evening meal but he had changed his mind when he considered that the late shift may well have hot drinks before the change-over at nine. Someone might realise and the plan would fail. Instead he chose the busy time to slip outside to the electrical plant room. He used his master key to let himself in, leaving the door slightly open to illuminate the room. He edged to the emergency generator and was about to pull out the fuses when the realisation struck him that he could leave his fingerprints there. He took out a handkerchief and covered his hand before pulling out all six plastic moulded fuses. As he had been told, he bent and disfigured the metal connecting pins and pushed them into an ancient pile of coal in the corner of the room. A quick check of the surrounding area revealed no spare fuses.

Wiping coal dust from his hands he went back to the door and listened for any activity outside. Voices could be heard but they seemed far away. When they could no longer be heard, he slipped out and quickly closed and locked the plant room door. He felt as though he had not taken a breath for two minutes. When his lungs did finally reactivate, they sucked in air at an alarming rate, sending his heart rate sky high. He had completed the first part, only one task remained and his part of the deal was done. He had to wait until after eight o'clock for that one.

*

Candice had thought long and hard about what she had done. At the time it had been on impulse, nothing planned, nothing considered, just two people finding a moment of closeness and allowing it to become a moment of intimacy. William too had thought about it a great deal. Handicapped since birth, he had been unable to function without help in many aspects of his life. He had always demonstrated a desire to expand his capabilities in any activity he had participated in. He had volunteered for everything, spotted opportunities his carers had missed and managed to control his frustration at his limitations with patience and positivity.

At the age of twenty-six, the evening in the day room with Candice had been the first significant sexual experience of his life. Whilst he was undoubtedly physically capable, expert clinical opinion could be divided as to whether William had the mental or emotional capacity to undertake or understand a meaningful adult relationship. William believed that he could. Candice also believed that he could. Although she accepted that there were many aspects of William's life that she could not, at that stage, comprehend. She had initially felt close to William because she felt that he needed her, and she needed to be important to someone in that way. There was more to William than that. Once the constant spillage of saliva was overlooked, William was clearly a kind and considerate young man, always stepping up to help people before he had been asked. He had initiative and used it to the benefit of others. In the deliberations going on in Candice's head, she rationalised that if William was capable of doing all of those things, showing the maturity to help others less able, comfort those who were upset, why shouldn't he be given credence for his own emotional welfare?

Candice was also aware that her stay at The Bowers was transitory as was her contribution to providing care to the patients of Heavem. Had it been a man in her position, embarking on a sexual relationship with a female patient whose capacity to consent was in question, he would have been in a most precarious situation. She could keep her own counsel, but could William? Her doubts were based on her lack of knowledge of his ability to realise the likely consequences of their illicit union. She knew that she made William happy, but could William be trusted to be discreet and keep that happiness to himself and share it only with her?

In group activities with the long-term patients, Candice made a special effort to avoid anything which might appear to favour William over the others.

Occasionally, William wanted to hold her hand which was a common practice. Candice did hold his hand but also held the hand of another patient at the same time in order to deflect any perceived unfavourable observations from the permanent staff. When they were alone, Candice began to explain to William that their liaisons would get them both into trouble with the hospital authorities, should they come to light. William appeared to realise this already, to her relief and surprise. He assured her that he would keep it a secret because he would never do anything that would make her unhappy. The longer term ramifications of their relationship were neither discussed nor otherwise considered.

On Friday evening, after the meal had been served in the day room in the main building, William helped to clear away the crockery for the patients who were less able to do so. Candice had been spoon-feeding stewed apple to a severely handicapped lady called Muriel. William went to Muriel's table and asked if they had finished.

"Yes, I think Muriel has had enough now, thank you," said Candice, wiping her hands on a tea-towel. Knowing that Muriel could not speak, William risked a covert word with Candice.

"Can we meet later, Ca'ice, please?" Candice looked around, there was nobody in earshot. William had picked his moment shrewdly.

"Sure. I'll be in the garden, at the stone bench, about ten o'clock." William smiled a soggy, wet-chinned grin before checking himself to appear unmoved by their snatched exchange of words.

Candice felt apprehensive. The risks were not to be underestimated but the tingle of an illicit liaison, a meeting that would bring a sense of intimacy, and planned this time, was a greatly uplifting sensation.

*

At 8.50pm Aberfoyle entered the side room off The Garrin's operations centre. None of the screen monitoring staff looked up to see him pass through. There was nobody in the tiny kitchen, so he set about swapping the items he had been given by the Rogersons. He took the teabags out first and tipped out the existing ones from a packet which was half full. He placed the drugged ones in the packet and replaced it on the shelf. He was about to do the same with the coffee when the kitchen door opened. In panic, Aberfoyle dropped the coffee jar which tipped out its legitimate contents onto the shelf. He moved his body across to conceal his error.

Glancing over his shoulder, he that saw a night worker, who Aberfoyle knew as Ian Page, had arrived early for work and was placing his sandwiches in the fridge for consumption later on during his shift. Neither of them acknowledged each other. Once Ian had left to attend the briefing and, finding himself alone again, Aberfoyle tried to control his fingers, involuntarily wobbling and slippery with perspiration. His brow glistened and he wiped it on the sleeve of his white, hospital tunic. He made the switch of coffee and replaced everything where it was supposed to be. His breathing was heavy and noisy. He took a moment to compose himself before going back to the staff changing room to prepare to go. He passed the briefing room where Ian Page had been joined by Alan Fell, Mohammed Halar and Frank Woan to complete the night crew. They were the intended victims of what he had just done. He tried not to connect his actions to real people. He told himself that the only people he should be concentrating on were Beverley and himself.

Aberfoyle drove home feeling apprehensive but better than he had felt for some time. He thought about Beverley and how there was nothing standing in the way of their happiness. He was going to take possession of the incriminating photographs and destroy them in a ritualistic fashion. It crossed his mind that it was a pity to be destroying pictures of the girl he loved. It didn't matter, there would be more pictures, a lifetime of them.

He parked the car under a yellow streetlight on the road outside his flat. It was 9.25pm. The night staff at The Garrin Unit would be hard at work bedding down everyone and administering medication before retiring to the control room where they would be taking some unknown medication of their own. He again shook that thought from his mind. It was not the time to dwell on negative things. He locked the car and walked along the pavement to the path leading to his door. Beverley was due to arrive at 9.30pm and he was keen to get the flat warm and welcoming for her. He put his key in the door but before he could turn it, a deep male voice close behind him said,

"Andrew Aberfoyle?"

He turned to see two people he had not seen before. The man was in his mid-forties and dark in both complexion and facial expression. His hair was military short, and his clothes were formal: a plain tie, a padded anorak over a dark suit. The woman with him was in her twenties, smart, upright, wearing a plum suit with a long jacket and sensible shoes. Her short, dyed-blonde hair gave her a no-nonsense manner.

"Erm, yes. I'm Andrew Aberfoyle. Can I help you?"

The woman took over for the introductions. Holding out an item Aberfoyle made no attempt to look at, she said,

"I'm DC Nixon, this is DC Williams. We are from the C.I.D."

Aberfoyle's heart stopped and his breathing did too. There was a possibility that their visit was about something other than his secret life. He hung onto that thought.

"Oh, if it's about a client of mine I must tell you that there might not be much I can say." He gabbled nervously, hoping to appear calm. The officers were calm, disturbingly so.

"Perhaps we could talk inside," said Nixon, more telling than asking.

"Erm, of course," he answered, finally turning the key.

They followed him up the stairs and into the flat. Aberfoyle turned on the main light and stood by the television. The officers assumed positions which effectively cornered him. He remembered that Beverley was due any time and he was keen to end their visit.

"Ask away," he said. Williams spoke.

"Andrew Aberfoyle. You are under arrest on suspicion of having sex with a minor."

He froze, chilled to the core. He went dry in the mouth and light-headed. Williams continued to caution him, but he did not take it in. He was more concerned with Beverley's imminent arrival. He snapped back to some logical thoughts.

"So, I have to come with you I suppose?" he said to Williams. Nixon answered him.

"That's right, but sit down there for the moment. We have to conduct a search of you and this flat."

They searched Aberfoyle's pockets and each of the three rooms that made up his home with reasonable thoroughness whilst the detainee sat in pensive angst.

"Can we go now and get this over with? I haven't done anything, you know. There's no truth in this."

The detectives ignored his plea and continued with the search. Nixon emerged from the bedroom carrying a clear plastic evidence bag. In it was a diary, an address book and a pad of writing paper. She put the bag down by the door and went back into the bedroom. When she came out, she had the bedding from Aberfoyle's bed in a larger plastic sack.

"We're seizing these items for evidence," she said before turning to Williams. "Ready?"

He nodded and placed handcuffs on Aberfoyle. They left the flat and headed for their unmarked police car nearby. Aberfoyle looked for Beverley approaching the flat. He was relieved that she had not turned up on time.

There was still a good chance that this could all fall away due to insufficient evidence. Those photographs, taken by those bastards who had double-crossed him, that was all they had. There was nothing on them that confirmed that his relationship with Bev was sexual. It was just being affectionate, harmless, supportive. They couldn't prove anything. He had done everything they had told him to do and when it was all over, they had given the pictures to the police. The low, despicable pair of criminal bastards. Who could believe them anyway? They were clearly criminals, they couldn't be trusted, they couldn't be believed.

"Where has this allegation come from please?" he asked from the back seat of the car. Williams answered.

"We had better save the questions until we're at the police station. You can have a solicitor present if you want one."

"Yes, well, I might, but I just want to know who has accused me. That's not too much to ask is it?"

Neither Nixon nor Williams replied.

On arrival at the police station they escorted Aberfoyle to the custody office and, finding it without a queue, approached the raised desk where an old sergeant sat on a high stool peering over his half-moon glasses at a pile of papers. He looked up at the detectives and nodded their cue to speak. Nixon explained their presence.

"This man has been arrested on suspicion of having sex with a minor. He's a counsellor at a children's home and the victim is one of the girls in his care."

The old sergeant looked impassively at the handcuffed man, but he spoke to the officers.

"What information or evidence have you got for grounds to arrest?" he said, as one who would say the same line a hundred times a day.

Aberfoyle's ears pricked up as the value of their source of evidence was about to be revealed in all of its unreliable and untrustworthy glory. Nixon wrestled a notebook from her coat pocket and flicked through the pages until she found what she was looking for.

"The evidence is from a complaint received earlier today. A statement has been taken which forms the basis for this arrest."

Aberfoyle's inner pain was reaching boiling point. The woman cop was talking about searching his flat and seizing potential forensic evidence. 'Get to the point!' He said inside his head. 'This is all going to collapse right now!' He hoped that the wise, old owl behind the desk would dismiss the allegation and let him go home. Nixon had more to say.

"We'd like to interview him as soon as he has had his rights, Sarge."

"Who has made the statement containing the allegation?" said the sergeant who had begun to write on the papers in front of him. Aberfoyle held his breath as Nixon looked at him and said,

"Beverley Louise Sharples . . . aged fourteen."

*

The stone bench at the edge of the wooded area was old and weathered but remained solid, built to outlive all who sat on it. Each human being who occupied it had their own unique story and the bench kept each story to itself and absorbed new ones every day.

Candice approached the bench which was illuminated only by moonlight. Clouds drifted by, changing the degree of illumination indiscriminately. William was sitting on it, apparently waiting but not looking at her. When she reached the bench, William spoke in hushed tones.

"There someone there," he said, looking into the blackened woods. Candice looked where William was looking but saw nothing.

"What have you seen, William?" she said.

"I 'eard someone. 'eeee move in there. I 'eard 'im cough."

Candice would have dismissed William's perception of an unseen being in the woods as fantasy, but he had never expressed such things before. His observations had proved to be accurate in most respects. She trusted him to tell the truth and to know the difference between the fact and fiction. She had no intention of identifying who was concealed in the darkness, but she also knew that she could not remain there with William and expect to keep their trysts a secret.

"Come on," she whispered, "we'll go somewhere else!" She led him away toward the garden centre where nobody should be at that time of night.

Once out of sight, the figure who William had heard emerged from the woods. He was dressed in black and wore a ski-mask. He ran across the grass to the edge of the side building where the lock on the electrical plant room had been recently repaired. He slid a black bag from his shoulder and pulled a cord to open it. With black-gloved hands he reached in and pulled out a pair of bolt croppers and a torch. He popped open the door and slipped inside, closing the door after himself before switching on the torch. He found the emergency generator as he had done before. This time, he removed the fuses and disposed of them, rendering the generator as useless as the one in The Garrin Unit had become earlier that evening.

Then he turned his attention to the main power supply.

CHAPTER TWENTY-TWO

The gate staff of The Garrin Unit had a routine which was tried, tested and functional. It did what it was supposed to do, fence the dangerous individuals inside where they could do no harm to people. Inevitably, their practices became predictable which, in turn, made them vulnerable.

Like the indoor night staff, there were four of them: Two occupied the gatehouse whilst the other two patrolled the perimeter fence, usually between the inner and outer fences. This was rotated hourly, but the changeovers could sometimes take ten or fifteen minutes, depending on the mood of the crews or what was playing on the radio at the time. They were unarmed, other than with handcuffs and nightsticks to defend themselves with in the event of a patient threatening violence. Communication was in the form of a two-way radio system, like the police one but with a shorter range and less reliable signal. At certain points on the perimeter, no signal could be found and as a result, dialogue over the air was nil. Communication with the staff inside The Garrin Unit was by phone only and that was carried out by the two who remained inside the gatehouse.

In the control room of The Garrin Unit, the evening's routine had progressed as usual. Friday in there was the same as on every other day. Once all of the inmates were bedded down for the night and with their usual absorption of medication, the four-man staff team occupied the kitchen next to the control room, occasionally peering round the door to look at the monitoring screens or going to answer the phone which rarely rang. A near-constant flow of tea and coffee had accompanied games of cards across the table and the radio set wafted out easy-listening tunes that everyone knew but were unable to name. If there was a need to attend to any inmate who activated their room buzzer, they would attend in pairs.

Alan, Mohammed and Frank had followed the time-honoured pattern of night duty whilst Ian Page had left the room to partake in a programme of exercise, a prospect deemed preposterous by his colleagues who chose more sedentary pursuits. Page was training for a coast-to-coast bicycle ride in aid of a local charity and he had chosen to enhance his stamina by use of a static exercise bike, reclaimed, repaired and replaced in the staff locker room by him for that sole purpose. This alternative regime, partly driven by boredom, also meant that Ian did not partake in the high-volume, hot beverage intake which his peers were rigidly sticking to. He was working up a sweat worthy of an endurance cyclist when the lights went out.

*

The custody sergeant had authorised Aberfoyle's detention and he was placed in a cell. Meanwhile, the duty inspector had decided that Nixon and Williams had more work to do before they could interview their man about the allegation. They were told to go to The Garrin Unit at Heavem Hospital where Aberfoyle had his main job and, with the consent of the staff, conduct a search of his locker. The purpose of this was to find any evidence which may support the allegation. The inspector was concerned that there was only the girl's word against his and therefore corroborative evidence was needed to make the case strong enough for him to be charged. Phil

Williams was getting ready to go when his trainee detective colleague Caroline Nixon offered an alternative suggestion.

"Why don't you stay here Phil?" she said, "There's no need for two of us to go and search his locker. You could stay here and book this lot in and package it up for forensic on Monday."

"That means you going up there on your own," he said without thinking before he spoke. Police station culture rarely allowed such things to go unpunished.

"Oh, you are good. Wow, nothing gets past you, does it?"

"Sarky bitch," he observed.

"Correct!" she agreed. "On both counts. Now, if I go to the secure bit at Heaven and look for incriminating stuff in our suspect's locker whilst you do this lot, it will save time. You can get off home and I'll be ready to interview him tonight. I don't want to leave it overnight. That's going to put us on the back foot tomorrow."

Williams was unconvinced. "We should ring Bernie and run it by him."

"Can you imagine his reaction?" she appealed animatedly, "Are we not able to organise ourselves without asking the D.S. whilst he's at home with his family on a Friday night?"

The older detective had to concede that his protégée had a point. He had been to Heavem Hospital countless times on inquiries, in both the secure side and the relatively normal side and each time it had given him the creeps. He was always reluctant to go, keen to leave and relieved when he did. He also came from the old school of coppers who felt obliged to protect female colleagues from imagined harm, such as not allowing them to patrol unaccompanied at night. It was when he considered the frosty response from the detective sergeant upon receiving that call that he had to agree.

"Alright, you win. You're sure you're alright going up there on your own?" she responded with customary sarcasm.

"All the bogey men are going to be tucked away in their beds, Uncle Phil. They can't get me if I keep very, very quiet."

"Get out and leave me in peace," he said, turning to examine the seized items in their bags.

She grabbed the car keys, blew an exaggerated kiss at Phil Williams and headed out.

*

Russell Warren had committed himself to Heavem for a period of twelve months and he had initially treated it as a sentence. Accepting it as a form of incarceration, he had also accepted the sense of isolation that came with it. Off duty he was at his lowest, preferring to go into work rather than determine his own leisure. It had been the same in his Drugs Squad days. He worked excessive hours and found in difficult to balance his time otherwise. He had occasionally gone to the hospital social club, but it had invariably been a flat experience. On one night he could be a customer, leaning at the bar drinking beer and chatting with anyone and everyone, and on the next one he could be taking action to contain and correct the activities of others there. The combination was a recipe for awkwardness and the result was that he spent his time either at work or in his flat, usually the former.

On that Friday night, Warren had chosen to go to work. It took his mind off his own loneliness which had allowed thoughts of his ex-girlfriend to re-enter his head. That ship had sailed long before, propelled by his inability to balance work and life. Work won. He knew where he was with work.

The social club was having one of its quiet Friday nights. It rarely had any busy ones. The last of the handful of customers drifted away after ten and the volunteer steward, who was also a member of hospital staff, locked up and departed by ten-twenty.

At ten-thirty, Warren decided to give it up for the night. He radioed through to the control room to inform them of the imminent end to his tour of duty. His message was acknowledged minimally by the radio operator. He switched off his radio and headed along the path to the row of staff houses. As he reached the short path to his own flat, he saw a shape dash through the darkness.

It was so fleeting that he was unsure whether or not had actually seen anything. He considered that that the solitude of life at Heavem and the unpredictable happenings there could have combined to play tricks on his senses. He erred on the side of making sure and he carried on through the gap between the houses and to the end of what used to be someone's garden. Across the bottom of the untended grass, a row of Leylandii trees lined the garden and protected the residents from the view of, and the viewings from, The Garrin Unit. He peered through the trees and saw the double row of high fences and beyond that the buildings of The Garrin. He had only been inside there once but that had proved sufficient to remind him that his own side of that divide was comparatively acceptable. Upon seeing nothing out of place he turned to go back to the flat.

He remained convinced that there had been somebody there, somebody he would have known if he had managed to get a better look at him. Once inside, he took off his coat. No sooner had he switched on the light and activated the television – all of the electricity went off.

Standing in the darkness, he waited to see if it came back on, but it didn't. Outside, scant light permeated through the broken cloud illuminating the room at intervals. When fully clouded over there was nothing. Warren went into his bedroom and looked out over the back of the flats. The area beyond the trees was also in darkness. A thought entered his head, a serious one. The Garrin Unit relied on power to keep it secure. The CCTV cameras would not work and the staff would be blind as to what could be going on there. The rest of the hospital would be affected too. He put his coat back on and fumbled for his keys. His torch was in the office in the main building. He was not exactly sure what he could do to help but it felt wrong to not be trying to do something.

Warren negotiated the tree-covered path from his flat to the main building by edging forward tentatively, sliding his feet and holding out his hands to protect his face from the hanging branches. In the open and allowing for moving cloud, he went across the site to the main building. The lack of light was eerie. Thankfully, some of the night staff on the wards had managed to ignite improvised lights in their staff rooms: stand-by candles and tea-lights left at the dusty bottoms of cupboards for that eventuality, but most of the windows remained in darkness.

In the far distance he saw The Bowers where there was no sign of life and beyond that was the children's unit which also looked devoid of activity. Hopefully, he thought, the power will all be back on before most of the residents were awake enough to notice. He let himself into the building and with the assurance of knowledge that there were no obstacles or hanging tree branches, he managed to find the operating centre which was unstaffed. Further along, he entered his office and found his issued torch which, thanks to the diligence of Police Cadet Christian Wood, was powered up and in working order.

He replaced the batteries in his police radio and switched it on. He tried a test call to the main station but there was no response. He knew that the radio was serviceable, it had been working only half an hour earlier. The inevitable conclusion was that the power cut had rendered his radio inoperable and he further developed the opinion that it was the rooftop aerial which required the main power supply to be able to operate. This added to the feeling of unease he was already acutely aware of. He picked up the office phone and put it to his ear. There was no dial tone. If something did blow up at Heavem that night, there was no way of getting any help.

*

Dean and Kenny Rogerson drove a pale blue, long-wheelbase, transit van up the rough and largely disused lane leading up to Heavem from the farmland behind. At the old concrete block, they turned the van around and, with the lights turned off, reversed it far enough back for it to be missed by any passing vehicles in the valley below.

In the back of the van were two lurcher dogs, a lamp on a strap with a large battery attached and several old, hessian sacks. In the event that they were stopped by a night police patrol, their presence in an out-of-town location could easily be explained as simply two blokes out poaching for rabbits, an activity usually too trivial and victimless for most coppers to bother taking action on. The van had been stolen the day before some distance away and was fitted with alternative number plates which, if checked, would relate to an identical van which was immobile on a farm in Cheshire and being used to accommodate chickens.

Once satisfied with their choice of parking space, the Rogersons equipped themselves with torches, several lengths of rope and roles of adhesive tape. Kenny also carried a blue-metal, cantilever toolbox. The other items were placed in a rucksack, black, to match their clothes, they set off through the woods keeping close to the buildings and high fences but remaining out of sight. When they reached a point where they could see the gatehouse to The Garrin Unit they concealed themselves and waited. They were in that position when the lights all went out. Kenny took a pair of night-vision binoculars from the toolbox and continued to observe the gatehouse.

The gate guards at The Garrin Unit were equally bewildered. Four uniformed men on a permanent night rota who carried out their vigil with a commitment to the ethos of routine rather than functionality. The team leader was Martin Maxwell, appointed on the longevity of his service at The Garrin Unit. His duties varied little from the other members of the team, other than his obligation to record any incidents in a ledger for the day team to follow up on where necessary. Maxwell had been a coach-driver until his bad back had dictated that he found employment whereby he could move his limbs more freely. His team consisted of Keith Bilton who had retired from the army after a twenty-two-year career, finishing as a sergeant, Dave Mockling who was twenty-one and had only worked there for three months and Norman Knox who was well over sixty and nearing retirement.

They had all experienced power interruptions before but had become used to the prompt activation of the emergency generator, restoring power within half a minute of it going down. This time there was no such respite. They also found that their telephone link and radio system had ceased to function. When the two outdoor patrolling guards returned to the gatehouse with their torches lighting up the animated conversation with their internally based peers, Kenny and Dean chose their moment to approach.

Slipping on workmen's jackets and hard hats from their bags, they took the metal toolbox and a torch and headed out to the gate. The four guards were too engrossed in their predicament to notice the moving beam of the torch as it wavered across the gravel to the gate.

"Hello!" called Dean. "Anybody there?"

The guards stopped talking and looked out, only able to see the sweeping beam of light. Two of them stepped out.

"Who is it?" asked Maxwell.

"We've come to get your power back on," continued Dean.

"Who called you?" enquired Knox.

"Our boss, Dave. I don't know who told him, but he sent us." Dean was enjoying the subterfuge. It played nicely into his fantasy world.

"Are you hospital staff then?" Maxwell was trying to find a reason to accept the unexpected visitors.

"Nah, electrical contractors. That's how they do it these days, I suppose." Dean looked at Kenny for approval. Kenny nodded.

The guards conferred in whispers, two in and two out of the gatehouse doorway within the high fence. Maxwell approached the fence and asked.

"Have you any identification?"

"Hah!" erupted Kenny, "Identification? No, just screwdrivers and stuff like that."

"We shouldn't let anyone in without identification," said Maxwell who felt awkward but obliged to say it.

Both Kenny and Dean picked up on the word 'shouldn't.' It showed that they willing to make an exception and were near to saying so. Dean turned to Kenny, neither of them in plain sight of the guards.

"Well, we haven't got any. So, if you don't want your electric back on for a while, you can make-do and we'll be off."

"No, it's alright," conceded Maxwell, who was being silently encouraged by the gesticulations of his team. "Come in. We'll make an exception, under the circumstances."

Kenny and Dean exchanged another glance as the keys jangled in the lock on the smaller part of the gate, the part that let in people and not vehicles. The gate swung open and the guard stepped aside to allow them through. He returned to the gatehouse and went inside where his colleagues were distractedly talking about the incompetence of the hospital administrators for that and many other organisational shortcomings. The torches were illuminated but placed on the table. Once all four guards were inside, Kenny and Dean entered. Without looking at them, Maxwell said,

"Let me just get you to sign in please lads."

He felt an arm come from behind and pull him backwards as the business end of a handgun was pushed under his jaw.

"Get down on the floor now or I blow his fuckin' head off!" said Kenny with unmistakable clarity.

The guards froze. Kenny raised the volume and spoke more slowly.

"So, you want me to shoot him then?"

The reality hit home for all of them at once. They sank to the floor with their hands behind their heads without being told to do so again.

"Face down, that's it." Kenny was completely in charge and everyone there knew it.

With no further word of direction, Dean took the lengths of rope from his bag and one-by-one he pulled the men's arms behind them and bound their wrists whilst Kenny held the terrified Maxwell, pushing the barrel of the gun into the soft flesh beneath his jaw. The traumatised guard lost control of his bladder and a rank smell permeated the room from his wet uniform trousers. When the other three were secure, the one with the wet pants was pushed down and secured too.

"This dirty bastard's pissed himself," observed Dean, "He stinks!" Kenny was having no unnecessary dialogue.

"Enough!"

He handed the gun to Dean who took up a position to oversee their captives and eliminate any unwelcomed movement. Kenny stepped outside the gatehouse and looked around. There was no sign of life either inside or outside of the gates. He reached into a pocket and produced a two-way radio. He clicked it into life and uttered into it,

"Gate's done, all four."

A similarly concise reply came back.

"Good!"

At that signal to proceed, the bolt croppers recently used to gain entry to the electrical plant room were set to work cutting through the outer perimeter fence. The man in the black ski-mask snipped away from the ground up, concealed from view by the tall Leylandii trees and the passing cloud overhead – or so he had thought.

Warren was convinced that the shadow he had seen was that of someone he had met before. He went to the main building and straight to the ward where the voluntary patients were being accommodated and treated. After gaining the attention of the two nightnurses, who were sitting in their office in candle-light, he asked them to check if any of the patients were unaccounted for. As though in a picture straight out of the Crimean War, the nurses went along the ward carrying lit candles. Warren stayed in the office with his torch on. There was no need to cause any undue alarm for the other sensitive souls in that ward by waking to see a policeman standing over them. After five minutes, the nurses returned, embarrassed and concerned to report that one of their patients was not in his bed.

"Who is it? Who's missing?" asked Warren. The nurse squirmed on the spot.

"It's Patrick, Patrick Miller."

CHAPTER TWENTY-THREE

DC Caroline Nixon drove the unmarked police car along the sloping, tree-covered road leading to Heavem. Moths and other creatures of the night flashed by in the beam of her car headlights, skimming their wings against the windscreen and taking her by surprise with each appearance. There was no street lighting and no other traffic. Her headlights were the only consistent source of illumination. She had overcome the annoyance and frustration caused by the night inspector's decision to have Aberfoyle's workplace locker searched rather than to get on with putting the allegation to him in an interview. She had put it down to her impatience, a trait that she had to accept needed some effort on her part to overcome.

She had been sent to jobs at Heavem several times, mainly when she had been in uniform, usually when the late PC Bob Tasker had needed a hand with something. Since taking up her detective post only two months earlier, she had only visited The Garrin Unit once and that had been during the day when the place was fully staffed and busy. She had not been there at night and whilst she anticipated that there would be no admin or medical staff present, she had no measure of what degree of staffing she should expect to find. All she wanted was someone who could grant her permission to gain access to one staff locker and lead her to it. The inspector had declined to give an authority for her to search the locker on the grounds that it was not Aberfoyle's home nor a place under his control. As a result, it could only be searched with the consent of the person who was in control of The

Garrin Unit. If that consent was declined, she would have to return to the main police station and ask for permission to start the interview without it. It seemed unnecessary and inefficient, but inspectors made such decisions and she had to accept that without questioning it.

The police car turned off the road and went by the main gates of Heavem. All was in complete darkness. She carried on to the parking area near to the gates of The Garrin and found that dark too. The situation was only fully apparent when she stopped the car and turned off the lights. There was nothing but a slight breeze and the rustling of leaves high above.

Nixon opened the car door and the tiny interior light came on to allow her to see the gravelled ground that she was stepping out onto. A chill in the air made her wish she had donned additional layers, but this was a visit she had not anticipating making when she had made that decision. All she had was her police radio, her notebook, handcuffs wrapped around her trouser belt at the back and a roll of clear plastic evidence bags. She did not even carry a torch. By the unreliable light of the moon through fast-moving broken cloud, she approached the gate. There was a discomforting silence about being there. There were no lights on in the building beyond the gates nor were any on in the gatehouse. There was a window at head-height to allow the guards to see any person of vehicle approaching. There was no evidence that the gatehouse was in use. She decided that it would do no harm to announce her presence.

"Hello!"

Kenny and Dean Rogerson crouched down on their haunches. Their manacled prisoners all lay face down on the floor of the area normally used to carry out searches of people entering The Garrin. Each guard was wondering whether whoever it was outside was going to help them or become one of them. Kenny gave them a graver alternative. In a whisper which carried more menace than a shout he said.

"If anybody tries to shout out, they get it - and so does she!"

After turning the volume on his two-way radio set down to zero, Kenny pushed the gun against the temple of the guard he had identified from the outset to be the most compliant. The guard's soaked clothing was testament to Kenny's judgement of character. Kenny lowered his head to whisper at him.

"Who the fuck is that?"

"I, I, don't know," he mumbled through trembling lips. Caroline answered the question without being asked.

"Hello, is anybody there please? I'm DC Nixon from the C.I.D."

The police! The police were outside the gate. If there was anyone who the tied-up guards wanted to turn up it was the police, but there was no way of getting that help which was so tantalisingly near. The woman who was shouting outside had no way of knowing what was happening in that small building. Everyone in there was thinking the same thing, but from different sets of priorities. Nobody said aloud what theirs were.

Nixon stepped back and surveyed the scene in front of her. She spun around and took in a full 360-degree rotation. She could not just give it up and go back, knowing the likely responses of her peers and supervisors were she to tell them on her return to the station that there was nobody answering the door at the high-security mental hospital facility. They would not buy that, and she was keen to avoid any suggestion that she was the type who cut corners and accepted everything at face value. She took out her radio and tried to contact her own control room in the hope that they could raise The Garrin Unit staff by phone. There was no response nor were there any other transmissions coming over the air. For a Friday night, that was unheard of. The radio was not working, and she put that down to being out of range of a signal. She let out a sigh, 'Brilliant!' she thought to herself.

Logic dictated that the guards must be somewhere nearby. Dark as it was, she decided to walk the around the perimeter until she found someone. She chose to take the route to the right, away from the fences bordering the rest of Heavem. The diminishing sound of her low-heeled shoes on the gravel was the only indication gained by the present occupants of the gatehouse that she was no longer out there.

Kenny turned the radio volume dial up two clicks and held it up to his mouth. He pressed the transmit button and whispered,

"There's been an, erm, development."

The voice, speaking through a woollen ski-mask, responded with a tone of disbelief. "What?"

"A woman from CID came here, on her own, I think. She's gone now. 'Don't know what it was about." Kenny winced in evident discomfort. He awaited a stern rebuke at least.

There was a silent pause, then,

"The CID, they've gone right?" said the voice over the radio. Kenny sensed that all was well once more. Dean read it on his face.

"Yeah, gone, right," said Kenny. Their remote conspirator added another recently resolved complication.

"There was another problem, some bloke. I've dealt with him. No problem now."

With nothing more to add, the man put away the radio and continued snipping the wires of the inner fence. When the aperture was big enough, he waited for the cloud to thicken then he slipped through it and ran across the grass in near total darkness to the back of The Garrin Unit. He edged along the building until he found the doorway he had been observing the movements in and out of for weeks. From his pocket he produced the carefully replicated master key and eased it into the lock. It clicked once, then again, and the door gave when the faintest of pressure was applied.

*

Ian Page swore in response to the realisation that the power had gone off and it was not coming back on. He had brought no form of portable lighting and there was no window to allow the moonlight in. Sweating profusely and out of breath, he fumbled in the dark to get his keys and felt his way across to the door. He guided the key into the lock and opened the door into yet more darkness. Working from memory, he managed to get back to the control room which was surprisingly silent.

"Alan? Frank? Are you there?" he called out into the abyss. Nobody answered. "Mo? Come on."

Page knew there was a torch in a drawer somewhere, but he could not go straight to it. Knocking over an assortment of domestic cleaning products, wires for appliances long rendered redundant and obsolete paper records, he finally found what he was looking for. It was a red, plastic lamp with a handle on the top. He clicked it on, and instant illumination made his eyes wince in the sharp contrast. Once accustomed, he scanned the control room and found nobody there. He crossed to the kitchen door and paused in a moment of disorientation, not fully wanting to proceed but knowing that he must. He called out again.

"Mo? 'You there?"

Page pushed the door with the back of his hand. It creaked open and allowed him a view inside. Alan was slumped on the table, his head on his hands, Frank was opposite him and in the same position and Mohammed was in the only upholstered chair, laid back and not moving.

"Oh shit!"

Page placed the torch on the table and checked his colleagues for vital signs. They were breathing but not responsive, deeply unconscious despite his best efforts to revive them. Page had no way to comprehend the situation before him. The darkness and the state of his colleagues could not be a coincidence. Something was going on and he needed to get some help. The first port of call was the outdoor and gatehouse team. He went to the master set for the radio channel. It was devoid of power and therefore dormant. The same had happened to the telephone system. Page decided to go out and speak to the gate staff but that would mean leaving the unit unstaffed internally. He had to check the inmates first.

He headed toward the rooms and let himself into the corridor. The torch lit up the single floor block, a strip with twelve rooms on either side. Normally, he would be accompanied on any visit to the block. It was odd and troubling to be there alone, but his task was simply to check the inmates and he could do that without opening any of the doors. Each cell had a spyhole but with no lighting it was unlikely to enable him to peep into them. A dark room is a dark room and any secrets therein would remain secrets.

His next act was to open the hatch and shine the torch in. Once each occupant was accounted for, the task was complete. He started at the first on the left, unclipping the latch and lowering the metal flap until it rested horizontally. Page shone the torch in and saw Bela Ferenquelar, sleeping noisily and unmoved, neither by the light nor the previous absence of it. The next few cells were the same but the sound of each hatch opening and closing had begun to disturb the inmates.

"What's going on?"

"What's happened to the lights?"

The block was beginning to stir. Page started to speed up the process. When he reached the cell containing Malligan, he expected it to follow the same pattern but Malligan was expecting the hatch to open and was standing ready for it. Page held the torch with his right hand and opened the hatch with his left, keeping hold of the flap in order to close it again without delay. He pointed the torch through the gap but before he could focus, he felt something grab his left hand. The shock made him lose all measure of what he was trying to do. In a second, his hand had been pulled through the hatch and his arm disappeared up to the elbow. He let out an involuntary scream of pain and fear. Malligan was gripping his hand and try as Page did, he could not get free of him.

"Get off me, get off!"

"Shut up and listen to me!"

Malligan's voice was low and laced with fired and unbridled menace. Page still held the torch in his free hand. He shone it into the void and tried to see Malligan. He could not see him because he was at the side of the door. What he could see was the shining blade of a machete. Malligan was holding it over Page's left wrist.

"Open this fuckin' door or I'll cut off your hand. Do it now?"

Page had no time to think or consider the consequences. He did not take in the ramifications of releasing a dangerous and mentally deranged man armed with a machete. All he could think of was that he would lose his hand if he did not do as he was told and do it quickly. He dropped the torch and wrestled his keys from a pocket. With vibrating fingertips, he steered it into the lock, reminded of the urgency by the grip of Malligan's hand and the feel of cold metal on the flesh of his left forearm. He got the key into the lock and turned it. The door opened outwards and Malligan came through it still gripping the blood-flow out of Page's left hand. He emerged into the corridor and put the machete to Page's neck before letting go of his hand. He gripped Page around his chest from behind and put the blade to his throat. He lowered Page down to reach the floor.

"Pick up the lamp, pick it up!" he demanded. Page complied. He took the torch and stood up still in the grip of Malligan and his machete. "Okay, you piece of shit," spat Malligan into Page's ear with venomous hatred, "get your keys and start opening these doors."

CHAPTER TWENTY-FOUR

With the entire hospital blacked out, Warren tried to decide where he could be of most use. It crossed his mind to get in his car and drive into town or at least near enough to be able to get a signal for his police radio, but something stopped him. It was the realisation that, of all of the buildings at Heavem, it was The Garrin Unit which gave him the greatest discomfort. He considered that it contained Gavin Malligan and a couple of dozen others like him. He decided to consult the guards at The Garrin Unit before leaving the site, for nothing more than his own peace of mind. The place was officially high security, the practices of which he had experienced for himself.

On his way to the gatehouse of The Garrin Unit, he shone his torch all around, looking for anything that was out-of-place. He had felt, almost constantly, that the only person who was out-of-place there was himself. Now he no longer felt that. Something was not right, and he was in the right place to do something about it. It was Patrick Miller who was out of place now. Each time he had come across Miller, he was somewhere Warren would not have expected him to be. It was likely that he was more of a danger to himself than to anyone else but, whatever he was doing, he needed to be found.

As he approached the darkened gatehouse, Warren cast his torch-beam at the high window, hoping to alert the occupants to his presence. Nobody appeared. He had not witnessed the abandonment of the gatehouse before. The lack of electricity there would not justify such a slack practice. Something was wrong and he had no way of getting in to investigate. He was five yards away from a loaded gun.

Warren made a similar decision to that which Nixon had made a few minutes before. The difference was that he chose to walk along the left side of the entrance. As his torch-beam left the gatehouse window, Kenny and Dean Rogerson listened intently, the gun sticking firmly in the neck of the petrified guard.

*

Inside the Garrin Unit, Ian Page began opening the doors at Malligan's directions, punctuated by the machete blade at his throat. The magnitude of what he was doing and what it could lead to was beginning to take shape in his mind. The possibilities made him tremble. If this was what it appeared to be, it was a mass break out and he hoped that it would be thwarted by the guards at the gatehouse and patrolling the perimeter. The selected cells were opened, and the torch-beam was pointed in the faces of the sleeping occupants. They were roused and guided out of their cells and into the corridor. Six cells were opened. Malligan didn't want six, he only wanted two, but he was unable to locate his preferred personnel straight away. Malligan had decided that killing Page would be counterproductive. He needed him to tell the story of the breakout, who was involved and how it was done. Page was pushed into Malligan's own cell and locked in.

Ignoring the unwanted ones but leaving their doors unlocked, Malligan took the two along the corridor and explained to them what they were being released to do. The first was Jeremy Pilkington.

"You have a job to do, as we discussed. Do you remember?" asked Malligan, knowing that Pilkington would have been thinking of little else. He was dressed in his pyjamas through which he began to rub his thighs in eager anticipation.

"Yes, I get to deal with a woman, where is the lousy, evil bitch?"

"She is in a building next to here. It's called The Bowers. Her name is Candice Kendal and she deserves to suffer, so make sure you do a thorough job, understand?"

"I understand exactly." Pilkington was by then fully awake. He returned to his room to get dressed. Malligan turned to the second of his willing conscripts, Bela Ferenquelar.

"I have fulfilled my side of our deal Doc, now what about yours?"

"I will perform surgery, but I must know patients are sick. I must know before I do this."

"They're sick alright. They live permanently in another part of this hospital. They'll never leave. They're just waiting there for you to cure them, in your own way. Your time has come."

"I ready for this," said the Hungarian as he too went to dress for the outdoors.

Malligan looked through the still-open hatch of his own former domicile. Page was sitting on the bed with his head in his hands. He did not look up when the torch was pointed at him.

He pointed the torch in the rooms of Ferenquelar and Pilkington to assist them to get themselves ready. Once they were, he led them out of the block and to parts of The Garrin Unit they had never been to. In the control room they were greeted by a man in black wearing a ski-mask and carrying a lit torch of his own. Malligan was the only one who was not surprised to see him.

"Any problems getting in?"

"There was but not now," said the faceless man as he slipped the bag from his back and opened it.

"What happened?" asked Malligan, who trusted his own judgement over everybody else's.

"Dealt with, one bloke, no threat," he said succinctly reassuring Malligan that the plan had in no way been derailed.

"And the guards outside?"

"Contained."

"Is the whole place without power?"

"Yeah, pitch black everywhere. Who are your new friends?" He flicked the torch light at Pilkington and Ferenquelar.

"They have jobs to do. You have to show them where to go."

"Fine!"

Malligan went into the kitchen to see the three unconscious night staff. They were totally out of it and would be for a while.

Malligan took the keys from the belt chains attached to all of the three. He led everyone out of the control room and locked the door.

"Here," he said handing keys to Pilkington and Ferenquelar. "Take these."

They took the keys but Ferenquelar did not like being told what to do. He did, however, want to get out of The Garrin. As Pilkington tucked the keys into his pocket, Ferenquelar placed his on a radiator and wiped his hands on his sleeves in disgust.

"What I use to conduct operation?" he demanded to know. "I need surgical equipment."

Malligan was getting impatient but he needed Ferenquelar and the pandemonium he was capable of providing. Some more cajoling was called for.

"You will be given all the gear you could want, when we get out of here. There's a great, big hospital right next to this, remember?" Ferenquelar accepted this and followed.

The man in the ski-mask led the way through the darkened corridors, occasional light permeating through wire-mesh reinforced sky-light windows, out of reach of the occupants of The Garrin. Doors normally locked and double locked had been left open as the mystery liberator had made his way through the building. Torchlight further facilitated the movement of the escape party. Once out in the fresh air, the tingle of freedom overcame a section of the party. It was Malligan who stopped to breathe it in. He composed himself and set forth behind the masked man.

They crossed the grass and soon found the hole in the inner fence.

"What about the guards – and the cameras?" asked Jeremy Pilkington in a sudden flash of reality amid the euphoria of the moment.

"They have been dealt with," Malligan assured him. "Come on, you have a job to do."

*

Once through the outer fence, Malligan stopped and held out his hand to their rescuer. Without any explanation, the man took things from his backpack and handed them over. There was a gas powered cooker lighter and a head-torch which Malligan switched on and off to test before putting it on his head.

"Take him to The Bowers and show him the room." he explained to the masked man whilst pointing at Pilkington without looking at him. He did the same with Ferenquelar. "And get him into the kid's unit, he'll do the rest. Understood?"

"I get it," answered the voice through the mask. He took a route without a path through the tall trees. Malligan took another direction. He headed off toward a part of the hospital grounds where no one was going to be. He had a fire to start.

With minimal sound and negligible light, Pilkington and Ferenquelar were taken to the main hospital building where they waited under a fire escape whilst the masked man told them what to do.

"You wait here," he said to Pilkington. "You come with me," he said to Ferenquelar, who was not prepared to take instructions which did not come with an acceptable degree of respect.

"Doctor, you call me doctor." He looked away proudly.

"Alright, Doctor, have it your way."

Even delivered with unmistakable sarcasm, Bela Ferenquelar accepted the use of his formal title and followed. Pilkington waited, rubbing his thighs with anticipation.

The children's unit was in total darkness. The occupants, seven kids and one nurse were all asleep and oblivious to the lack of electricity and the threat posed by two men who were approaching the building. In the sheltered doorway, Ferenquelar was handed a small bag with a zip around it.

"Everything you need is in there," he said. Ferenquelar took the bag, it looked as though it should contain toiletries for a holiday. He unzipped it and peered inside. There were new scalpels, a bottle of chloroform, surgical gloves and face mask. The masked man turned to the door and with a jemmy retrieved from his bag, he prized open the door with minimal exertion and consummate burglary skill.

"It's all yours, Doctor!" he said with undisguised contempt. Ferenquelar stepped inside and closed the door after himself.

The man returned to find Jeremy Pilkington standing under the fire escape, excitedly rubbing his legs and breathing heavily as would a bull about to enter into combat.

"What took so long?" he appealed.

"I said I would come back, and I have." His abrupt tone put an end to Pilkington's protest. "I have to take you to The Bowers, there's a woman there who needs your attention." He gave him a head torch and told him so put it on but not to light it up. He slid it over his head and straightened the lamp in readiness.

"This Kendal woman, she is an evil bitch, isn't she? I have to give her what she deserves." His masked guide did not answer.

Pilkington was taken to The Bowers and up the fire escape to the first floor. Outside the window he was given his instructions.

"Inside this bedroom is the woman you have to kill. You'll need this."

He produced a long-bladed kitchen knife and handed it to Pilkington. "That's what you wanted isn't it?"

Pilkington smiled. He had thought it was all a dream until then. His dreams had mostly gone in the same direction as this but the reality of feeling that magnificent weapon in his hand had awakened every part of his mind and body. He could finally resume his campaign against the evil of humanity, those twisted, malicious, manipulative harridans who had teased and tortured him with such ease all of his life. They had to pay, they deserved it, it was his mission in life to deliver what he could upon them, to belittle them, destroy them.

"That's perfect!" he said whilst salivating over the wide blade of the knife.

The masked man took his jemmy and gently popped open the sash window. Jeremy climbed in. The window was slid down.

As the masked guide stole away into the night, Jeremy Pilkington stood and allowed his eyes to become accustomed to the darkness. The thin curtain, which was barely noticeable as he had climbed inside, had fallen back across the window. It was insufficient in density to keep out light but there was barely any ambient light outside to see by. Pilkington could make out the shape of the room. He was next to a tall wardrobe which smelled of old, treated wood. He was standing on a carpet which had no bounce left in it. Near the window was an unoccupied bed. Across the room was another bed and beyond it was the door, which was slightly open. He stealthily moved with silent footsteps along the bottom of the empty bed then he saw that there was a human shape in the second bed. He heard light breathing coming from the shape. It was her, that horrible woman he had been told about, it was her!

He moved to close the door, not wanting to be disturbed. He pushed it closed and eased the latch without making a sound. He felt for a lock to turn but there was not one fitted. It didn't matter, soon he was going to do what he did best, before those fools put him away again in that ash-pit of a place and surrounded by mad people. It was his mission to kill women and how he did it was up to him. There, in the dark of that room, it was not perfect. He wanted it to be perfect, he needed it to be perfect. He had waited too long to settle for anything less. How disappointing would it be if he couldn't see the terror in the eyes of that bitch, see the despair as life was torn from her.

It was payback for all of the unwarranted anguish she and all of her kind had brought upon him though his entire life, shaping him into the one strong man who was prepared to stand up to them, challenge their devious ways, gain justice for all of their sins against him and all innocent men. He had to watch her die, savour the power of life and death that he wielded, and she had to show him that she felt that power. He gripped the handle of the knife and felt the adrenaline rush through him. With his free hand he reached up and turned the head-torch to light the beam. He looked down at the sleeping form on the bed, directing the beam to the foot of the bed and steering it up along the outline of legs, curled in foetal comfort and slumber, so soon to end.

He ran the blade of the knife lightly over the outer blanket, bringing the tip within millimetres of the condemned woman. Pilkington's breathing became deeper and louder. He was aroused in every part of his body. His eyes flared and spit flew in sprays with every heavy exhalation. The beam reached the torso. That was where he would stick his knife first, into the organs, not the heart, not so swift an end. She didn't deserve any mercy. What mercy had she and her kind ever shown him? Pierce the guts but don't kill with the first incision, that was the way, make the most of it, maximise the pleasure for him and the torture for her.

He saw that her head was covered by the blanket, only the top of her head was showing. 'Don't try to hide from me, you evil cow!' He mouthed without speaking aloud. He was desperate to see the horror in her eyes. He wanted her to see the knife that was going to do all that damage, the knife that was to put an end to all of her lies and greed. He took hold of the edge of the blanket with his fingers throbbing with anticipation. He pulled in down to reveal his victim, in all of her weakness and vulnerability. The dormant figure lay there. The sleeping breaths fell silent. Eyes opened, mouth opened to speak, the knife rose above with its blade pointing downwards. Light from the head-torch glinted off the steel blade. One, single, poorly pronounced word was uttered from the prone form.

"Ca'ice?"

Pilkington froze in bewilderment. He was unable to comprehend that the form before him was a man. He had no way of dealing with this new revelation. He shook all over, still brandishing the knife over the bed.

William also froze in disbelief. He had fallen asleep whilst waiting for Candice to bring a candle and matches from the kitchen and now, there was a figure with a light emitting from the top of its head, wielding a knife. He could only think of Candice, she was the only person who should be there, and he was unable to contemplate the presence of anyone else. When his eyes were able to give some confirmation that there was a large knife above him, William managed to let out a monstrous scream.

It could be heard all over The Bowers and beyond. Screams in the night were commonplace at Heavem, but Candice heard it and knew straight away that it had come from William. She had been told that he could have such episodes, but she had not witnessed one for herself. She had lit the candle and was headed up the stairs.

Warren had also heard the scream. He too recognised that it was different from the screams often emitting from the wards of Heavem Hospital, there was a life-threatening tone to it. It was even louder when it happened again. He ran from the perimeter fence of The Garrin and headed to where he had perceived it to have come from. The darkness had punctuated the sound which made its origins easier to follow.

Candice had also detected a new immediacy in the screaming. She hurried along the landing, hot wax dripping from the candle onto her hand. She could not feel it. She opened the door of her bedroom to see an explosion of frantic activity which she could not comprehend. A giant struggle on and off the bed was unfurling before her. By the light of her candle she saw the back of a man. Above his head was the knife blade, trembling in the erratic light of a head-torch. William was still screaming incoherently but still at ear-splitting volume. He was holding the wrists of the attacker and was locked in a struggle for his life. The man was also making noises, pained growling, peppered with utterances of 'Get off me!' and 'No, no, no!'

Warren followed the screaming to The Bowers. He found the front door locked and he banged hard on it with the palm of his hand.

"Open the door, for god's sake, open this door!"

As William was being pushed slowly down onto the bed, Candice found sufficient rational thought to realise that he was losing the fight. She put down the candle on the dresser and reached for the stool. Holding it by its feet and raising it high, she brought it down on the shoulders of the knife-wielding figure. It resulted in the cessation of his efforts to force William backwards. William dropped on the bed and fell down onto the floor on the far side of it.

The man turned to see who had impeded his struggle. It was the woman.

Warren tried to shoulder the front door in, but the old, oak door was heavy and solid. He made no progress with it. He was about to try to find another entrance when the door clicked open. Not waiting to express any of the varied emotions he was feeling, he pushed past the dishevelled resident whose room was downstairs and nearest to the door.

"It's upstairs," said the man, also finding it difficult to understand what was going on.

Warren ran up the main staircase three steps at a time. The screams and shouts had become intermittent, so he dashed toward where his disjointed thoughts were telling him to go. He was using instinct rather than logic and it did not help him to find the seat of the chaos. On the first floor landing he shone his torch at the rooms and tried the doors. All were unlocked and he pointed his torch inside finding nothing more than people in their beds in relative calm. At the third room he heard another higher pitched scream from further along the landing. It lasted long enough for him to find the room he was looking for. He dashed in to see a gladiatorial scene. Candice, in a long T shirt used for nightwear, was standing in a defensive pose, holding a footstool high in front of her. The shape of her adversary was confused by the light emitting from the top of its head. Only when Pilkington raised the blade higher did Warren take in the full reason for the screaming. He drew his truncheon and stepped forward to protect Candice.

Flooding through Warren's head were thoughts of a drugs debt being the reason for this attack. He focussed with high concentration on the blade and the individual who was brandishing it.

"Police! Drop it, drop the knife, now!"

Pilkington could not handle confrontation with men. He was only able to exercise power over women and he was still desperate to kill this one. A few seconds of intense stand-off ensued. Nobody was prepared to back down: Candice still clutching the stool, Warren holding his wooden truncheon out in front of him and Jeremy Pilkington gripping the handle of his steel-bladed knife. The impasse was interrupted by a sharp, thrusting kick to Pilkington's back which knocked him flat on the floor and the knife out of his hand and out of his reach. William had got to his feet and managed to negotiate his way around the foot of the bed and delivered the crucial blow to Jeremy Pilkington's lower back.

Warren wasted no time. He dived on the prone figure and wrestled his hands behind his back. By the light of his own torch and Candice's candle which were both placed on the carpet. He manacled the attacker then pulled off the torch from his head. Everyone heaved deep breaths, wordlessly composing themselves from a bewildering and adrenaline-fuelled experience, life threatening and life-affirming at the same time.

Several of the residents of The Bowers had come to the door, tentatively seeking reassurance that the horrific incident was over. The door was pushed open and three timid faces peeped around it. Warren was in no frame of mind to be polite.

"What does it take for you people to step up? Huh? Someone could have been killed in here and you just do nothing!"

The residents of The Bowers had to accept that they could have done something to help. They looked at each other then turned to leave. Warren stopped them.

"Wait, there's something you can do. Come in here." They shuffled inside the room, lit with an assortment of inadequate forms of illumination.

"What do you want us to do?" asked a man in a dressing gown from the 1930s.

"Look at this guy, anybody recognise him?" He pulled Pilkington's head around to face the group. Candice had gone to comfort William but they both looked at his face.

"No, we don't know him," she said after nodding at William's assent to that.

"Not me either," said one of the men standing in the doorway. Warren took the direct route.

"Who are you? Why did you come here?" he shouted in Pilkington's ear, releasing only a tiny fraction of the anger he was feeling. Pilkington said nothing. Warren began to consider what he could do with the guy when there was no way of contacting the main police station for help. The man in the old dressing gown had more to say.

"Erm, I think I can suggest something, erm, about him!" He pointed at the manacled man on the ground being held there by Warren.

"Go on then!" said Warren with undisguised impatience.

"His clothes, that jumper and trousers, yellow stripe on the sleeves and legs. I work in the laundry, I know where they're from, where he's from."

"Where?" said Warren wishing that he would just say what he knew without dithering.

"It's what the inmates wear in the Garrin Unit."

CHAPTER TWENTY-FIVE

Caroline Nixon was regretting her decision to walk around the outer perimeter fence of The Garrin Unit. The absence of any light made it a challenge to negotiate the terrain and offered no help in locating the patrolling guards who she was looking for. The only light that she could call upon came from her digital wristwatch which gave off greater light than was needed to enable the wearer to tell the time. At certain points, the overhanging tree branches obscured the path around the base of the high fence which resulted in her having to hold onto the fence to get to a point where she could proceed without assistance. It was also much further than she had anticipated, and she had lost her bearings. Where she was in relation to the gatehouse was a mystery.

She knew that the main part of Heavem was the other side of the Leylandii trees and she could simply head through them and find someone to ask, but her intention was still to find the guards and she was unlikely to do that by leaving the fence. Her shoes were also unsuitable for traversing rough and dirty ground. She indulged in some unprofessional language in the solitude of her situation but through her frustration she remained determined to finish what she had set out to do and get back in time to interview Aberfoyle about the allegation made by Beverley Sharples. She was thinking about the strengths of the case against Aberfoyle when she found something that changed the whole purpose of her presence there.

She caught her arm on a protruding edge of the fence. It was nowhere near any feature which would explain it. There was a part of the fence that had been damaged and the jagged edges were curled outwards. She felt it and used her watch light to see that there was a gap in the fence, cut top to bottom and big enough for a person to pass through.

Whilst trying to comprehend this, she heard William screaming for his life from somewhere on the other side of the trees. Having been to Heavem before, she was aware that such noises could be considered part and parcel of life in a large mental hospital. However, like Warren had done at the same time, she recognised a particular degree of urgency and desperation in the screams, an immediacy which distracted her from her current predicament. Someone was in acute distress and she could not ignore that. She put this information, together with the human-sized gap in the fence and the absence of guards at the gatehouse, and she knew that she was in the eye of a storm - a break out at The Garrin and no way to summon help.

Her body froze and her thoughts darted in directions she could not control. Her heart raced and sweat appeared on her brow. 'What to do, what to do!' She said almost out loud. Finally, she took a huge breath and let it out slowly. She left the relative positional safety of the high fence and headed through the trees.

The screams continued as, with arms raised to deflect the branches from her face, she made frustratingly slow progress through the woods. She had not managed to progress fifteen yards when she tripped on something. It was bigger than a tree root and it did move when her foot came into contact with it. The impact made her stumble and lose balance. She fell forward breaking her fall with her hands and settling on her elbows. She looked to the side and saw something that made her activate her watchlight. It was a pair of shoes, and someone was still wearing them.

Her eyes darted to the other end of the motionless form she was lying next to. She scrambled to her feet, partly to see better and partly to be able to defend herself from whatever threat may be directed at her. It was a man, unconscious and bleeding from a wound on the back of his head. The blood was fresh and wet and there was no indication that he had been there long. She crouched to feel for signs of life, still aware of the distant screams she had been moving towards. She detected a pulse in his garrotted artery and his chest was rising and falling but in a shallow way. At least he was alive.

She steered him into the recovery position and chewed her lip for a logical course of action as to what to do with him. She realised how reliant she had been on the lifeline that was a police radio. She had not realised how vital that commodity had been up until that moment. Again, she made a conscious effort to compose her breathing and hoped that her heart would get in line too. Finally, she decided that there was nothing she could do but get help for the guy and she stood up and headed off in the direction she had originally chosen. Counting the strides to twenty-two, she emerged into the relative space of the path which led past the garden centre and to the main hospital building. She looked for a point of recognition in order to find the man again once help had been sought. She spotted a yellow plastic box marked Grit Salt which would be used to clear frozen paths in the winter. That was it. Find that again and go across the path and twenty-two steps into the woods.

Now able to step up her pace unencumbered by obstacles, Nixon ran up the path to where she had perceived the screaming to have come from but at the point where she reached the darkened buildings, the screams stopped. She stood still, breathing heavily from running, and listened for some more indication as to what could induce a person make throat-damaging noises like that.

After a period of silence, she heard shouting coming from one of the buildings. It was not the main building, it was further away, across the open green expanse, a shadow of a building, only two floors high. She ran to it and heard a man's voice, enraged and contemptuous. She ran to the door of The Bowers and pushed it open. In the hallway was the resident who had initially let Warren into the building. He was standing at the bottom of the stairs looking up at where all of the drama was unfolding. He turned his head to see the figure of a young woman emerging through the doorway. She leaned on the heavy wooden door as though she was trying to push a broken down car.

"Police!" she announced with as much authority as she could manage in her frantic state. "What's going on in here?" The man pointed and said.

"Upstairs!"

Nixon could see by the ambient light coming from the window above the main door. She ran up the stairs, ill-equipped to be able to engage in any physical restraint should the situation call for it. On the landing she saw people gathering at a doorway and headed to them.

"Police, move aside please, Police, thank you!" She reached the doorway and stepped inside. The torch and candlelight made the scene surreal, like an arty film from Eastern Europe. There was a woman, hugging a man on the floor at the foot of a screwed up bed, both were crying and shaking all over, another man on the ground being restrained there by a man in a black coat who broke her train of bewildered thought by saying with unequivocal authority.

"Good, about time. Give me a hand with this fellow."

She realised that Warren was in police uniform and felt some instant relief that she was no longer alone in this bizarre place. She stepped forward and took one of Jeremy Pilkington's arms. Between them, the two police officers lifted him to his feet. Warren turned to Candice who was holding William's head to her chest.

"Don't touch anything, leave that where it is." He nodded toward the knife which lay on the threadbare carpet where Jeremy had dropped it. Candice nodded and resumed comforting William. Warren recognised William but he had not seen him inside The Bowers before. He was too occupied to linger on that.

"What's happened?" she appealed, trying to make sense of the mass she had become embroiled in.

"He's come into here with that knife, hell bent on killing someone."

"Who was screaming? I heard it from miles away," she said.

"The couple on the floor on the room, it was them he was trying to get at." After using the word, he considered for the first time that Candice and William might actually be a couple.

"Who are you?" he asked his new helper.

"I'm Caroline Nixon, I'm new on C.I.D. Who are you?"

"Russell Warren, I'm the beat officer here."

"Oh! I've heard of you," she said.

"We can chat later. We need to get this guy somewhere safe. Have you summoned a van?"

"No, I can't get my radio to work," she said, feeling that she was the first police officer in history to whom this misfortune had happened. They walked Pilkington out of The Bowers and across the grass to the main building. Once inside, they went to Warren's office and secured him to the radiator whilst they went to the far end of the room to talk. Warren was about to begin but Caroline had more urgent things to reveal.

"There's something you need to know. There's a guy in the woods, been hit on the head with something. He needs medical help. Are the phones working?"

"No, nothing. There's no radio signal anywhere on here."

"We have to get him some attention, he's bleeding from the head."

"Can you find him again?"

"Yes, I'm sure I can. What are we going to do with him? I have a car but it's over at the front of The Garrin."

"I have an idea," said Warren. "Stay with him a minute, I'll be right back."

Leaving the head-torch provided by Pilkington, Caroline stayed by the door and shone the light on him, determined not to miss any efforts by him to escape. Warren returned within a minute. With him was a male nurse.

"This is Terry. He's a nurse in the ward upstairs," he explained. "He can put him in one of the padded cells for a bit while we see to that fellow you found."

They unfastened the handcuffs, unwrapped them from around the radiator and reapplied them to Pilkington who was by then mumbling incoherently. He uttered some passages about it being a man and how some woman had made a fool of him again. The rest was like the ramblings of a person who talks in their sleep. He was taken up a flight of stairs to a ward which was heavily secured by at least four forms of lock. Terry assured them that they were experiencing a quiet period on the special ward on which he was deployed. Warren conducted a thorough search of Pilkington who seemed not to notice. Leaving the cuffs on him, Pilkington was placed in the padded cell and a nursing colleague of Terry's took responsibility for him. The nurses noticed that Pilkington was wearing the standard issue clothing of the inmates of The Garrin Unit. Once out of earshot of Pilkington, that brought more of Nixon's recent experiences back to her.

"I found a gap in the fence, the fence of The Garrin. That must be how he got out."

She explained her reason for going to The Garrin Unit and how the gate-staff had left the place unmanned.

Warren concurred that he too had found it in that desolate state. Somehow, the guards at The Garrin had been made to disappear. The calibre of the inmates was such that they had to consider the real possibility that Pilkington had done grave harm to one or all of them in his bid to get away. Heather Fellhouse's words came back to Warren, ringing in his head like a church bell. 'A disaster waiting to happen.' It was happening right now.

*

Terry recruited another male nurse from another ward, reassuring Warren and Nixon that they were trained in more than just the nursing of mental disorders. They acquired a large first aid box and headed off to where Nixon had noted the Grit Salt box on the path past the garden centre.

A trek through the woods in a wide line and with the benefit of numerous lamps they soon came across the injured man. The nurses examined him and quickly confirmed that he was alive but had lost a lot of blood. The injury to his head appeared to have been caused with some blunt force and could have damaged the brain but they were in no position to tell. What was clear was the need for him to be taken to a hospital which was fully equipped to handle such trauma cases. A bandage was applied to the man's head whilst Warren and Nixon stepped aside to form a plan.

"Where is this gap in the fence?" he asked intently.

"Through there," she pointed. "I found it and when I heard all the screaming I came through this way and tripped over him. What do you think he was doing here? He's not one of the guards, is he?"

They went to where the nurses were working on the patient. He had been turned over and they were ready to carry him out of the woods. Warren pointed his torch at the man's face. Most of it was covered with blood, but Warren could make out enough of it to know who he was.

"I know this guy," he said, still trying to work out what had led to him being there and being injured.

"Who is he then?" enquired Nixon impatiently. "Is he one of the guards from The Garrin?"

"No, he's a patient from this part. His name is Patrick Miller."

Miller was carried out of the woods and up the path to the main building. The nursing pair assured Warren and Nixon that they could take care of him until an ambulance could be contacted. Warren explained to them that Miller was an informal patient so that they could speak to the staff on his ward and find out more about him.

It was time to find out what had happened to the patrolling guards of The Garrin Unit.

*

Meanwhile, at the back of the main building where the maintenance crews had left their machinery, the giant incinerator was fully lit and the temperature inside it was increasing. Malligan knew that it was not yet hot enough to be capable of performing the function he had in mind for it - but it would be soon. He had climbed onto a ledge connecting the building to the top of the incinerator and crouched out of sight of the path below. Feeling the increasing heat come through the metal casing, he silently urged it to accelerate its increase in temperature. He had waited for months for this night to come. He was unwilling to wait any longer than necessary.

He heard footsteps approaching. Concealing himself from unwelcome attention, he extinguished his light and watched the path. When he was satisfied that it was who he wanted to see, he raised his head and greeted his co-conspirator. The man in the black ski-mask came up to the incinerator and saw him.

"Climb up here, out of sight," ordered Malligan. The man in the mask went to the side and negotiated his way up to the raised platform. Malligan wasted no time on pleasantries. All he wanted to know was about the plan that he had devised and how it was unfolding in reality.

"Did you get them to the right places?" he demanded to know.

"Yeah. Those crazies are doing what they do best. I suppose you heard the screams, Mally?"

"Yeah, it's just as I planned. That's the distraction I wanted and settle a few old scores at the same time. Give me that radio."

His liberator handed over the walkie-talkie. Malligan took it and pressed the transmit button.

"You got everything under control there, have you?"

The deep Welsh voice came as a sign of a successful mission to the Rogerson brothers. Kenny answered.

"All good here, good to hear your voice." Malligan was in no mood for chatting. "Is the van in place?"

"Yes," Kenny assured him, "keys are in it as you wanted."

"Stay there, I'll tell you when to move."

Kenny nodded to Dean. Soon it would all be over and they would be in the money, big money. Mally would cut them in on the large fortune he had stashed away. They knew what was coming in on a daily basis and for how long. They were due a split of a vast sum of money because they were the ones who had carried out his instructions to the letter. They were the team that had got him out of there. He would see them right. He was good like that.

Malligan kept the radio set and turned to his helper.

"You mentioned some trouble earlier, what was it?"

"Some nutter in the loony bin here, he followed me out. It was bad enough me having to live here for these past few weeks, pretending to be one of them. He saw me cutting the hole in the fence. I had to knock him out. Did him with a brick, back of his head as he was trying to run off. Couldn't afford to let him go and shout his mouth off, could I?"

"He's dead then?" enquired Malligan impassively.

"He won't have survived that. I hit him hard enough."

"No loose ends?"

"I dragged the fucker into the woods. They won't find him for ages."

"You've done a good job, I'm pleased with what you and the lads have done. We're out of the country before the morning guards turn up."

"I gotta hand it to you, when Purcell told me what you had planned, I thought this idea of yours was mad, but it's worked."

"Nearly finished. There's something else I have to do with this incinerator."

"What are you doing with it?" asked the masked accomplice.

"I need to make it look like I've been put in it. They won't be looking for me if they think I'm dead. All I need is a body for them to find some bits of later."

"You're a fuckin' genius Mally. That bloke I finished with the brick, I could find the body and use that."

"You could, but I have a better idea."

Malligan let the machete slip down from up his sleeve and the handle fell into the grip of his hand. With one swift, smooth motion he raised the weapon and brought it down into the shoulder of the man who had taken huge risks to rescue him from a lifetime of incarceration. The man dropped to his knees, feebly clutching at his shoulder as Malligan drew the blade out and stood with it poised and ready to deliver another blow. With his free hand, Malligan pulled the mask off him. To the police and the hospital authorities he had been known as Roger Reid, unfortunate, homeless, former soldier who had been a voluntary patient at Heavem for the past few weeks. To Gavin Malligan he was his second-in-command and the man entrusted to run his affairs and carry on his business in his absence, Dermott Conlon.

Conlon's breathing became frantic, shallow, erratic. It was the action of a man who knew that he was going to die but he desperately wanted to know why. His plaintive eyes turned to look at his executioner, standing over him as an axeman or the operator of a guillotine.

"What . . . why?" he uttered, "I got you out, you . . ."

"Don't play the fuckin' innocent, Conlon. You know as well as I do that you only got me out so that you could get at the money, my fuckin' money! As soon as you got at that, you were going to do the same to me. I never trusted you and if you trusted me, then you're too stupid to live anyway."

"I was . . . loyal!" he spluttered through spasms of intense pain.

"Loyal? Were you fuck, loyal! What happened to you when I got arrested for doing in that little twat on the tip? You just fucked off and left me to take it. You should have got me out of there, that's what you were paid to do. Now, all you want is the money I made. You don't get it. What you are going to do now is what you should have done that night - help me to get away."

He looked at the incinerator then back at the suffering Conlon. Without another word, he swept the machete across horizontally and connected the blade to the side of his neck above the first wound, severing the main artery but not separating his head from his body. It instantly separated Dermott Conlon, alias Roger Reid, from the living world.

No sooner had Conlon's lifeless frame fallen onto the hot metal flat roof, Malligan began removing his shoes. He took off his Garrin Unit issued shoes without laces and put on those worn by Conlon. He placed the shoes under the aperture to the hopper chute. Anything he could do to indicate that the body in there was his was a good idea.

*

Bela Ferenquelar felt supremely empowered. He had been given the opportunity at long last. He did not dwell on the whys and wherefores of his good fortune. His life's work was more important – he was more important. Only he could cure the suffering of the sick, only he had the skills and the will to go straight to the heart, sometimes literally, of the afflictions of his patients and take out the malignant entities therein. But he was even better than that. He was ethically superior as well as surgically. He knew deep within his being that the patient had a right to know what was going on, what was happening to him or her, through every stage of the operation, even though conventional medicine had considered them too young to be able to listen and comprehend it.

In the darkness of the children's unit at Heavem, he edged his way around the corridors and landings, peering into the rooms of the children and forming plans as to who was the most in need of his expertise. Using the torch provided sparingly, Bela worked out that a children's home such as that would be staffed by adults responsible for the welfare of their young residents. He could not allow anyone to interfere with his work and his incarceration in The Garrin Unit had confirmed to him that he could not trust the fools who thought that they knew how to help sick children better than he did. He had to take steps to eliminate anyone who stood in his way.

When he found the bedroom where the night cover care assistant was asleep, he prepared a cloth with chloroform and applied it to his face. There was to be no interference from anyone that night.

With the night staff rendered incapable of interfering in his plans, Ferenquelar returned to the kitchen where he had first explored the facilities. He had decided that it was the most suitable room for his crucial work. He set about preparing it for surgery. He cleared the free-standing table normally utilised for the preparation of meals and found the cupboard containing cleaning materials. The tabletop was scrubbed thoroughly and dried with towels stored in drawers beneath it. Ferenquelar rolled up his sleeves and scrubbed his hands and arms with soap and a weak solution of bleach. He felt like a high priest, supreme master of his temple of medicine, the greatest healer the world had ever known.

CHAPTER TWENTY-SIX

Warren and the newly acquired trainee detective had to work out what to do next. It was the first moment they had found to rationalise and share their thoughts. Nixon explained about investigating an allegation of illicit sexual activity against a therapist from The Garrin Unit and the reason she had been sent there that night. Warren explained about the previous occasions he had encountered Miller and how his activities had been suspicious, even by the standards of Heavem. Eventually, Warren made a suggestion.

"You've got a car here, right?"

"Yes, I have. What are you getting at?"

"I'm saying that you should go back to town and get some help."

"Erm, No!" she exclaimed without raising the volume. "I'm not leaving you here on your own. You might not have noticed, but at least one homicidal psycho has got himself out of there tonight and the gap in the fence is still open for more."

She had made a valid point, but Warren had his doubts about what two of them could achieve, unarmed, ill-equipped and without the prospect of any back-up from the town. She had been thinking further ahead than he had.

"We have to get in through the gap and find the guards. If they are alive and tied up or something, they can help us." Warren could not summon to his mind any counter argument though his reservations remained. He agreed to go to look for the missing guards.

They slid sideways through the gap in the outer fence and dashed, with the urgency and stooped gait of escapers, across the narrow strip, normally monitored by elevated cameras, and straight to the hole in the inner fence. Repeating the process, they emerged onto the grass of The Garrin and hurried to the building. Having no bearings and in poor light, they edged along the building line until they reached a doorway. A gentle push on the door caused it to open. Even though they knew that Jeremy Pilkington had escaped, it still brought a chill to both of them to see the door open and the darkened aperture within. With torches lit, they cautiously entered and commenced a search of the interior.

All doors were locked until they reached the control room. It was like the Marie Celeste, eerily devoid of life, abandoned inexplicably whilst appearing functional and normal. They were about to go out of the room when Nixon noticed the door ajar at the back of the room. Pushing it open with an invisible orchestra warming up to a frenzy inside her head, Caroline Nixon scanned the kitchen with the torch.

"Oh shit!"

*

Several miles away, in the custody block of the main police station, a senior constable on jailer duties saw that a small red warning light on the wall be a cell door had become illuminated. It indicated that the occupant was in need of some attention. Because it was a Friday night and arguably the busiest period of the week for people getting arrested, he had other more pressing duties to attend to before answering the summons. When he remembered that the cell contained the only prisoner who was recorded as having not consumed any alcoholic drink prior to his arrival, he considered that there may be a reason for the activation of the red light. The old cop took the keys and headed down the corridor to extinguish the red light. He did so then he opened the hatch in the cell door.

"You pressed your buzzer, was that on purpose?" he asked, knowing that there was usually no justification.

"Yes. It's important. I have to tell you something."

"Can't it wait until you are interviewed. It won't be long, so they tell me."

"It can't wait. It couldn't be more urgent."

The cop saw something in desperation of his voice and the tearful eyes of that detainee that made him believe what he was saying.

"What's your name again son?"

"Andrew Aberfoyle, and please hurry."

*

Fully expecting to find the night workers of The Garrin Unit stone dead, Warren and Nixon were relieved and amazed to find that they were breathing and very much alive. Attempts to revive them were futile, giving rise to the assumption of involuntary, chemical inducement. That explained a small part of what had gone on there. The full story was yet to be revealed and the remainder of The Garrin Unit was yet to be explored. They left the sleeping night staff and continued into the building, finding doors unlocked when they should have been locked indicated the correct direction to go in. The torchlight afforded some reassurance as did the presence of each other, but the atmosphere was charged and prime for an explosion.

The nature and purpose of The Garrin Unit together with the antecedents of its occupants were factors impossible to remove from their minds. Conversation between them was minimal, nothing needed to be said. They passed the office of Ron Jeaver, where Warren had been on his only previous visit. It provided him with a reference point on which to establish his bearings, although he had approached it from a different direction previously. Finally, they reached the block which, under normal circumstances would be the hub of the entire security arrangements for the unit.

With torches raised, they stepped beyond the threshold, through a doorway which should have been locked and into the corridor where the dangerous and the deadly were housed. They paused without a word of discussion, then they stepped tentatively on. The first few doors were closed and evoked no additional concern but the third one on the left was wide open. Their torches pointing inside, they scanned the interior and saw the trappings of long-term incarceration and evidence of individuality within limits, but no occupant.

Further along they found the same worrying absence in another room. As they egressed that room, a voice from behind a door opposite called out.

"Hey, over here, I need help here!"

They stopped to gather some composure. Both Warren and Nixon were becoming increasingly aware of the gravity of their situation. To them, that voice was a faceless representation of everything inhuman about the building they were searching, hideous and terrifying without being visible. All logic told them to ignore it and hope that whoever had spotted their torch beams would give it up and go back to sleep without any need for further conversation. It was not to be.

"Help, please. Frank? Alan? Mohammed? Is that you? I need help, come on, please!"

Warren let out a deep and thoughtful breath. He was not prepared to try to open the door, not that he had a key to do so, but there was something in what the man behind the door was saying that he was unable to ignore. Nixon said nothing, leaving this call to her new partner.

"Who are you?" he said.

To Ian Page it was the sound of salvation, being brought back from the gates of hell.

"Ian, Ian Page." It then struck Ian Page that he was not talking to a member of The Garrin staff. It didn't matter, he was ready to be rescued by anyone. "My colleagues have been doped or something. There's been a breakout and I got locked in here by them. Please get me out."

Warren raised the torch to the spyhole and pointed it through. Page shielded his eyes with a raised arm them stepped back to allow his rescuers to see him.

"I.D." said Warren, "We need to see some I.D."

Page frantically tried to gather his thoughts. The urge to cry was hard for him to fight. He traced his earlier movements in his mind and came up with the solution.

"It's in the locker room gym, on the exercise bike."

"Where is that?"

Remembering that the person he was talking to was not on the staff but still not considering who they actually were, Page offered directions for them to go to the gym and find the I.D. card which bore his picture. Caroline went to find it and Warren waited at the cell door. Meanwhile other occupants of the corridor had begun to stir. The voices and flashes of light from the torches had resulted in the light-sleepers amongst them to rouse and take an interest.

Caroline returned within a minute with the I.D. card and handed it to Warren. He pointed his torch at it and nodded his confirmation to her that the man he had seen through the spyhole was Ian Page of The Garrin Unit nursing staff.

"Okay Ian, we are police officers and we need a key to get this door open. Can you tell us where to get one?"

"Yes, yes, oh god, thank you, yes!"

"Shhh, keep your voice down," said Warren in hushed tones, "Where's the key?"

"Okay, okay." The tears flowed down Page's cheeks now, "There's a key to the internal doors, an unofficial spare. It's in the bottom of the first aid box in Mr Jeaver's office, please hurry!"

"I know where that is," said Warren to Nixon, "Stay here."

He darted up the corridor and to the office he had been in before, but it was locked. Feeling around and pushing the edges of the door, he could tell that the door was not as strongly constructed as the cell doors. He put down the torch and put his shoulder against it. The door lock sprang off and scuttled along the floor. He recovered the torch and entered. The first-aid box was on the filing cabinet he had been reading the contents of only a few weeks before. He popped it open and pulled out countless surgical dressings until he found the key and darted back to the block with it.

Nixon was just beginning to take in the situation she was in: standing alone, unarmed and in the dark inside a building where psychopathic killers could escape from their cells. Warren's return alleviated some of her fears, but not all of them. Warren went straight to the door and Nixon raised the lamp to facilitate his access to the lock. The door swung open and Ian Page dashed out as though it was ablaze within. He struggled to take in air and gain sufficient composure to speak but after a few seconds he brought himself back to the here-and-now and remembered his role.

"Make sure all these doors are locked," he said indicating the ones which had been left open. "I need to work out who has gone, your torch please."

Nixon held out the torch and Page raised it to each inspection hatch in turn, moving to the next one once the occupant had been confirmed as being present. He took two minutes to return to Warren and Nixon with a preliminary situation report.

"There's definitely three missing. All the others are in bed so it could be worse. What about my colleagues, have you seen them?"

"They're out cold in the little kitchen, drugged with something I expect. Sleeping it off," said Warren, partly in an effort to keep Page focussed and in control of his emotions. Page led them back along the corridor and up to the control room where the situation was as it had been when Warren and Nixon had found it but not as Page had seen it. Mohammed and Alan were in the same positions as before, but Frank was not there. Attempts to revive the remaining pair were still futile but they were breathing and apparently unharmed. It was agreed to leave them where they were. Page took them to Jeaver's office where he tried his phone which was also out of use. Warren tried to identify their options.

"Where's Frank?" asked Page.

"Who's Frank?" asked Nixon.

"He's the fourth one of our night team. He was there out cold with the others when I came out of the gym, but he's gone."

"Maybe he came to and got himself out?" suggested Warren applying what logic he could muster in such bizarre circumstances.

"I can't see that," pondered the perplexed Page. "He wouldn't have just gone. He would have at least gone to check the block. He'd have seen all the doors open and I would have been able to get out. I just don't get it."

"I'm sure he'll turn up," said Nixon without any better purpose than blind optimism. Warren brought them back to the matter in hand.

"Okay, we know that there are three inmates missing?"

"It appears so, yes," said Page with a heavy sigh. "If they got out over two twenty-foot fences and past the patrol guards. Nixon explained to Page that the fences had holes cut in them and the patrol guards were nowhere to be found. Page was experiencing new depths of despair.

"They might not have gone far," said Warren, "We could initiate a search."

"What, with two of us?" said Nixon who was trying hard to avoid being negative. "We don't even know who we are looking for or where they might be headed." Page went to the filing cabinet and opened it.

"All the information we have is in here."

He placed the torch on the files and flicked through to find the relevant ones, stopping first at the thick file for Bela Ferenquelar. He pulled it out and placed it on the desk before searching for the others. Warren and Nixon started leafing through it. Page found Malligan's file and Pilkington's and he placed them both on the desk with Pilkington's file on top. Each file had a photograph of the subject attached to the front with a staple. Warren glanced at the photograph attached to Pilkington's file and said to Page.

"We've caught that guy already. He tried to kill a woman in The Bowers with a bloody big knife. We've got him in one of the old padded-cell wards next door."

"That's what he does," said Page, "He hates all women and wants to kill them. It looks like he has gone for the first woman he could find."

As Nixon examined the file, Ferenquelar stared back from dark, sunken eyes set behind thick eyebrows. The records of his medical and psychiatric assessments were skimmed through but when his criminal activities prior to his admission to The Garrin Unit were summarised, a cold feeling ran through her body.

"Oh shit! This bastard has killed thirteen people claiming to have been curing some sickness that only he knew of," said Nixon without looking up from the papers.

Warren moved Pilkington's file away and looked at the file beneath it. It was his turn to feel a change of body temperature.

"Malligan!"

Page picked up on this. "You know him? Gavin Malligan?"

"Yes, it was me who got him put away. Big-time drug dealer and dangerous nutcase. He likes to use a machete and he kills without giving it a second thought."

Images of Luke Gould's lifeless body swam through his mind. He had to physically shake his head to get rid of them. Page had more up-to-date information to offer.

"It was him, it was his doing, all this. He had a massive cleaver-type thing, he was going to cut my hand off. He planned this escape and he's taken these two out with him."

"Why would he want these two to go with him?" asked Warren, thinking aloud. Page joined in.

"He could have taken any or all of them, it doesn't make any sense. It's not as though they were his friends."

"He needed them for something. A smokescreen maybe? Take out more dangerous prisoners than himself and where do all of the efforts to catch them go first?" Rationalised Warren.

"If that was true," interjected Page. "He would have let them all out, make a bigger smokescreen."

"Yes, but he was choosy about his fellow escapers. A fellow who has killed only women and a mass-murdering doctor."

Both men began turning the pages of Malligan's file, looking for something that explained his alliance with Pilkington and Ferenquelar.

"This Pilkington guy was in an upstairs bedroom in The Bowers, trying to kill –" Warren's words failed him as he made the links he was looking for.

"What is it? Who was he trying to kill?" asked Page, feeling the tension of Warren's silence. He put his thoughts into words again.

"He went straight to a woman called Candice Kendal. She was the main witness for the prosecution at Malligan's trial. He knew how much Pilkington hates women, Malligan sent Pilkington to kill her."

Page pointed out something in the file. "Look, this is recent. Malligan complained that someone was planning to kill him."

"So, he sees himself as a victim?" said Warren in disbelief. "And he claims that Bela Ferenquelar is the one who's going to do him in." They looked up from the page and at Nixon who was still intensely scrutinising the file of the Hungarian doctor. Warren asked her.

"Does it say anything about this in his file, Caroline?"

"No, but it does say more about the patients who 'Doctor Death' here has killed. They were all children, all thirteen them." She looked up and added, "If he took Pilkington out so that he could kill a particular female on his behalf, why would he take a child killer out too?" Warren thought of what was beyond the fences and why Malligan would hand-pick this monster to leave with him. When he made the link, it hit him like an express train.

"Oh God! The children's home!"

CHAPTER TWENTY-SEVEN

The guard house had been silent for over an hour. Dean was getting restless. Kenny felt it and it was making him restless too. The four guards lay on their stomachs on the floor, each tied at the wrists behind them. Former soldier Keith Bilton had read the situation more quickly than his peers and had the presence of mind to make some provision. At the point he was being tied up, he had managed to pull both cuffs of his shirt over the base of his hands and Dean had applied the rope around the cloth. Keith had, when he was sure that Kenny and Dean were watching the others, wrestled his cuffs out of the binding rope and allowed some movement in the resultant space. He worked at the rope, taking care to avoid making it tighter. The crossed-over position of his wrists also proved advantageous.

With cramped and numb fingertips, he pushed and pulled the folds of the rope until there was a clear loosening of the knot. Once he felt that he could slip one hand out of it he stopped working the knot and concentrated on exercising his muscles all over his body without any visible movement of limbs. Lying motionless on the ground, he looked for some change or lapse in the vigilance of his captors. He was aware that the door to the gatehouse had not been locked when the Rogersons had entered but that the main gates were locked. Not being able to locate any of the keys that had been taken from him and his colleagues, he dismissed the idea of getting to the gate and out of the confines of The Garrin Unit to get help. He further rationalised the risk to his colleagues, should he make a break for it. There was no reason for the armed pair to do harm to them, it was to be him who would be taking the risk.

Long, deep breaths, ready to act. Not hasty, not impatient, wait . . . wait.

Dean's restlessness manifested itself verbally.

"What's taking so long?" he whispered. Kenny was eager to cut out any unnecessary talking.

"Shhh! It's cool, it's fine." He hoped that would be sufficient assurance for Dean, but it fell short of addressing his needs.

"But, what if –"

"Shhh!" Kenny repeated in a more purposeful tone of whispering. Dean felt that their respective positions at either side of four, prone and captive men on the floor did not allow for effective communication. With the old revolver still in his hand, he stepped over them one at a time to get across to where Kenny was standing by the door. Kenny bridled in anticipation. He didn't like what Dean was trying to do. There was nothing to say and Dean should just shut up and accept that. They would get word over the radio when they had something to tell them and not before. Keeping the torch switched off, only the moonlight from the high window and the glass panel in the unlocked door allowed any vision of the room.

Keith Bilton knew where the threat was coming from. He knew where the gun was, and he focussed his attention on the man who was carrying it. As Dean Rogerson stepped over him and lifted his foot to step over the second man, Keith seized his moment. He slipped his hand out from the loosened bind and sprang to his feet. He pushed Dean forward making him trip on the men lying on the floor and fly headlong into Kenny. Both men were taken completely by surprise as were the bound guards on the floor.

Dean and Kenny were in a combined heap at the side of the door as Keith dashed to the door and yanked it open squashing the floundering brothers in a tangled heap on the ground and partly trapped in a space under the desk beneath the window. Keith exploded through the doorway and began sprinting away. Without a set of keys for the gate, he had no way of getting out of the Garrin so he took off across the tarmacked forecourt toward the building, hoping that the night staff inside would be in a position to help him.

Dean had managed to keep hold of the gun. He scrambled to his feet and pointed it at the three men on the floor. Kenny got to his feet and said aloud to Dean.

"Not them. Get him, stop him!"

Dean pulled the open door out of his way and darted outside. He saw, in half light, the figure of Keith Bilton, zig-zagging across the open space. Dean took off after him, his heart pumping to bursting point, his mouth dry and wordless. He had to stop that guard from getting away and raising the alarm. He raised the gun and tried to aim it at the moving target. Dean's hand was unsteady, he wrapped his left hand around the fingers of his right and brought the gun under control. Keith Bilton was back in paratrooper training. He was reliving it all over again but this time there was a real enemy and a real gun threatening his life. With luck he could get to the building, get out of sight. There were people in it. There were trees and bushes around it to conceal him in their darkness. With luck he could survive this. Dean let out a breath, as he had been shown by Kenny, and trained the gun on Keith. He squeezed the trigger.

Keith could have darted left or right at that moment. His zig-zag movements, intended to confuse the assailant and make him a hard target, gave him at least a sporting chance. He had a chance, with luck he could get away. His luck had held out so far, it could see him safely to the darkness of the building and all of its concealed places. With luck he would be fine.

As the bang of the revolver rang out across the night air, his luck ran out.

Keith fell to the ground, face first, his arms splayed out in crucifix fashion. His hands offered no impulse to break his fall. The momentum of his running and the force of the bullet pushed him along the hard ground, scraping his chest and face against the tarmac. What light of life there had been in his eyes only seconds before, went out as though a rapid eclipse had passed over him but there was no re-emergence on the other side. He had been a soldier, an elite soldier. Now he was a fallen hero.

*

When the facilities in the kitchen of the Children's Unit were as clean and serviceable as they could be, Doctor Bela Ferenquelar laid out his newly sterilised instruments. The sharpest knives the room had to offer were sharpened still further on a worn, granite block and he utilised several thin, cotton towels he had taken from the drawer beneath the table. He tied a cloth around his mouth and nose then he gathered his bottle of chloroform and a clean flannel and headed through the darkened building for the landing with bedrooms on either side. His earlier reconnoitre of the rooms had provided him with the opportunity to select his first patient. He slipped inside the bedroom with a weaker solution of chloroform on the cloth than he had used on the adult, taking particular care to avoid inhaling it himself. He stepped up to the side of the bed of the diminutive child, sleeping and oblivious to the stone-face and heavy brow of the doctor of delusion. He placed the cloth over the face of the child.

Sally Imsworth jerked awake, opened her eyes and took in the dark shape leaning over her, pressing her head down on the pillow. Petrified and under the control of the huge man, a giant to her, she was unable to put up any resistance and within seconds, the chloroform took over and snuffed out all conscious activity. Her tiny body fell limp.

Ferenquelar held the cloth in place for a further twenty seconds. Unlike when he put the adult members of staff to sleep, he had purposefully reduced the dosage for his preparation of Sally's operation. He had to ensure that she was unconscious and silent, at least until he was ready to begin the procedure. Letting go and placing the face cloth in his pocket, he pulled the bedding away to reveal the pyjama-clad child, completely under his control. He lifted her with minimal effort and held her like a baby in his arms.

At the door, left closed upon his entry, he released a hand and pulled it open. Peering out to check for any activity, he satisfied himself the he was the only conscious soul there before he stepped out and headed along the landing, pausing briefly to close Sally's bedroom door. Unexpectedly, the door lock emitted a sharp and metallic sound which reverberated across the open landing. Ferenquelar paused. Nobody stirred so he continued with careful and deliberate steps to the stairs and down to his kitchen operating theatre.

He placed Sally gently down on the table, lifted her wrist to check her pulse and placed his hand on her forehead by way of testing her temperature. The child lay on the table, devoid of activity but breathing in a shallow and near-silent fashion. Ferenquelar took the tea-towels laid out earlier and tore one into five strips. He tied one to each of Sally's wrists and ankles and secured them to the legs of the table. The fifth strip of cotton was tied around her mouth and knotted at the side beneath her ear.

Once he was content with his arrangements, he went to the window and looked out into the sporadic darkness of the night. He closed his eyes and breathed deeply and slowly, mentally preparing himself for the forthcoming exercise of his unique surgical skill. Only he, Doctor Bela Ferenquelar, of all of the doctors in the world, was capable of performing this operation. Only he, Doctor Bela Ferenquelar, had the supreme ability to identify this condition, missed and beyond the range of all other medical minds. Only he, Doctor Bela Ferenquelar, physician and genius could save this unfortunate child, but there was more to it than his professional skill. He was the most ethical of all of the world's doctors. The patient had a right to know what was happening to them at every stage of the procedure and for that they must be conscious.

The dose of chloroform applied to Sally's face had been administered with high precision. The adults along the corridor would sleep for hours but the impish form behind him, ritualistically tied to the table, should be regaining consciousness soon. Until then he must wait and ready his mind.

CHAPTER TWENTY-EIGHT

Warren and Nixon were running between the inner and outer fence when they heard the shot ring out like a cannon through the night sky. They stopped in their tracks and tried to rationalise what was happening. Dangerous criminals on the loose and now gunfire, the night was taking a turn for the worse. They snapped back to the moment and continued into the woods beyond the outer fence.

Ian Page heard the shots too. He thought about his missing colleague Frank Woan and a shiver ran through him. His emotions were in turmoil and his eyes filled up once again. Telling himself aloud to 'get a grip,' he went back to the control room kitchen to do what he could to accelerate the recovery of his other two workmates.

Gavin Malligan also heard the shots. He knew that the Rogerson boys had a gun. It had been his idea for them to have one in order to take out the guards. It was not in the plan for them to use it. Maybe someone else had shot at them. The guards were not armed as far as he knew. No, it must be the boys who had fired it, but at what? Either way, something had gone wrong. He picked up the walkie-talkie and pressed the transmit button.

"What's happened?"

Kenny was frozen on hearing Malligan's gravelly Welsh voice. Whilst Dean was traumatised at having ended a life, Kenny knew that Mally held no such reservations. He would end theirs without sparing either of them a thought. He spoke into the radio.

"S'alright, we had a bit of trouble, but it's all sorted now."

"Don't leave any loose ends," said Malligan, leaving no doubt as to what that meant. Kenny looked at the three men tied up on the floor.

*

Ferenquelar's cerebral deliberations were curtailed at the muffled sound of his patient's stirring on the table. His judgement in calculating the dosage of chloroform and the size of the patient had been perfection. He strode around the table and gazed down at the child. Sally was regaining consciousness, but had she known the full horror of her predicament it would have been enough to make her remain out for the count. The moonlight afforded sufficient light to be able to make out the shape of the man standing next to her. She pulled at her bindings, but she was only able to move her hips slightly in any given direction. Ferenquelar fitted the torch strap around his head and switched on the light. He turned his head and the torch-beam down toward Sally. She stopped moving when she saw the glint of light bounce off the steel blade of the knife. In a voice that could have come from the centre of the earth he said.

"Ah! You are wake. This good, we can begin."

From inside the gag, Sally tried with all she had to scream for help. All that came through it was a dull and barely audible murmur of protest and desperation. He ignored the wriggling and muffled groans of his patient. She was truly very sick and in dire need of his expertise.

"I cure you of serious disease," he said. "Only I, Doctor Bela Ferenquelar, can perform this surgery. Soon, your suffering will be over."

Sally tensed every sinew and muscle in her petrified body. A nightmare – all of her nightmares, happening for real and nobody was there to help. She was determined to resist, there was still fight left in her. She twisted her head around, squirming in all directions. The huge man had to hold her head still before continuing with his explanation of what was to happen.

"I make incision here," he growled with practiced calm and professionalism as he traced a line across Sally's forehead with the knife blade. "I remove cause of problem, all is to be fine, not worry."

Sally screwed up her eyes in the hope that when she opened them again it would be different. It wasn't. Ferenquelar began murmuring from behind his facemask, unintelligible sounds, mainly in his native language. He examined the knife in the beam of light emitting from his head.

He suddenly stopped his murmuring and became silent. Sally was bracing herself for what was going to be inflicted on her, but the knife remained raised over her, then it dropped with a deafening clang on the kitchen floor. Ferenquelar soon followed. He slumped onto Sally then slipped down and out of sight. Sally was aware that something, someone was pulling at the cloth binding her right wrist to the table leg. When the first bind was removed, she saw a figure in the half light. Whoever it was moved to free her other hand. When it was untied, she sat bolt upright and saw that it was Christian.

"Oh Christian, he was going to kill me with that big knife." Sally was crying tears of relief.

"I heard him upstairs Sal, I couldn't see what he was doing at first. I went to get the staff, but I couldn't get him to wake up. I saw what this fellow was doing to you, Sal. I had to hit him with that."

Christian was also in his pyjamas and he was wearing his police cadet baseball cap. He nodded toward a thick piece of painted wood, as long as Sally was tall. It was from the banister rail at the top of the stairs and had been worked loose by the residents of the home. One carefully aimed blow to the back of Ferenquela's head was enough to put him down. He lay face down on the kitchen floor, the facemask still in place. Christian and Sally worked on the knots of the cloth around her ankles. As soon as they were off, she swung herself around and slipped to the floor, narrowly missing the prone figure of her attacker. Her arms and legs were still wobbling as she tried to stand up. She wrapped her arms around Christian and held on to him and the tears gushed freely from her eyes. Christian was keen to get out of the kitchen and find the staff. As they released from their embrace and stepped sideways around the motionless giant, a fat hand in a surgical glove shot out and grabbed Sally by the ankle.

Sally let out a scream, an uncontrolled high-pitched eruption of sound containing all of the fear she had felt before. Christian dived onto Ferenquelar and tried to pull his grip from Sally's leg. Ferenquelar reached across with his free hand and tried to grab the knife.

"The knife Sal, don't let him get the knife!"

He shouted to her, but her screams drowned him out. Ferenquelar scrambled his body across the floor toward the knife. Christian let go of the arm that was holding Sally and grabbed Ferenquelar's free hand in an attempt to prevent him from recovering the knife back into his possession. The presence of a small boy on his arm was enough to prevent him from moving forward. Still groggy from his recent blow to the head and subsequent period of unconsciousness made all movement hard for him. He had done little physical exercise for years which added to his labours. He remained determined to get to that knife and carry on with the vital work he was put on earth to do. Now he had two patients to operate on.

He inched forward, touching the edge of the knife's handle and inadvertently nudging it further from his outstretched fingers. Christian held on with all of his might, displaying strength beyond his physique.

"Sal, the knife, the knife!"

Finally, Sally realised what Christian was saying and she reached down to pick up the knife. She composed herself sufficiently to take the handle in her small hand. She had prevented Ferenquelar from getting it, but he was still holding her by the ankle. The first thought was to get him off her and the way to do that was to stick the point of the knife into Bela's hand. It was his turn to let out a scream. He let go of her leg and she jumped clear of further contact.

"Christian, come on! Let's go, get help!" More light came upon them and a familiar voice brought a much-needed sense of safety to both of them.

"Okay, we've got him," said Warren. "Cuff him please, Caroline."

*

Kenny Rogerson stood in the doorway of the gatehouse staring in disbelief whilst telling Dean to get back inside. Dean stood on the tarmac still holding the revolver out in front of him with both hands. He had never killed anyone before, and he was unable to take it in. He was also not taking in what his brother was saying to him. The three captured guards lying on the floor of the gatehouse did not need to see what had happened to know what it was. Their colleague had not made it out. One shot told the full story. What lay in store for them was vying for prominence in their scattered thoughts. Keith was not going to come back with help to free them. Keith was not going to come back at all. Dean stared at the dead man on the ground ahead of him.

"He was running Kenny, I had to stop him, you said I had to stop him."

The mention of his brother's name within earshot of their captives brought a new urgency to Kenny's mind. Those men in there were a liability and what to do about it left few options.

"Get back in here, now!" demanded Kenny more forcefully.

Dean lowered the gun and stumbled back, stooped, round-shouldered and broken. He reached the gatehouse and stepped inside. Kenny took the gun from him and closed the door.

*

The moonlight was consistent since the clouds had dispersed. Visibility had improved as a result. On the top of the incinerator, Malligan had replaced his own shoes with those previously worn by Dermott Conlon. He had intended to change clothing with him but the blood on the jacket had made him reconsider that. He did need some alternative clothes because of the broad yellow stripe along the arms and legs of his hospital issue jacket and trousers. It was also important that Conlon would, in death, make a convincing substitute, convincing enough to make the police accept that he was dead and not go looking for him.

Once he had carefully placed his own shoes near to the hopper chute of the incinerator, he dragged Conlon's lifeless form to the aperture and pulled open the metal lid. The heat emanating from the chute was intense. It made him reel backwards and steel himself to proceed. Wiping sweat from his brow, he lifted Conlon under his arms and heaved his head and shoulders into the square gap. One more shove and his upper body weight took his legs down the chute and into the body of the incinerator. There was an angry roar of leaping fire as the mortal remains of his former partner in crime were devoured by the furnace.

Malligan was about to close the heavy lid when something took his attention. He turned to look over the flat roof of the incinerator. He looked around for his machete, but it was not at his feet or nearby. Broadening the range of his search, he looked up and saw the missing weapon. It was in the hand of someone his plan had not accounted for.

CHAPTER TWENTY-NINE

Warren and Nixon had got Ferenquelar under control as Christian was holding the crying Sally. Raised up to his feet, Ferenquelar made noises of complaint but not in English. He was taken outside and across to the main building. The nursing staff of the padded-cell ward were surprised to see another escapee from The Garrin Unit, nevertheless, they agreed to house him in the cell next to that containing Pilkington. Christian and Sally were examined for injuries by the nurses but, although traumatised, they were physically unharmed. Warren left them with the nurses and headed outside with Nixon.

"That leaves Malligan," said Warren. "These two didn't get very far, let's hope he didn't either."

"Did you say that it was you who arrested him?" asked Caroline.

"Yeah, for murder. He likes to use a machete."

"I've had a thought and you might not like it." Caroline felt that their shared experiences of the night allowed her to speak freely.

"Go on!"

"It looks like Malligan sent Pilkington to kill that girl, the one who gave witness evidence against him at his trial. He might be harbouring thoughts of revenge against you too. Have you considered that?"

"Not recently I hadn't. It is possible I suppose. It would mean that he is still here somewhere."

At that moment the sound of a high-revving engine interrupted their train of thought. Through the trees they saw the headlights of a vehicle approaching the hospital and a blue flashing light. A second, then a third came into view, all with emergency lights fully utilised. Warren and Nixon ran toward the main gate to see that there were two marked police vans and a car, one of the vans contained the seven-man support unit. The driver of the leading van spotted them and pulled the convoy to a halt. Warren dashed up to the van and spoke to the front seat passenger, Sergeant Vinnie Davies.

"There's been a breakout from the Garrin and the power has been cut," said Warren.

"Yes, we know. A bloke in the cells called Aberfoyle told us. He knew all about it, he's the inside man." Explained the sergeant as he climbed out of the van.

"He's my prisoner," said Nixon. "I came here to search his locker."

She went on to explain that police radios were out of use. Davies was aware of that and he had bought short-circuit radios which did not rely on the main aerial. He gave one to Nixon.

"Sarge, we heard gunshots about ten minutes ago," said Warren. "We've caught two of the escapers, they're in the main building now, but there's another still out here somewhere. It's a proper job. A lot of planning has gone into this."

"Aberfoyle told us everything: he drugged the staff, knocked out the back-up generator and made a duplicate key. He was being blackmailed by somebody about his underage girlfriend. When she dumped him by making her complaint, he came clean about the whole thing. He had lost everything and had nothing more to lose."

"Did he say what happened to the outside guards?" interjected Nixon. "They have disappeared."

"No, he didn't say anything about the guards," said Davies. "We had better start a search for them. I've sent for a firearms team already. Those gunshots you heard makes their arrival more urgent."

A plan of action was put in place, but the absence of the firearms officers made the range of it somewhat limited. As they were discussing their options, a car arrived, and Ron Jeaver climbed out. After Jeaver had announced that he had called out an emergency electrician in a manner which suggested that this measure would solve all of their problems, Warren put him in the picture about the night's events. Jeaver's expression changed instantly.

"So, there's no sign of my external team?" said Jeaver as he chewed his thumbnail nervously.

"No, and your indoor staff have been drugged and are unconscious. One of them is missing too. Ian Page wasn't affected by the sedative. He's still in there guarding the ones who didn't get out. Pilkington and Ferenquelar have been apprehended trying to kill people in the main hospital. There's only Gavin Malligan unaccounted for."

"Malligan!" exclaimed Jeaver, "He told staff that another patient wanted to kill him and put him in the incinerator. Has anyone looked there?"

"Not yet," said Warren, "Sarge, we can go and have a look for Malligan without waiting for the firearms team, right?"

"We can have a look, from a distance. Show me where it is."

Warren, Nixon, Davies and two other uniformed constables headed off through the gates of Heavem and toward the incinerator. The Support Unit organised themselves into a search formation and headed off to form a loose cordon around The Garrin Unit, deploying two officers to remain watching the entrance. When any of the missing guards appeared, they were to tell Davies over the radio.

The first hint of daylight was emerging over the trees when the impressively equipped police support team filed across the edge of the parking area near to the gatehouse of The Garrin Unit. Inside the building Kenny, Dean and their three surviving captives could hear the marching sound of multiple footsteps on gravel. Dean was shaking and jabbering incoherently after the realisation of what he had done had sunk in. Kenny was anxious and undecided as to what to do. He climbed onto the table and peeped out of the high window. After seeing the line of cops on the other side if the fence, Kenny ducked down again and went back to sitting on the floor with Dean.

"What is it Kenny? What's making that noise out there?"

"It's nothing, just someone going past, they haven't seen us, it's okay."

Kenny picked up the radio and pressed the button.

"Mally, are you there?"

*

On the roof of the giant incinerator, a tense stand-off was underway. Malligan was burning up inside at his own inability to account for what stood before him. A miscalculation, an error in judgement? No. He had been partly correct in his assessment. The issue was how he could put that error right. He had learned the hard way never to show weakness, display unerring strength at all times. This time, he needed that more than ever.

"It's you. You got out too, eh? That's good, I wanted you to get out. We're mates, you and me, aren't we?"

The machete rose up then slowly lowered in the hand of his unexpected accomplice. In all of their exchanges, it had been Malligan who had gained the upper hand, dismissive of anyone who he had judged to have been of no use to him, but not now. Malligan was in the hot seat, facing his own preferred weapon being brandished by another man.

"Well? Aren't you going to say anything?" demanded Malligan, giving away the desperation he had tried hard to conceal. He had hoped for some indication that an accord could be struck. His tormentor was in no mood to be conciliatory.

"You Nazi bastard!"

Arthur Elevand seemed taller than before. He was composed and determined as he passed the machete from his right hand to his left then back again.

"What? No mate, that's not me. I'm no Nazi!"

"I know what you are. I've been hunting your type for years. You are a Nazi clone."

"No, you've got it wrong. I'm nothing like that. I'm just a bloke, like you."

"You are nothing like me." Elevand's voice rose sharply in an acute but momentary burst of anger. His eyes remained firmly boring into those of Malligan, standing small as though he was prey, trapped and helpless. Lowering his tone again he continued, "I am onto you. I have been on your trail for some time. You are a clone of Hitler, just like those others. I got them, all of them – and now I've got you!"

"Mally, answer please!"

Kenny Rogerson's tinny voice of panic came out of the walkie-talkie, placed near to Malligan's feet. "We've got the coppers outside! What are we going to do?"

*

Dean was oblivious to the radio messages. Kenny gave up trying to speak to his boss when he had first heard the sound of car engines. At the front of The Garrin Unit, two marked police cars and a small police van spun across the car park and came to a halt next to the two support unit officers posted there by Vinnie Davies. From the cars, out stepped four police officers who went directly to the rear of their cars to open the tailgates. Whilst talking to the two patrol cops, they took black-handled rifles and matching handguns from the car and checked their chambers in a regimented and efficient manner. They were police officers, but they looked and behaved like soldiers.

From the van emerged another cop with a heavy beard. He produced a German Shepherd dog from the back which obediently remained at the handler's side without a lead. A radio message was sent to Vinnie Davies, informing him that the armed boys and the dog handler had arrived. His response was to inform them of the earlier gunshots and to stand-by for further instructions. When access could be gained, they were to enter The Garrin Unit and sweep it for threats before Jeaver and his staff could enter and assess the situation. The objectives were recapture any escapees, to prevent any further escapes and find the members of Jeaver's night team who were unaccounted for.

Dean Rogerson heard the activity outside the gatehouse. It brought him in to a comparatively rational state.

"What's going on Kenny? Who's out there? I can hear talking." His brother tried to offer some reassurance.
"It's alright, they can't get in. We have all the keys. It's fine, we're the fuckin S.A.S remember? We'll think of a way out of here."

It was what Dean had wanted to hear. He had all but dismissed the shooting of Keith Bilton less than half-an-hour before, preferring instead to dive into his fantasy world of heroic combat and excitement.

"Yeah, we're the fuckin' SAS, Kenny. We'll get out and we'll win, yeah!"

The incapacitated guards looked at each other as they lay side-by-side on the floor. They sensed a change of composure amongst their captors after the shooting of their colleague, but not a word was exchanged between them. Nobody wanted to give any reason for further shooting. Because of this, no effort was made to communicate to whoever it was outside. Dean was enjoying the mood Kenny had created for him to exist in.

"We'll get a helicopter, eh Kenny?"

"Sure, yeah!"

His brother continued to reassure him whilst hoping that the radio would bring forth a solution from Mally who always knew what to do. He picked up the radio and put it to his ear. He had set the volume to its lowest audible option. He turned up the dial in the hope that it would bring the message he so desperately craved. The result was a high-pitched whine which was heard by the cops outside the gate. The police dog yelped and howled at the sound.

"What was that?" asked the dog handler.

"Dunno. It came from over there," answered one other firearms officer.

All seven cops advanced to where they perceived the noise to have come from. Surrounded by trees and high fences with open spaces beyond, they narrowed the possibilities to the gatehouse and the area just beyond the fence. A powerful torch was shone though the netting and began to scan the gatehouse and open space toward the main building. A flash of light swept over the high window, momentarily illuminating the inside of the gatehouse giving hope to the captive guards whilst causing

Kenny's and Dean's breathing to stop. Dean reached for the gun which lay on the floor in front of both of them. Kenny placed his hand over Dean's on the gun, silently indicating that he should take no action. They should wait.

The police officer holding the torch spotted the upturned heels of Keith Bilton's shoes forty yards away across the open ground. He moved sideways to get a better view.

"Oh shit! There's someone there, not moving."

His colleagues moved to join him and confirmed that the man appeared to be dead. Weapons were drawn and raised in anticipation. A radio message was passed to Sergeant Davies.

"Is it the cops Kenny?" asked Dean.

"Yeah, it's the cops, bro. But they don't know were here so keep down and keep quiet."

"But it's only cops, Kenny. We've got a gun. Cops don't have guns. We can get out of here."

"No Dean, we have to keep down, shhh!"

"We can do them Kenny, we're the fuckin' SAS, they're just cops. They'll be scared of us Kenny. I can get us out." He stood up and dashed to the door.

"No Dean, come back!"

Dean swung open the gatehouse door and darted outside with the old revolver in his hand. The cops outside the fence spotted him and turned their lights on him.

"He's armed!" shouted a firearms officer with his rifle raised to his shoulder. "Armed police! Drop it!"

Dean could not see through the torch beam and, in his excited state could not comprehend what was being shouted. He had no idea that the cops were armed. He raised his revolver and called out.

"We're the fuckin' SAS!"

He had lifted his gun arm to an angle of forty-five degrees before the double-tap to his torso knocked him off his feet. With the weapon still in his hand, he writhed on his back, his lungs filling with blood. Kenny ran out after him, crouching down to lift his brother's head.

"Step away, get back, now!" called out the marksman.

Although his instructions were unmistakable in an atmosphere of clarity, they went unheard by Kenny. His thoughts took no usable shape and all logic had left him. He felt the life slipping away from Dean's body and he saw no further than that. Despite repeated demands for him to step away, he wrestled the gun out of Dean's hand and, with the feelings of a man who had no way of rationalising that situation, he stood up as though he was alone and faced no threat to his life. The next two bullets from the police officer's gun were to the head. Kenny fell to the ground next to Dean.

The shots were heard by Warren and the others. They carried a different sound, deeper and stronger than the one they had heard earlier. It made them all stop and make silent judgements about where these had come from and whether they should proceed with their current aim.

"I bloody hope that was our lads doing the shooting," said Vinnie Davies raising the radio to his ear.

"Situation report!" he exclaimed. A uniformed cop at the other side of the building answered, his tone was unnerved and concise.

"Two suspects engaged, armed with a handgun. Proportionate action taken, two casualties, believed fatal. One other already down before we got here. Can't get inside to carry out examination to assess further threat level."

Davies, due to retire in a matter of weeks, let out a long breath and tapped the radio against his teeth.

"There's a way in Sarge." said Warren. "The gap in the fence where the breakout happened."

Davies nodded an acknowledgement before ordering the firearms team to make their way to the gap in the fence, using Warren's directions from the main gate. Davies left Warren and Nixon to check the incinerator whilst he went to the scene of the shootings.

CHAPTER THIRTY

In the glimmer of morning light, Elevand showed no indication that he was prepared to reconsider his assessment of Malligan's true identity. He did, however, seek to make the most of his victim's undivided attention having been dismissed by Malligan as a worthless fool so many times.

"You thought you were so damn clever, didn't you?" he snarled.

"No mate, you've got me all wrong. I've never done you any harm. I defended you, against those others in there. It was them who treated you bad."

Malligan was buying time and using it to work out what Elevand's Achilles heel might be. Elevand didn't seem to be able to feel fear so he opted for the only other approach he knew.

"I could do you some good right now. I've got twenty million stashed away overseas and I'll cut you in on it. Just think man, you could be rich. Go anywhere do anything, disappear, think about it, how good your life would be."

Elevand stared dispassionately at him. No emotion was displayed.

"You lying, Nazi scum!"

Elevand ran at Malligan with the machete raised over his head, bringing it down with a wild, thrashing movement at his prey. Malligan stepped sideways and avoided the fierce blade but Elevand swept it around at him as though trying to fell a tree in a high wind. Malligan was able to grab Elevand's arm, then the hand that was holding the machete. It became a battle of mind and body, to the death, one hell bent on surviving and the other convinced he was saving the world. They edged toward the aperture of the incinerator, locked together, neither conceding an inch to the other, their movements were sideways and lurched and shuffled in an intense struggle. Malligan made enough room to head-butt Elevand who reeled backwards without letting go of his quarry. Hands not gripping the machete swung wildly in attempts to land meaningful punches, but they were too close together for any to have much effect.

Warren and Nixon came running around the edge of the next building to see the epic battle unfurling on the high stage of the incinerator. Taking in the scene, all that the unarmed cops could do was to surround the huge metal box at a safe distance and hope for the best.

The embattled pair edged toward the open hopper chute which had so recently consumed the mortal remains of Dermott Conlon into its belly. Malligan felt his foot touch the raised lip of the aperture and the desire came over him to try to steer Elevand toward it. Neither man had any awareness that they were being watched by police officers.

Warren had no idea of the identity of the man who was fighting with Malligan, although the yellow stripes along his trousers and sleeves told his story very clearly. He recognised Malligan without hesitation and the memory of the death of Luke Gould was made all the sharper for seeing a machete wavering above and around their heads. Nixon snapped him back to the present. Having recognised Gavin Malligan from his picture on the file in Jeaver's office,

"Is that the guy who wanted to put Malligan in the incinerator?" she asked, trying to make some sense for herself amongst the frantic madness of the night's events.

"I don't know. I suppose it must be."

He was not really thinking about that. He was trying to decide what, if anything, could be done to get this chaos under control. Apart from climbing up and joining in, there were no obvious courses of action and Vinnie Davies had ordered everyone to observe from a safe distance.

The struggle on the huge, metal box edged over the gaping square leading to the furnace below. Malligan swung Elevand around and over the hole. Elevand's foot slipped into the gap and his weight took him lower into it. Realising from the heat what Malligan had been trying to do, Elevand found renewed vigour and used his grip on Malligan to extract himself from the deathly hole. He got both feet back onto the roof and pushed Malligan backwards. Both men failed to control the momentum and although they twisted and thrashed around wildly, they were off balance and stumbling toward the edge of the roof. The machete was somewhere out of the view of the watching cops, between them or behind them, but it was still there somewhere. The pair lurched off the roof, still locked together, and soared through the air, landing in a heavy and bone-breaking heap on the tarmacked path.

The police officers ran to them, Warren with his wooden truncheon in his hand, ready for further combat, but it did not come. Both men lay still, entwined and interlocked. Up close, laboured breathing could be heard. Five cops formed a cautious gauntlet around them, waiting and ready for another outburst of violence.

Neither of the two moved.

"Where's the blade?" asked Nixon, knowing where the threat was coming from and hoping that Warren had a better view. He didn't answer. Sounds of people running could be heard nearby. The firearms team came into view, sprinting up the path with weapons raised and ready. Spreading out into the gaps left by their unarmed colleagues, they braced for further conflict but there was no movement at all.

Finally, a leg moved slightly, and then an arm. One of the men was shuffled off the other and was left slumped onto the ground. The other slowly got to his knees then to his feet. Both men were dressed the same and their faces were out of sight. The only unequivocal fact was that only one of them was moving.

With nothing in either hand, it was Gavin Malligan who was recovering from the fall. He raised himself upright, lifting his head to the heavens. As though only one leg was functional, he swivelled around on the spot until he settled his gaze on Warren. Malligan began laughing, pained and standing up in clear difficulty, he laughed with a twisted cruelty in his voice. It was as though nothing in the world applied to him, and it never had. Nixon's warning about the blade took shape in the view of those in front of Malligan. The handle, and only the handle, of the machete was visible. It was sticking out of Malligan's ribs. The whole of the blade was still inside him. He stopped laughing abruptly, dropped to his knees then onto the ground, lifeless and still.

Arthur Elevand hauled himself to his feet, winded at having fallen but otherwise unharmed. Warren stepped forward and, without any undue physicality, took Elevand by the arm and guided him into the care of the uniformed officers who applied handcuffs to his wrists behind his back.

"I got him!" said Elevand, steadily recovering from his exertions and the fall. Warren, Nixon and Davies approached the prone form of Gavin Malligan. His eyes were fixed open and a snarl remained on his lips. Over half of the blade of the machete was buried in the side of his torso. Elevand was jubilant and eager to share it.

"I've been tracking the last clone for years. I knew it was him when he arrived here. That's it, no more clones of Hitler, this was the last one. My work here is complete."

He adopted a facial expression of peaceful accomplishment, as though in prayer, as he was led away.

CHAPTER THIRTY-ONE

With the threat abated for that critical moment, the firearms team divided up to escort Warren and Nixon back into the Garrin Unit, to guard the lifeless form on the ground and to cover the gap in the fence. The police patrols regrouped and entered the Garrin Unit once Elevand was properly detained. Inside the building they called out to Ian Page who came out of the control room to greet them with good news. He reported that his colleagues were now awake and recovering and all of them, Frank Woan included, were present and accounted for. Frank had been found locked in the room of Arthur Elevand who was believed to have escaped along with the other three. It was assumed that Elevand must have dragged the unconscious Frank into his own cell in order to make it look as though he was still in it before he went.

Warren reassured Page that Elevand had been recaptured as had Ferenquelar. He broke the news that Malligan was dead. Leaving no other inmates on the missing list, the episode, as far as escapees were concerned was over. It remained imperative to locate the outdoor team of guards. A search by armed and unarmed cops of the outer sections of the Garrin Unit, revealed and released the three tied-up guards and still terrified inside the gatehouse and one guard dead nearby. Once Jeaver and his electrician had restored power, the early crew began to arrive along with police reinforcements, Warren went back to his office in the main building to try to summarise the night in some readable form. As he sat down at his desk, exhausted and close to breaking down, there was a gentle tap on his door. Candice Kendal came inside.

"Are you alright?" she asked, although it was clear that Warren's welfare was not the main reason she was there.

"Erm yeah, I think I am. And you?" he enquired. She nodded and dipped her eyelids momentarily. Warren added "What about William, how's he?" Candice let out a sigh.

"He's recovering. He's dealing with it very well. He was petrified when that man came at him with the knife. He was lucky to survive that."

"Yes, a few of us can say that about tonight," mused Warren. "From what I have learned about him, he only wants to harm women. That's probably why he didn't kill William, it was you he was after."

She sat on the chair with customary finishing-school elegance and looked down at her shoes. She looked up with renewed resolve and said,

"You found William in my room. I want to talk to you about that. It's not anything, you know, improper. He's capable of making his own mind up about his life, and so am I." Warren sensed what she was hinting at and nipped it in the bud.

"Candice. What the hospital authorities may want to do about it is not my concern. As I see it, you are both adults and both able to make your choices. I can't see anybody being a victim here. I try to uphold the law and I haven't seen anything to make me think one has been broken. If you and William are happy, that's fine." He paused and looked away for a moment then added, "I let you and Luke down badly. I'm not going to add to your suffering."

"Thank you," she said stifling a tear. "I can leave in a week but I'm going to stay on, as a volunteer. The families of patients can contribute in many ways here. William has no family. I am going to fill that gap for him. He needs this and it's what I need too."

"Good!" said Warren smiling. The door swung open and Superintendent Brian Henville entered the room as though he owned the hospital. Warren felt it right to object.

"Do you mind? I am having a private conversation here."

Henville was in no mood for niceties.

"It is less urgent than what I have to say, continue it later."

Warren reluctantly nodded to Candice for her to go which she did without further discussion. Henville closed the door after her and, remaining standing, turned to speak to the seated Warren.

"What bedlam has been going on here last night?"

"A well-planned jail break from the Garrin, amongst other complications," summarised Warren. Henville moved the discussion on swiftly.

"Tell me what you know about Patrick Miller."

"He's a voluntary patient, been here a couple of weeks. Habit of straying off from where he's supposed to be but that's nothing unusual around here. We found him with a head injury. Is he alright?"

"He is making a recovery, no long-term effects, I believe," explained Henville

"What's your interest in Miller?" pressed Warren.

Henville ran his tongue across his upper teeth in contemplation before explaining.

"Patrick Miller is a pseudonym. He is an undercover operative, placed here by the Regional Crime Squad's Asset Recovery Team."

"A cop? What was he doing here?"

"He was watching a man called Roger Reid."

"I know Reid," said Warren, piecing together the unfolding information along with his own. "He came here as a voluntary patient too."

"Reid is really Dermott Conlon, a close associate of the now deceased Gavin Malligan."

"I know about Conlon from when I was on the Drugs Squad, but I couldn't even get a picture of him. Where is he now?" asked Warren. Henville was unable to answer that.

"His whereabouts are presently unknown. When Conlon was identified, the R.C.S. believed that he was here to get close to Malligan and try to either spring him from The Garrin Unit or find out where he had stashed the proceeds of his criminal empire."

"So, the R.C.S. think they have a million quid salted away?"

"They know they have several millions in offshore accounts. The proceeds of a drug importation and supply on a massive scale and over a long period. The strand you were investigating on the Drugs Squad was only the tip of the iceberg."

"And you didn't think it necessary for me to know about all this?" said Warren in undisguised annoyance. "This is going on in front of me and I'm kept in the dark about it."

"Oh, don't be so naïve Warren! You've worked on enough covert jobs to know the score. A need-to-know basis: you were better off being out of that loop. That is why I instructed my officers not to come here unless it was urgent. A minimal police presence was required in order to avoid compromising the undercover operation being carried out by Miller."

Warren had to concede that point. When he had got over his initial resentment, he accepted that he would have done the same. Henville changed the subject.

"I understand that trainee detective Caroline Nixon conducted herself with some credit throughout this episode."

"She did, she should be commended for her actions, at least," opined Warren before he was asked.

"As should you Warren. It would have been an almighty mess if you had not been here to take the action you did. I know that a commendation probably won't mean much to you so I'm also going to recommend an immediate return to detective duties. I take it that would be agreeable to you?"

Warren stood up and walked to the window. A wasp was hovering on the outside of the glass, trying to find a way to get in. He looked out beyond the wasp and saw the movement of patients and staff on the grass along with police scenes of crime officers and uniforms liaising with nursing staff and hospital managers. The patients were all making their own noises and customary gestures. Away to the left he could see the edge of the Children's Unit and, further round and out of sight was The Bowers. Heavem was just being what it always was: a place to put everyone who did not fit in with the rest of humanity. On seeing that, more clearly than he had done before, he saw the depth of raw humanity being played out before his eyes. That brought a new and uplifting outlook upon him. He turned to Henville and said.

"I said I would do a year here. I want to finish that."

Henville was taken aback and his face made no effort to hide it. "Are you in command of your senses Warren? I'm offering you the role you had before, probably a move onto R.C.S. on the back of your performance last night, I shouldn't wonder. You're choosing to stay here?"

"For the time being, yes."

"May I ask why?"

"It's done me good to be with people who aren't living like rats in a sewer. Drug users and dealers? They suck the life out of everything they come into contact with: their loved ones, each other, themselves and me included. Here? I've been able to help decent people. Those who life has dealt a poor hand to, but they don't feel sorry for themselves, they just get on and make the most of it. I'm not saying I want to stay here until I retire, I just want to finish what I started. If it's alright with you, I'd like to hold off on you offer of a transfer, at least until next year."

Henville shook his head in disbelief then nodded in acceptance. He turned to reach for the door handle then stopped and looked back at Warren who remained gazing out of the window.

"You may be right but staying here too long could be equally harmful. I think poor Bob Tasker stayed too long. Don't forget that."

"I won't."

Henville left the room and Warren sat down to slip blank paper into his typewriter.

He had no recollection of switching on the hospital radio set, but he noticed that it was still operating and emitting its quiet entertainment across his desk. The Beatles' 'Fool on the Hill' came to its conclusion and the velvet voiced presenter began his link.

"It's been quite a night, here in Heaven, with all the burns, bangs and break-outs. We here at Heaven Radio offer our sincerest condolences to the folks who waved goodbye during the night. But, like life itself, you'll be

lucky to get out alive. Never a dull moment in Heaven,
who would want to be anywhere else? A big thumbs-up for
our own PC Russell Warren and his friends. A job well
done. Thanks for looking after us all. Here's local boys
10cc with 'Life is a Minestrone.' So true, so true."

Warren stood up and felt a determination to hunt down whoever that voice belonged to. Curiosity outweighed his many emotions at that moment, not least of which was fatigue. He set off to the door then stopped himself. He thought about what he would do when he tracked down the mystery broadcaster. Would he challenge him to explain his cryptic messages? Try to put a stop to his mischief? He reached the door and paused. He realised that he liked Heaven Radio and what it did. He should leave it as it was. He didn't want to know who the voice belonged to. It all added to the colour, the life and the madness and was probably keeping him from losing his grip when so many things around him made no sense.

Heaven Radio could carry on doing what it does without his intervention. It was a part of the madness that came with the job.

■■

Other titles by Barry Lees;

This City of Lies

It is 1959 and war veteran turned San Francisco private eye Kerrigan takes on a routine matrimonial case in which those involved are not what they appear to be. Events take a dangerous turn when he finds that he too has become a target, but for who? When he witnesses a murder, his instinct to survive takes over. Alone and struggling with the memories of his war experiences, Kerrigan must find the killer before the killer finds him.

The Governor's Man

It is the Fall of 1959 and San Francisco Private Investigator Kerrigan is hired to find a missing person. A name from the past evokes painful memories which force him to challenge his own judgement and question his loyalties. Cast into a complex web of deceit, politics, religion, theft and murder, he has to investigate and eliminate many suspects, each with equally compelling motives, to uncover the truth, catch a killer and put right an old injustice.

By Sword and Feather

It is 1960 and San Francisco Private Investigator Kerrigan reluctantly accepts a job as a bodyguard to foil a kidnap plot. Whilst trying to avert a diplomatic incident, he becomes involved in an investigation into a murder with a bizarre yet familiar modus operandi. Made to relive old traumas of the Burmese jungle, he is driven by the need to avenge the death of an old friend.

Exiles from a Torn Province

Belfast 1978. Catholic James falls in love with Protestant Lizzie. Knowing the risks, they keep their identities secret from each other. When both suffer the loss of a family member in violent circumstances, their respective communities whisk each of them to safety overseas - but to different countries, whilst Darry, an ambitious I.R.A. operative, is caught and jailed for one of the killings. Although neither knows it, all three are set on a collision course. The clash of peace against violence is taken to the extreme. The result is an audacious, terror-plot aimed at the heart of the U.K. establishment.

Track and Eliminate

When destruction and death strike the picture-postcard village of Eckscarfe, Inspector Imran Bhatta and PC Mel Sharpe are called upon to investigate. Inexperienced, ill-prepared and poorly supported, they probe what appears to be a tragic accident, but it soon becomes a much more shocking and demanding enquiry. They must follow every lead, examine every item found and challenge every witness account to get to the truth.

Many suspects, motives, alibis and half-truths come to light, and yet the question remains. Who, in that idyllic setting, could be behind that murderous act?

The Blue, the Green and the Dead.

When a company fracking for shale gas are found to have caused earthquakes, the community forms a strong objection and large-scale protests follow. Amidst the protesters, one of them has a secret. An agent of a powerful player is trying to inhibit the fracking operation, but for different reasons. Highly trained, ruthless and a seasoned killer, he will stop at nothing to achieve his aims. Among the police lines is another secret, a cop with a past and the skills to equalise this situation.

Violence and rancour grow and deaths soon follow. When the anti-fracking campaign takes a dramatic and catastrophic twist, it creates a flashpoint that really does shake the ground beneath.

Printed in Great Britain
by Amazon